CW00738823

CIRCLE
DANCE

CIRCLE DANCE

ANTHEA COURTENAY

Copyright © 2022 Anthea Courtenay

The moral right of the author has been asserted.

Apart from any fair dealing for the purposes of research or private study,
or criticism or review, as permitted under the Copyright, Designs and Patents
Act 1988, this publication may only be reproduced, stored or transmitted, in
any form or by any means, with the prior permission in writing of the
publishers, or in the case of reprographic reproduction in accordance with
the terms of licences issued by the Copyright Licensing Agency. Enquiries
concerning reproduction outside those terms should be sent to the publishers.

This is a work of fiction. Names, characters, businesses, places, events
and incidents are either the products of the author's imagination
or used in a fictitious manner. Any resemblance to actual persons,
living or dead, or actual events is purely coincidental.

Matador
Unit E2 Airfield Business Park,
Harrison Road, Market Harborough,
Leicestershire. LE16 7UL
Tel: 0116 2792299
Email: books@troubador.co.uk
Web: www.troubador.co.uk/matador
Twitter: @matadorbooks

ISBN 978 1803132 143

British Library Cataloguing in Publication Data.
A catalogue record for this book is available from the British Library.

Printed and bound in Great Britain by CMP UK
Typeset in 11pt Adobe Garamond Pro by Troubador Publishing Ltd, Leicester, UK

Matador is an imprint of Troubador Publishing Ltd

MY THANKS

to all the friends and relatives who have encouraged
me during the writing of this book, especially:
      Patrice Chaplin for regularly telling me to finish it,
      the members of my Writing Group, past and present,
      including Caroline, Cordelia, Eamann, Lindy, Lynne,
      Maureen, Miranda, Nick and dear Henry, for their
      interest and thoughtful feedback,
      and to Robert and Erica for their special support.

CONTENTS

PART 4
NOVEMBER: BATTLING WITH THE WITCH

PART 5
INTERLUDE

PART 6
SPRING: RENEWAL

PART 7
SUMMER: ENDING THE DANCE

CIRCLE DANCE

BEFORE

It was all her own fault, of course. As usual. The memory of it woke her in the night, so urgent she had to write it down.

She had spent the evening with her friend Fiona, and they had been discussing the general unsatisfactoriness of life and their childhoods and their difficult mothers.

Fiona remarked, 'It's not as if we asked to be born.'

And Miranda heard herself saying, 'I don't know, I sometimes wonder if I did. I can just imagine myself sitting up there saying "It's my turn now!" and zooming off before anyone could stop me.'

And then, something clicked in her mind. She woke in the night thinking about it – no, not thinking, remembering. And the more she remembered, the more she knew that this was how it had been.

There she was, sitting on a cloud or wherever one sits up there, raring to go. There was something terribly important she had to get on with, and she was bouncing up and down on her cloud saying, 'My turn now, my turn now!'

And They said, 'Why don't you hang about a bit till something nicer comes along? This lot won't be easy.'

'I can cope,' she said, her toes twitching and itching. 'D'you think I've learned nothing up here? I'll get it right this time!'

They sighed and shrugged their ethereal shoulders. 'On your own head be it.'

'Yes, yes, I know it's my choice.'

'Just remember that when you're in trouble,' They said.

'I'm not getting into any trouble!' she retorted. 'I learned enough about trouble last time!'

They made no reply. They gave her a gentle, kindly shove, and down she slid.

She was nearly there when she realised she'd left half her luggage behind. She shouted at Them to send it on after her, but couldn't tell whether They'd heard.

*

They were right, of course, as always. The minute she arrived she knew she'd done the wrong thing. For a start, in her eagerness to arrive she'd forgotten about the travel arrangements. The accommodation was not only cramped but positively hostile. This conveyed itself to her quite clearly in the dark, overheated environment that was supposed to provide a warm and tender shelter for Miranda's embryonic self. Her host's emotions pulsed through the blood vessels that joined them, producing a constant discomfort, a sort of anxious itch, from which there was no escape.

The woman was scared: Miranda could feel the waves of fear pulsating around and through her, entering her tiny system like a poison that would pollute her for a long time to come. And it wasn't just fear. This woman was furious. She did not want to be a mother.

At one point, indeed, there was some question of a separation. Miranda's intrusive presence made her host ill. Four months from conception, and already she made her mother sick – there's power for you! There was a bumble of medical voices, probings and proddings, discussions about possible termination. But by then she had decided to stick it out. For one thing, she'd have looked an awful fool going back again so soon. And there was this – this thing, this project she had to get on with. Using all her unborn strength she willed the medics to decide in her favour, and they agreed she should stay.

Birth was when war was declared. Mother and child were locked in battle for two whole days. Halfway through Miranda got fed up with the whole thing, so she wasn't altogether helpful. And when she finally emerged, she was the ugliest baby anyone had ever seen, as well as the most difficult baby any mother ever had to put up with. She knew this, because when she was six her mother told her so.

Up there in the clouds she had forgotten about all this birth and baby bit. She had forgotten the helplessness. She was picked up and put down without a by-your-leave. She couldn't control her bodily functions and her eyes wouldn't focus. She couldn't speak, though she could understand – oh, she could understand all right. There was a tone of voice that told her clearly she was surplus to requirements.

And there was so much to relearn. What were these things waving about in front of her? Oh, they must be her arms. Someone put a finger in her little fist and her little fist closed over it, quite automatically. Very irritating, that; she preferred to be in control. And the corner of the blanket had come off her small foot, which was getting cold. 'Excuse me, someone, would you mind covering my foot, and incidentally I have wet myself again.' All that would come out was: 'Waaa!'

As for eating, she just couldn't do it. There was this angry nipple shoved at her, exuding drops of dislike, and she wouldn't have it. Her mother told her later that she'd sent her back to the nursing home, like a faulty appliance, to be taught to eat. They must have succeeded, for she survived to become rather fond of food.

After a few months, Miranda got fed up with the whole thing. Some people quite liked her – the father did, but he wasn't always there. Perhaps it wasn't too late to go back after all. With so little autonomy, she was interested to discover that she could control her breathing. She began holding her breath until she went rigid and blue in the face. This simply led to shrieks of alarm and a sharp slap or two that made her gasp – and set a trend for the future.

What with all the battling and not eating and failing to hold her breath for long enough, Miranda became quite depressed. Coping with her current environment was as much as she could manage, particularly as it showed no signs of improving, and she quite forgot that she was here for a reason.

As she wrote this all down in the middle of the night it became clear to Miranda that, dream or memory, it would account for an awful lot. If she had taken Their advice and waited, picked a different landing stage, she might have had a warmer welcome. As it was she had had to do her waiting down here, wondering what she was here for, trying this and that and usually getting things wrong. All her fault, all her own fault for being in such a hurry to get her own way. As it was, she had had to wait to catch up with living and for her life to catch up with her.

It wasn't until her thirties that one night, on her way into sleep, she remembered that there was something important she had come to do. What on earth was it? It was ironic; she had been in such a hurry to get born, and now she couldn't for the life of her remember what for.

It really was time for a change.

PART I

SPRING: SAP RISING

1

THE KNIGHT OF CUPS

'My, lots of changes,' said Cassie, as she laid out the cards. Through the smoke of her small cigar she peered at the colourful pictures. 'What a busy lady! Yes, lots of changes. Shuffle again.'

In London in the late 1970s anyone wanting to change had no excuse not to. Over the past two years Miranda Fleming had been to workshops and classes on creative visualisation, Psychosynthesis, the Alexander Technique and Natural Dance, and regularly attended the Festival of Mind, Body and Spirit. She meditated morning and evening. She had joined a self-development Support Group where she was learning the value of positive thinking and expressing her feelings – though she did neither very well as yet – and she, who had always felt an outsider, was beginning to feel acceptable in groups. She had even begun to believe that it might be possible to be happy.

It was at the latest Festival of Mind, Body and Spirit that she had met Cassie, who gave her a tantalisingly short tarot reading and informed Miranda, between shuffling cards, that she herself was a former actress, who still did bits and pieces for television. At the end of fifteen minutes, during which she hinted at all kinds of excitements to come, complete with happy ending, Cassie leaned towards Miranda and remarked confidentially:

'This is the last festival I'm doing. All the psychics elbowing each other to get the front tables – you wouldn't believe it! I can't be bothered. Healing's what I like doing, anyway. You could do with some healing. Come and see me at home.' And she gave Miranda her card.

Miranda liked Cassie. With New Year approaching, she decided to treat herself to a full tarot reading. She didn't want healing; she wanted to be told about happy endings. So here she was in Cassie's attic flat in Muswell Hill, crowded with cane furniture, candles, theatrical photographs, silk flowers billowing out of shell-encrusted vases, and three cats, Alpha, Omega and Zack.

'You want to be careful with changes,' Cassie went on, leaning back in her chair. 'When you start heading for the light, everything gets stirred up: there are dark forces around that try to put the boot in. When I started doing all this my life did not get easier, believe you me. I didn't ask for it – I suddenly started seeing spirits and hearing voices all over the shop – I thought I'd gone barmy, so did everyone else. I've sometimes wondered if it's all worth it. But you have to follow your true path.'

'The trouble is, I don't know what my true path is,' said Miranda.

'Well, let's see.' Cassie tapped the cards, nodded and gazed at an invisible television screen beyond Miranda's right ear. 'You haven't found it yet. It's there, but you won't touch it till you let go of the past.'

'I am working on it!' Miranda responded. Cassie had told her about her past at length, with surprising accuracy. But she didn't need to be told she had had a horrible childhood and some messy times since.

'Well, they're saying you've got to keep at it!' said Cassie. Miranda wasn't sure whether 'they' were the cards or Cassie's spirits. 'Trouble with you is you got out of the womb on the wrong side. You've been squashed. You've had lot of pain, but it can be used, you know. Recycled!'

'Any love life in there?' Miranda wanted to know.

'Shuffle,' said Cassie. 'Men,' she said, as Miranda shuffled the well-worn cards, 'are more trouble than they're worth, my duck, tell you that for nothing. Now cut, with your left hand. Pick seven. And there, ' with a flourish she turned the first card face up, 'there he is!'

There he was, the Knight of Cups, the young prince on his white horse, bearing a golden chalice. Cassie grinned. 'There's the lover,' she said. 'If that's what you really want.' She laid out the six remaining cards. 'There's a tricky woman here, disrupting things.' She tapped the Queen of Wands. That, thought Miranda, had to be Daphne, a marketing consultant for whom she occasionally worked and a regular source of disruption in her life.

'And here we have … hmm. This is powerful, the Tower Struck by Lightning.'

The Tower looked rather like a pepper pot: its roof, riven by lightning, was flying upwards, and two horrified people were being flung out of it. On the next card rode Death, his horse striding over the plains, trampling the noble and the powerful and the religious.

'Oh dear,' said Miranda.

'That's symbolic,' said Cassie. 'Doesn't mean a real death. It's good, actually, it's about transformation. Letting go of old values. It looks like this chap,' she tapped the Knight of Cups – 'is going to bring about some positive change in your life. But it won't be all plain sailing. This chap,' she pointed to the Tower, 'is the old order breaking down. It can mean a disaster, but not here, it's more like some sort of breakthrough, throwing out old garbage, stuff you don't need.'

She looked at Miranda over her half-moon specs and said, 'These are very strong cards. You're not using your full potential, you know.'

Miranda knew. For most of her life she had been hiding. Safest to hide, not to try anything, in case she got it wrong. But now she was coming out, a little step at a time.

Cassie screwed up her eyes against her cigar smoke. 'Airy-fairy bloke, the Knight of Cups, could be creative. Could be someone you know already, or else he's just round the corner.' She looked dubious. 'I don't know what you want a man for, I've given them up. Well, the last one gave me up, but that was no great loss.'

I want a man to love me, of course, Miranda didn't say. *Because I want to know what it is to be loved. And because if* Cosmopolitan *is to be believed, everyone in the world is enjoying an amazing sex life except me.*

'They're a distraction,' said Cassie. 'You'll have better things to do. There's a lot of books and papers around you – d'you work with books?' Suddenly, she swept the cards together. 'You're going to be fine. There's lots of good things happening for you, but there'll be some shenanigans first. It's all part of the game.'

'How d'you mean?'

'It's only a game, life, you know. Remember that, when it gets tricky – don't take it all so seriously. There'll be a few bumps along the way, but everything will fall into place, you'll see.' She packed the cards together with an air of finality. 'I don't like getting into predictions,' she said. 'People always have options, you make your own life.'

She looked at Miranda sharply. 'You're fizzing!' she exclaimed. 'Too much thinking! Stop trying to work everything out. You need to learn to trust more, trust Spirit.

Trust your own intuition, you've got plenty. Now, shall I give you some healing?'

*

Miranda floated home on a euphoric cloud, feeling as if her soul had had a car wash. She had tried healing at previous festivals, but had never experienced anything like the powerful waves of peace that poured through her as Cassie's hands moved over her head and shoulders and down her spine.

She was also buoyed up by the promised arrival of the Knight of Cups. Someone she might know already... Mentally she scanned her regular haunts. The Natural Dance class – mostly women. There was a fair sprinkling of men in the Support Group, but it was against the rules to socialise outside meetings. Clearly, it could be risky to start a relationship with someone who habitually witnessed you in a howling heap.

A better source might be the Friday evening Writing Circle she had joined the previous autumn. She had been introduced to it by her friend Fiona, whom she'd met while temping for the charity where Fiona worked. There were plenty of men in the Circle: sensitive, writing-type men, Fiona had commented somewhat dubiously, liable to be more in touch with their feelings than the average. 'Though whether they'll be in touch with yours is another matter.'

Fiona, tall, bespectacled, divorced, was less than starry-eyed about life. But, she informed Miranda, Jocasta – who ran the Circle – was a good teacher with some interesting ideas. She had formerly taught in an evening institute but disliked its bureaucracy and now gathered her flock privately in a room above a pub in Marylebone.

Miranda had written as a child, fairy tales, attempts at poems. In her twenties she had even sold a couple of short stories to a women's magazine. Soon after meeting Daniel, the last man in her life, he declared (having read none himself) that women's mag stories were trash. After that, she didn't feel like writing any more. But when Fiona told her about the Circle, she felt an urge to try again, less for the lure of the sensitive, writing-type men, than as another potential path out of the wood. Of course, it was always possible that the Knight of Cups would ride his white horse up the pub stairs to the chamber where Jocasta presided over her circle.

*

At thirty-four, Miranda still believed in fairy tales. It was perhaps surprising that she still believed that being in love would bring her happiness when all the evidence to date suggested that this was the last place to be happy in. As Fiona once remarked: 'Knights on white chargers are all very well, but you still have to scrape up the poop.' Nor did Miranda see herself as a fairy-tale princess. In her un-magic mirror she saw a passable but unremarkable smallish person with straight brown hair and brown eyes in a pale face. Moreover, most of the knights in her life had been lame, and none of them had horses. The secretly lame ones were the worst, she never saw them coming – Daniel had been one of those. But still she longed for the strong, kind, clever man who would take her by the hand and unlock the hidden potential she was sure she had about her somewhere.

She knew what other women would say, the ones who ran groups and wrote articles on self-esteem. They'd tell her she must rescue herself and not expect a man to do it. Don't be so feeble, they'd say: these days Sleeping Beauties have to wake up and hack their own way out of the wood.

But when you have been a prisoner for a long, long time, you need a little help in breaking out. A long time ago Miranda had been locked in a tower by a wicked witch. She couldn't see her (though she often heard her voice) but every time she tried to step outside, the witch was waiting, disguised in some innocent human form – as a flatmate, or an employer – just waiting to pounce and turn Miranda's life upside down.

This year, though, she was armed: she had her Support Group and her meditation and allies like Fiona and Cassie. Even the current witch in her life, Daphne, was only a spasmodic presence, and somehow she would cope with her.

*

Jocasta had such obvious pretensions to witchiness that Miranda could not sense her as a real threat. The Circle itself had something of the atmosphere of a secret society – a coven, even. The participants sat round the room in a ring with Jocasta as the jewel. She occupied her throne like a presiding goddess surrounded by her acolytes; sometimes she lit incense to offset the smells of beer and cigarette smoke rising from the bar below.

Most of the group were long-term regulars; they were writing novels or poems or plays, two or three extracts of which were read and discussed every week. Sometimes Jocasta read her own poems, but her main role was to utter penetrating criticisms of her students' work and surprising pronouncements about the arts of writing and living and sex – about which she clearly knew a lot. With her long, ethnic skirts, her trailing, silky red hair and pale, heart-shaped face bare of make-up, she was not an obvious femme fatale. But she habitually left the pub with a man, by no means always the same man.

After the meeting, when they all descended to the bar, she would enact a kind of royal round of her attendants, asking intimate questions about people's private lives in her clear, little-girlish voice. 'How old are you? Do you have a lover? How many lovers have you had? Do you get cystitis?' Rumour had it that at three in the morning she would rise from her unchaste bed and fill a red notebook with the information gleaned during the evening. Writers must take notes, constantly, she commanded.

Fiona said blow that for a lark: what she really wanted was to write a Mills and Boon and earn lots of money and stop being a secretary. She had begun a romantic novel without informing Jocasta of its intended destination. Jocasta's comments about it were tough but so was Fiona, who remained uncrushed.

Miranda was less resilient. When she finally produced a story, about a lonely old lady befriending a homeless, slightly odd young man, Jocasta halted her after a page and a half.

'You're not writing from your experience,' she said. *Well, of course not*, thought Miranda, *this was supposed to be fiction*. 'And all this internal monologue holds up the flow. As for this schizophrenic character – do you know any schizophrenics?'

'Well, he wasn't meant to be exactly—'

'If you're going to write about a schizophrenic you need to follow one about with your notebook for at least three months.'

The impossibility of doing any such thing, combined with a further catalogue of criticisms, left Miranda completely downcast and she was unable to write anything for several weeks, though she obediently began filling a notebook.

Just before Christmas Fiona announced that she was considering leaving the Circle; she was fed up with Jocasta's undue interest in her students' private lives. Judy, a well-off divorcee in her mid-thirties, had invited the entire Circle to a pre-Christmas party. Shortly beforehand, Jocasta declared to Fiona that in the interests of note-taking she intended to inspect the contents of Judy's cupboards and wastepaper baskets. This, said Fiona, was carrying research too far. She and Miranda spent much of the evening tracking Jocasta to safeguard Judy's privacy.

In the end, Fiona stayed. Whatever Jocasta's personal habits, Fiona found her teaching useful, and her Mills and Boon was developing into something more in-depth. And perhaps she shared Miranda's feeling that – whether despite or because of Jocasta – there was a kind of magic about the Circle. In that upper room stories and dreams and the echoes of many different lives were offered up and woven into an ethereal tapestry that lingered in the air and in the mind.

As for sensitive, writing-type men, there were a number of eccentrics, and one or two that Miranda liked. The only one who had made any approach, however, was Julian, who was not at all Miranda's idea of the Knight of Cups. In his late thirties, thin, with a Byronic profile, a mane of dark hair, and large, grey eyes, Miranda at first found him rather daunting. The first time they met she had the odd sensation of having known him before; in fact, she found him quite hard to get to know. He carried about him an air of touch-me-not. Yet his combination of good looks, writing talent and slight remoteness gave him a kind of charisma: he clearly had hidden depths.

Julian was writing an avant-garde novel, poetic and mysterious stuff rendered the more mysterious because the extracts he read at the Circle came in no sort of order. Jocasta, who approved of experimental writing, clearly thought highly of Julian's talents. She also appeared to think highly of Julian. At Judy's party she had summoned him to dance with the unlikely cry of 'Come on, sexy-socks!' Julian had never struck Miranda as a sexy-socks. He was far too cerebral.

The first time they talked was the evening when Jocasta laid waste to Miranda's story. Earlier in the proceedings Julian had read a poem about the ghost of a child. It was flowing and lyrical and Julian read it beautifully in a dark brown velvet voice; Miranda was not surprised to learn later that he had for a time been a professional actor.

At the end of that painful evening Julian approached Miranda in the pub. 'I thought she came down on you far too heavily,' he said. 'I really liked your story – will you let me read the whole thing?'

Miranda was surprised and flattered. 'Yes, sure. Thanks. I really liked your poem.'

'Thanks. It needs more work, of course.'

He bought Miranda a beer and made to offer her a cigarette, but found he had only one left; during the ensuing conversation he smoked several of hers. He hadn't managed his budget very well that week, he explained. He was living on the dole while writing his novel; he believed that the State should support the arts. Unfortunately, this support did not stretch very far.

That was the start of a Friday evening friendship which Miranda found puzzling; they never met outside the Circle and Julian displayed no signs of wanting to. He seemed to be a loner, sufficient unto his poetic self, who enjoyed pub conversations about writing, the theatre and music – he played the piano, though he did not own one. He had no telephone, professing a deep dislike for them. Miranda was extremely surprised one evening when, after she had left the Circle early with a headache, Julian actually phoned to ask if she was all right.

That act of concern aside, their friendship was mainly built on discussions of matters spiritual and psychic. Miranda enjoyed having someone to share these topics with, though Julian often challenged her about her interest in self-development. 'Why do people want to be sorted out?' he would ask. 'It's like cutting down a forest and leaving the landscape bare. You take all the mystery away.'

Steeped in writers like Carlos Castaneda and Aldous Huxley, Julian's metaphysical interests leaned towards flights of supernatural fantasy which were echoed in his novel. At times Miranda found his approach rather trying; though he often expressed a desire for spiritual experiences, he saw no need to do anything to achieve them. Miranda pointed out that people who had ecstatic revelations usually dedicated a great deal of time to prayer and meditation, but spiritual ecstasy, it seemed, was supposed to come to Julian unaided.

'Does your meditation really do anything for you?' he once asked.

'Yes… it's very relaxing. It makes me peaceful I suppose.' She didn't think she was very good at meditation; it was supposed to put one in touch with Infinite Being, but she never quite got there.

'I don't think I want to be peaceful,' said Julian. 'I'd rather try LSD, only I don't know the right people.'

'You might meet a load of giant spiders,' said Miranda, recalling a bad trip an acquaintance had described to her. 'It's not necessarily a shortcut to God.'

'I don't know that it's God I'm looking for… why – do you believe in God?'

'Well, not an old man with a beard,' said Miranda. 'But there must be something – some creative force. Don't you think? If there is a god then he, she, it, is a sort of life force, part of all of us. So somewhere inside, I'm God, you're God.' This was the theory taught by the Guru Chakrao Fellowship, with whom Miranda had learned to meditate, and it appealed to her.

'Maybe. Actually, I feel as if I walked away from God at some point in my life. As if I had to demonstrate my independence.' Julian gave one of his small, enigmatic smiles.

Miranda's early brushes with God had been unsatisfactory. She had tried Christianity at school, hoping it might solve her permanent unhappiness. It hadn't. 'The Kingdom of God is within,' the Christians said, but when Miranda looked within, all she could see was murk. God wasn't Love, God was Guilt. When she left school she dropped God without difficulty. Now, though, she wanted to sort out what she actually did believe. At least her conversations with Julian were helping her to clarify her ideas, since everything Miranda proposed Julian liked to test, query or oppose.

Clearly, the Knight of Cups was not someone she already knew. Which meant that if Cassie was right, he was just round the corner. She wished he'd hurry up and arrive.

2

RESOLUTIONS

On New Year's Day Miranda sat at her desk reading her notes on her session with Cassie. 'Lots of changes,' Cassie had said. Well, she'd started on those. Living alone was a big change, following an increasingly acrimonious flatshare with someone she had thought was a friend. Growing plants was also new to her, but now the green spears of spring bulbs were spiking through the black January soil of her window box.

Below her notes she wrote:

Resolutions:
Find love.
Be happy.
Find God?

Hmph. These were ambitions rather than resolutions, and she wasn't even sure there was a God to find. Still, why not aim high?

Find out what I'm here for, she added.

Miranda's ground-floor flat in West Hampstead was small but bright; its large bay window overlooked a quiet, leafy street dominated at one end by a Victorian church. Here Miranda had placed her desk; although looking out could be a distraction from work, she loved the light and the trees. Another pleasant distraction was stroking the cat, Rollo – so-called because of his habit of rolling onto his back displaying a soft, tickleable white tummy; she had inherited him from the previous tenant; his change of ownership didn't seem to trouble him.

At her window Miranda typed reports, attempted short stories, and indexed books. Indexing is a curious occupation; some of Miranda's new friends were surprised to learn that it was done by human beings. She was good at it, she enjoyed organising words and ideas into logical patterns, creating order from disorder. And while the orderly part of her mind was occupied, another part could wander off and dream.

The downside of indexing, which is also its safety, is that nothing ever happens to the person doing it. Whereas, judging by their stories, the other Circle members led lives full of events – affairs, dramas, break-ups, breakdowns. Miranda was, she realised, seriously short of source material for writing. Her twenties had been an anxious blur of boring jobs and unsuccessful relationships, interspersed with black depressions. At thirty there had been the disaster of Daniel, her one attempt at real love – though afterwards she realised that she had not really loved him; rather, she had responded to what she thought was his love for her, until this revealed itself as a desire for total domination, which had finally driven her back into her solitude with all doors bolted.

Over the last year she had been venturing out again, not only with her groups but by offering her services as a freelance secretary. This had brought her into contact with Fiona and hence the Circle, and with Clive, a cheerful local property dealer who employed her on an ad hoc basis. And, less fortunately, with Daphne.

A Bristol-based market research consultant in her mid-thirties, Daphne needed her reports typed during her visits to London, and a friend of Clive's had recommended Miranda. Daphne's fingernails were long and bronze, her clothes and accessories expensive. She had a deceptively pretty round face and silky blonde hair which she wore glamorously loose or sleeked back in an efficient bun, according to which client she was meeting. She had enormous confidence, apparently limitless energy, two ex-husbands, several lovers, and multiple sclerosis.

At the end of their second day's work in the Knightsbridge hotel where she was staying, Daphne remarked, 'We seem to work well together. I don't often come across women who can work with me.'

Miranda was flattered. She should have been warned. Over the next few days it dawned on her that what Daphne meant was that she had found herself an intelligent doormat. Miranda had never worked so hard for someone so autocratic and demanding, and did not intend to repeat the experience. On their last evening, however, Daphne celebrated completing her report by buying Miranda an expensive dinner in the hotel restaurant. Following a lengthy inquisition of the waiter about the temperature of the wine and the tenderness of the steak, she remarked lightly: 'I believe in getting the best out of everything, while I can. I may not have long to live.'

Echoing Daphne's tone, Miranda responded equally lightly. 'Why – are you planning to die of overwork?'

'No. I've got MS. It's in remission at the moment, but every time I have an attack it gets worse. I'd rather die of overwork than crumble away in a wheelchair.'

Miranda was shocked, both at Daphne's frankness about her imminent demise and also because Daphne looked much healthier than Miranda felt. Daphne went on, 'MS doesn't kill you, but the complications can.'

Tentatively but truthfully, Miranda said, 'I've always thought dying must be quite nice. If you're ready to go, that is.'

Daphne said, 'Oh, I'm not frightened of dying. But I'm not planning to do it just yet.'

Daphne's illness put an end to Miranda's resolution not to work for her again; it created a sense of obligation. Over time, this turned into a feeling of entrapment, especially when Daphne began referring to their relationship as a friendship. Perhaps she truly saw Miranda as a friend because she could talk to her openly about her illness, which she tried to conceal from her clients. At the same time, by calling her a friend, Daphne obliged her to be one.

Over the next few months Daphne had employed Miranda at regular intervals, not just as typist, but as confidante, theatre-ticket-buyer and, eventually, speech-writer. She would fling Miranda some scrappy, badly spelt notes, with the command: 'Just get this into some sort of order and I'll write it up properly later.' It was a while before Miranda realised that the some sort of order she produced was Daphne's finished presentation, and even longer before Daphne admitted to being dyslexic.

Daphne's forays into London usually involved a week's intensive work during which Daphne simply took Miranda over, body and mind, leaving her totally drained of energy. Miranda consoled herself that Daphne didn't come to London that often; she paid well, and at least her life was interesting. Oh, but it was time Miranda led an interesting life! She was tired of living on the sidelines; half-sick of shadows, like the Lady of Shallot, she wanted to break the loom and leave the room and join the real world. Recently, for the first time in her life, a dance teacher had said, 'Good, Miranda!' It made up for all the excruciating school dancing classes at which she had invariably started on the wrong foot. For nearly thirty-four years she had waited to get the steps right. It was time to join the dance.

*

At her desk on New Year's Day, Miranda sucked her biro, wondering whether to go back to the Support Group, which would soon be reassembling. When she had joined it the previous summer she had been enchanted by the warmth and acceptance, and the freedom to say what she felt, to be listened to and truly heard. Now, in the cold light of January, she realised how irritating she found the jargon that accompanied all the hugs and mutual appreciation.

Just then, her attention was caught by the sound of a child crying. Across the road a youngish woman with dandelion-yellow hair was pulling along a small, howling boy, yelling at him to shut up or she would give him something to cry for. He was little, he stumbled on the curb, and the mother pulled him up sharply by the arm. Miranda winced. The child fell suddenly silent, but the woman went on shouting until he started crying again.

Miranda's heart began to thump. She wanted to run out into the street and say, 'Stop, you must stop! Can't you see what you are doing?'

Then she realised that what she really wanted was to hit the mother. Since this was not possible, she started crying herself. One thing the Support Group had taught her was that it was OK, in fact desirable, to cry when present events re-activated past memories. *That was definitely a reactivating event*, Miranda thought – damn this jargon! But it reminded her what the group was about.

She remembered the depressed elderly woman someone had brought to a Support Group open day. She couldn't cry. Her mother had forbidden her to cry, she told the group. 'She was a very kind woman,' she kept saying. 'She told me I was no good, and she was absolutely right.'

Liz, the focaliser, began explaining the group's philosophy that everyone is born good, happy, creative and loving.

The depressed woman said, 'Oh, no, they're not, dear.'

The group did their best to feed back good things about her, and she rejected them all. They told her it wasn't too late to have a happy life. She said, 'My father always told me that if you expect the worst, you'll never be disappointed.' But she was disappointed. She never came back.

Watching the mother and child disappearing round a corner, Miranda thought about disappointed lives, about the wounds inflicted on little children by parents who didn't know what they were doing, and she cried some more and hugged Rollo, and realised that she did need the group after all.

*

Two weeks into January, the Circle resumed. Miranda was looking forward to it; despite Jocasta's discouragement, she enjoyed the gatherings and the company. She arrived early at the Pig and Apple to meet Fiona for a drink. Fiona was not yet there, but several others had already arrived. The pub was furnished with high-backed church pews; in one of them she spotted Julian, deep in conversation with Fergus, a good-looking young Scot who wrote like an angel – though Jocasta regularly chided him for not being in touch with his feelings. Seeing Julian after the break, she once again experienced an odd pang of recognition, as though something within her resonated with something in him. It was elusive, however, like an escaping dream, and she let it go.

As Miranda went to the bar, two more regulars came in: Flaxman, a tall, flamboyantly eccentric man in his thirties with a tendency to long hair, boots and cloaks, and Trevor, small, intense and skull-faced, with a predilection for wearing women's clothes – which he had not as yet indulged in the Circle.

There were enough men around, Miranda thought, as she ordered a cider. Why would none of them do for her? Fergus and Flaxman were particularly beautiful to behold, but Fergus was much too young and Flaxman too weird. Julian was certainly attractive, but too remote for intimacy. She was heading towards him when Trevor nobbled her, an Ancient Mariner gleam in his deep-set eyes. 'Miranda, I have something to tell you!'

'Oh, yes?'

'I got married over Christmas!'

'Married?' This seemed extremely unlikely.

'Having been unable in thirty-six years to persuade anyone to marry me, I decided to marry myself. I put on a long red velvet dress and stood in front of the mirror and went right through the wedding service. It felt wonderful.'

'Congratulations,' said Miranda. 'I hope you'll be very happy.'

'It's utter relaxation,' said Trevor. 'Utter and complete relaxation. It's the best form of marriage there is.'

'I suppose it must be,' Miranda agreed. It sounded quite profound; perhaps she should try it. Trevor went off to tell someone else the good news, and Miranda joined Julian and Fergus, who were discussing the difficulties of getting down to writing. Fergus announced in his precise Scottish voice that his solution was to write three pages a day, no matter what. Miranda wondered why she didn't do that. Everyone seemed to have their act together except her.

Julian greeted her. 'How was your Christmas?'

'Oh, all right.' Miranda had spent Christmas as usual with her Aunt Phyllis, her Uncle Tom and her cousin James, trying not to be depressed. Christmas always revived memories of her terrible childhood Christmases, which her mother used as occasions to behave even more appallingly than usual. Conscious that her aunt was her mother's sister, Miranda always felt a little uncomfortable with these perfectly nice relatives. Their method of dealing with Christmas was to invite hordes of people round and to be extremely bright, determinedly ignoring any less cheery feelings that might be lurking underneath.

'How was yours?' she asked Julian.

'Rather depressing, actually. Parents, you know. My mother kept trying to fatten me up and my father still wants to know when I'm going to get a proper job. Honestly, they're so limited.'

After giving up acting – he had never told Miranda why, though he had hinted at a tragic love affair – Julian had had several 'proper' jobs; the last was in the small ads department of a newspaper. Boring though this sounded, Miranda thought it brave of him to throw it up in order to write. But she could understand his mother's desire to fatten him up.

'It's been difficult getting back into the novel,' Julian went on, 'but I've made a bit of headway. There's a new chapter I'd like you to look at before Jocasta sees it. Have you written anything?'

'No, I meant to, but I've been busy with work.'

'You do too many things,' he said, not for the first time. 'You must make time to write.'

'I don't know that I'm really a writer anyway.'

'But you have talent!' he said earnestly. 'You mustn't waste it.'

Fiona arrived at last, and they were shortly joined by Judy, their Christmas party hostess. Judy plumped herself down on their bench wailing, 'Oh, God, I'm so depressed!' Blonde, petite, with perfect skin and a large divorce settlement, Judy was not an obvious candidate for depression. 'Christmas makes me feel so lonely!' she sighed.

Fiona had enjoyed Christmas because her daughter had been home; now she was depressed because Franny had returned to boarding school. 'It breaks my heart every time,' she said. 'But she loves boarding. And since my ex pays for it, and it means I can work full-time, I suppose it's for the best.'

At ten to seven Jocasta swept in, one of her regular swains at her heels, and the group trooped upstairs. Miranda looked hopefully round the room, but there were no new faces, no Knight of Cups that evening. In fact, the numbers had thinned out slightly, with the loss of one or two people who were no loss – like the woman who had written a lengthy and highly personal account of her hysterectomy. Jocasta had dealt with her severely. 'This is not a therapy group,' she declared.

Oh, but wasn't it? thought Miranda. There they all sat, baring their souls, or veiling them thinly under the guise of fiction. Nakedness of soul was encouraged. 'Have you had a lesbian relationship?' Jocasta asked Judy when she read out what Miranda assumed to be a totally imaginary account of a female twosome. Judy had gone very pink, and made no reply.

How daring Jocasta was, how fearless in her criticisms of people's tender little offerings. Wasn't she afraid of being disliked? Evidently not; most people came back for more.

Miranda left that evening with the latest section of Julian's novel, which she had offered to type. She read it as soon as she got home. Beautifully laid out in Julian's elegant script, it had the usual dreamlike quality of his work. Miranda looked forward to discovering where it was all leading. Though the story was unclear his writing echoed the preoccupations Julian so often voiced – a desire for ecstasy, a frustrated spirituality, a fascination with the occult. Miranda looked forward to typing it. It would have to be after Daphne's forthcoming visit, though. Which, despite all her efforts at positive thinking, she now realised she was dreading.

*

It was not just that Daphne was demanding: she made Miranda feel small. Her psychology degree was a powerful weapon for putting others in the wrong. During one of their weeks together, Daphne had taken a break to ask Miranda about herself, and had been dismissive when Miranda mentioned the Support Group.

'These things are such a rip-off!' she declared.

'It's not expensive,' protested Miranda. 'You pay according to your means.'

'Look,' said Daphne. 'There are far too many of these untrained people running groups, exploiting people's vulnerability. I spent four years getting a degree in psychology. I do know what I'm talking about.'

'I don't feel exploited. The whole idea is that we help each other, it's mutual. Anyway, the focalisers are trained.'

'Focalisers!' Daphne snorted and rolled her eyes. 'What do you need a group for, anyway?'

Miranda hesitated. 'Well… I've never had a lot of confidence.'

'Oh? Why, do you suppose?'

'Oh, my mother was very hard to please,' Miranda said with a small laugh. She hoped Daphne would leave it at that. But under relentless cross-questioning she found herself speaking of the childhood she did not care to remember: her mother's constant anger, her father's absences and early death.

There were times as a child when Miranda wondered whether her father had actually existed. Perhaps she had dreamed him. She couldn't remember his face. A few small, smudgy black-and-white snapshots showed hazy features, often shadowed by a hat. He could have been anybody. She was eight when the news of his death arrived. A civil engineer working at the time in Canada, he had been killed in an accident. Miranda's mother clearly expected her to have no feelings about it; obediently, Miranda had none. For her part, Mrs Fleming reacted as though he had died on purpose to annoy her. In fact, accident compensation and a good pension left her well provided for, with an interesting role to play: widow, victim and martyr, burdened with a difficult daughter. ('Do stop sulking, Miranda, nobody likes sulky little girls! Smile, for God's sake!')

'It's difficult to feel self-confident when you've been criticised all your life,' Miranda now summed up.

'Still, at least she didn't hit you!' said Daphne.

Miranda stared at her. 'Of course she did.'

'Oh. I'm sorry.' Daphne pushed her round spectacles on top of her glossy head. Miranda could almost see her psychologist's notepad. 'All that must have affected your relationships,' she commented. 'How's your love life been?'

'Messy, mostly.' Why was she letting Daphne interrogate her?

'It's not surprising you attract bullies,' commented Daphne after dragging from her the story of Daniel. *And not just men,* thought Miranda, deciding that this really was the last time she would work for Daphne.

'I must say, it all sounds extremely damaging,' Daphne summarised. Miranda instantly felt extremely damaged. 'If you ask me, these encounter groups are thoroughly dangerous, rootling around in people's psyches and stirring up emotional pain.'

Since Daphne herself had been rootling around in her psyche for the last twenty minutes, Miranda responded with some heat. 'It's not an encounter group, it's about getting rid of pain, not stirring it up! You feel better at the end of a group.' Instead of perfectly ghastly, which was what she was feeling now.

'Oh,' said Daphne. 'That's interesting. Well, back to the grindstone, I suppose.'

But she had breached Miranda's defences. That night she woke with a thumping heart from a dream in which she was still living with her mother. This dream had recurred with slight variations ever since she removed herself from her mother's orbit many years ago, and it always culminated in a row. The best variation had been immediately after she started meditating: on that occasion the row ended with Miranda chasing her mother out of the house, throwing after her a book on Buddhism. But now, here they were again, sharing a tiny claustrophobic flat and engaged in actual physical combat.

At one of the lectures run by the Guru Chakrao Fellowship, Miranda had learned that a common effect of meditating was to trigger the kinds of situation that had not been fully dealt with in the past, thus speeding up the process of karma. The beneficial energy of Guru Chakrao would help meditators to work through their karmic debts quickly and easily, thereby achieving fulfilment and happiness. Daphne was an undealt-with situation with a vengeance, and showed no signs of being worked through quickly or easily. Still, according to Warren, the Australian lecturer, every difficulty in life had an underlying spiritual purpose. Miranda looked forward to discovering the spiritual purpose of Daphne.

3

CREATIVE BLOCK

At the end of January Daphne swung into London on crutches; shortly before Christmas she had suffered a serious attack affecting her lower half. She had decided that rather than a hotel it would be easier for her to stay at a friend's flat in the northernmost peaks of North London, which entailed a complex journey for Miranda. From here Daphne sallied forth by taxi to her various appointments, managing to make even crutches look stylish.

On their first morning, Miranda's spirits lifted when Daphne proclaimed herself a reformed character. 'It was a really scary attack, I can't tell you! When I was in hospital, the psychiatrist came to see me. He really laid into me about how hard I work. He said, "I'd hate to come home to you", and that really hit me hard. I don't want to be the sort of person people can only take in small doses.'

What a splendid psychiatrist, thought Miranda. She had further cause for optimism over lunch, when Daphne remarked, 'I was thinking about what you said about your Support Group – about encouraging people to say something appreciative every day. I've been trying it with my home help, it works!'

Daphne now dutifully made appreciative comments to Miranda at the end of every day. She needed them: it was a tough week. With no hotel service on tap, Miranda was expected to produce lunch and sometimes supper on top of her day's work, and to pop out at intervals to the cleaner's, the chemist's, the grocer's, the post office. Since Daphne never managed to produce a comprehensive shopping list, this involved many poppings.

Work crept later and later into the evenings. Margery, who owned the flat, often arrived home before Miranda left, looking no more pleased about Daphne's presence than Miranda felt. Miranda began suffering from a grumbling, insidious ache in her front teeth, whether from genuine tooth trouble or as a psychosomatic reaction to Daphne, she couldn't be sure. Both teeth were root-filled, surely they shouldn't be hurting?

Their days together were considerably lengthened by Daphne's frequent pauses to talk – about her illness, about Miranda's lack of love life (clearly Miranda's own fault) and about her own love life which remained unaffected by her disabled state. 'Fortunately, I still have one orifice in full working order!' she remarked on the first day. She currently had a lover in London and another in Bristol. Miranda suspected that the Bristol lover was married.

On Thursday, when Miranda said tentatively that she would like to get away early next day for her Writers' Circle, it was the original, unreformed Daphne who said, 'Oh Miranda, not another group! For heaven's sake! These amateur writing groups are so self-indulgent! And, surely, your forte is editing other people's writing, not original stuff.'

'Well, you may be right, but I happen to enjoy it,' Miranda said quite tartly.

'Goodness, Miranda, you can be so brusque at times. I had hoped you could finish typing the report on Friday.' Daphne sighed. With an inner groan, Miranda reconciled herself to forgoing the Circle.

The reason for Daphne's own brusqueness became clear over a salad lunch at the kitchen table. The previous night's outing with her London lover had not gone well. In the restaurant they had bumped into a colleague of his, and his embarrassment at being seen with a girlfriend on crutches had been only too evident. And although he had helped her to bed on their return, he had not stayed to share it.

'Fortunately,' Daphne told Miranda, smoothing back her already smooth hair, 'I don't depend on him for my sexual identity.'

Miranda could have felt sorry for her, but knew it was not pity she wanted.

'Have you ever thought about having healing?' she asked.

Daphne said, 'Actually, I did go to a healer once. When my first marriage was breaking up I got ill – I think now it was the first MS attack, but it wasn't diagnosed at the time. I went to see this chap in Bath, but I never went back. He scared me, actually. I didn't tell him anything about myself, and just as I was leaving, he said, "You should be looking at your marriage!" Spooky.'

'The thing is,' said Miranda, 'it's just that I know this very nice woman healer, she might be able to help.'

'MS isn't curable,' said Daphne.

'Maybe not, but healing can make you feel better, it can relieve pain. And you'd like Cassie, she's a character!'

'I'll think about it.'

That Saturday night, having finally waved Daphne off, Miranda flopped into bed wondering whether it was Daphne's doing that after a week with her she felt like a non-person, or whether she actually was a non-person and Daphne simply brought that out? Cuddling Rollo for comfort, she experienced a sharp pain in her front teeth; she really must see her dentist.

*

'Where were you last week?' demanded Julian, as they took their usual corner in the pub after the Circle. Miranda explained that she had been a prisoner to Daphne. 'You shouldn't let people exploit you,' said Julian.

'I can't afford to turn work down,' said Miranda. 'Anyway, Daphne relies on me. And it's not that often. How was last Friday?'

'It was good. Jocasta was quite benign, actually, letting people read at length for once. She asked me where you were,' he added crossly. 'I said, "How should I know?"'

Miranda digested this. Fiona had mentioned that some Circle members thought Julian was her boyfriend; perhaps Jocasta did, too. Julian evidently found the idea distasteful. To cover her embarrassment, Miranda fished in her shoulder bag. 'I did find time to type your chapter.'

She had stayed up late to do it. Since Daphne's departure she had had to catch up with her other work, juggling her hours between some last-minute typing for Clive and a complicated index on Irish history.

'Oh, thanks. What did you think of it?'

'It's beautifully written,' Miranda said. 'Very atmospheric.'

'I don't know,' said Julian. 'I feel very unsure about it, sometimes.'

Julian often expressed a gloom about his life and his writing which Miranda suspected to be partly a pose. She sometimes felt he had been born into the wrong age: he would probably have been happier being unhappy as the kind of Romantic poet he physically resembled.

'It's very original,' she encouraged him. 'Jocasta likes it a lot.'

'She seems to... she's invited me to her place to discuss it in depth,' he said. 'I'm not sure I'll go, though. I don't really trust her.'

'You can trust her literary judgment, I'd have thought.'

'I meant more... personal stuff. She does probe people. I mean, all that about writer's block this evening – when did she last write anything? But she thinks it's OK to have a go at other people.'

During the evening, Flaxman had announced that he was quite unable to write. Jocasta responded: 'A block in writing means a block in life. In what area is your life blocked, Flaxman?'

With some dignity, Flaxman replied, 'I think that is a private matter.'

Jocasta had backed down – temporarily. Miranda could see her now over Julian's shoulder speaking intensely to Flaxman, who was shifting uneasily from one long leg to the other.

'Have you written anything new?' Julian now asked.

'I've been too busy.'

'You do too much. You ought to drop some of this self-improvement stuff, I'm sure it interferes with your creativity.'

Miranda said, 'I've been busy with Daphne!'

Ignoring this, Julian continued: 'Creative people need their hang-ups. You don't want to end up boringly normal.'

'I didn't think I had any creativity till I started on the self-improvement stuff,' Miranda responded. 'Anyway, I'd rather be normal than unhappy.'

'You always seem happy to me,' Julian said, adding, 'That's one of the things I like about you.'

Startled at this unusual declaration, Miranda said, 'But I used not to be. Anyway, the stuff we do in the Support Group is supposed to make you more creative, not less. It helps you change the way you see things. It's all about changing your beliefs really.'

Changing your beliefs was also an ongoing theme of Warren's monthly talks to the Guru Chakrao Fellowship.

'Thoughts and beliefs,' Warren had expounded at the last meeting, 'are forms of energy which attract events: negative beliefs attract unpleasant events, and vice versa. For example, if you believe you are unlovable, life will play this belief back to you, and you will not be loved. But empty your mind and heart of that belief, and you will become a valley for love to flow into.'

It was an uplifting idea. Did she really believe she was unlovable? Was that why she was still alone? She was probably quite loveable, Miranda decided, it was just that no one had noticed it.

'Changing your beliefs?' queried Julian now. 'That sounds like brainwashing to me.'

'No, no!' exclaimed Miranda. 'The idea is that you've been brainwashed by all the put-downs you've had through life. So, for example, you're only allowed to say positive things about yourself and other people.'

'That sounds terribly artificial to me.'

'Actually, it's quite liberating. And it's no more artificial than believing you're no good because that's what you've been told all your life by your parents and teachers and people.'

'Is that what happened to you?' he asked.

They rarely discussed their backgrounds. She hesitated. 'It seems to happen to most people, one way or another! My mother was a bit, well, very critical, and my father died when I was eight. I don't really remember him.' After her grilling by Daphne, she had no wish to go into detail.

'Poor Miranda, that's sad. My father was away in the war, when I was small,' said Julian. 'But he came back.' He lit a cigarette.

Miranda concluded: 'Anyway, my mother's not in my life now. She ran off with a married man, a Frenchman, they live in the south of France. I haven't seen her for years.'

'My mother has always been kind,' said Julian. 'A bit too kind, at times. My father used to be rather fierce. But I had a happy childhood, really.' This statement seemed at odds with the dark tone of Julian's writing. He went on, 'My grandmother was lovely to me, we had a very strong bond. She's dead now, but sometimes I think she's still keeping an eye on me.'

'My grandparents were nice,' said Miranda. 'I used to spend my summer holidays with them.'

Her late grandparents had been a gentle couple; in their red-brick Victorian house in Twickenham she knew peace. How this quiet pair had managed to produce her loud, hysterical mother was a mystery to her. Their daughters had been mainly brought up by a series of governesses; at the age of three Miranda's mother had severely bitten one, according to Aunt Phyllis.

It was at her grandparents' house that Miranda first entered the world of fairy tales. Up two flights of stairs was the attic floor which in pre-war days had contained the maids' bedrooms. In one of these were stored shelves of children's books that had belonged to her mother and aunt: old *Tiger Tim* annuals, novels like *The Secret Garden* and *The Little Princess* with their awkward heroines who somehow won through. And there were fairy tales galore – *The Blue Fairy Book*, *The Green Fairy Book*, and a collection of Grimm with dark, scary illustrations. As soon as she arrived, Miranda would race up to the attic to luxuriate in these other worlds. She had been happy there.

She was about to return to the theme of changing one's beliefs when Jocasta passed by on her way out. 'What are you two so deep in discussion about?' she asked.

Julian said, 'We were discussing whether we'd rather be happy or creative.'

Jocasta said, 'Oh, I'd rather be happy any day.' At the door she turned, assumed a sweet smile and said, 'Well, goodnight, lovebirds!'

Julian went very pink and Miranda felt a stab of irritation. 'Julian is not my lovebird!' she snapped. 'I'm sorry,' she said to Julian as the pub door swung closed. 'That really annoyed me.'

'Me too,' said Julian. 'You see what I mean? She has to interfere.'

But Jocasta had flung Miranda an invisible dart. On the bus home, she found herself wondering what Julian would be like in bed. Rather bony, she decided. As for Jocasta, she had never struck her as a seeker after happiness, unless she was confusing happiness with power.

*

Power was the theme of the Support Group that term, and Miranda was not comfortable with it. The new group was very unlike the one she had attended last summer, run by Liz, a comfortably built woman with a motherly approach. Liz's small house in Richmond had been a safe haven in which people could release the less cosy emotions that most of them had been sitting on for years, through self-revelation, psychodrama, One-to-One counselling, many tears and much hugging and mutual appreciation. It was at that group that Miranda had encountered at least two other contenders for the title of ugliest baby ever born.

Now Liz was in India, and this term's group met in a dusty community centre in Camden Town. Al, the new focaliser, was a fresh-faced young American who opened the first evening with the enthusiastic announcement that this semester they were going to do some really exciting, in-depth work on power.

Miranda's stomach immediately knotted up. Liz had often talked about self-empowerment but, enunciated in Al's earnest Californian tones, the word 'power' acquired an oddly scary ring. He continued: 'I am here to offer this group my total commitment. And what I want from each and every one of you is your commitment to find your personal power. I want this to be a really powerful group.'

Miranda quailed. She was glad to see some familiar faces, including that of Rosa, a small, lively, Jewish girl who had a quality of listening which enabled Miranda to be completely open with her. When it was time for everyone to pair off for ten-minute One-to-One sessions, it was Rosa whom Miranda grabbed.

'I don't want power!' she began. 'And I don't want people telling me what I ought to be and feel!'

'What do you want?' asked Rosa.

Miranda closed her eyes to sense what she really wanted. 'I don't know… it's as if – there's something in me that feels trapped.' She felt slightly light-headed. It was odd how these One-to-Ones opened up secret areas of oneself. 'I want to get out. Yes, that's what I want, I want to get out.'

'Keep repeating that,' instructed Rosa.

Miranda repeated hesitantly, 'I want to get out, I want to get out.' Something was stirring inside her, a sense of energy, moving, uncoiling. 'There's something in here that wants to get out, but I'm afraid of letting it out.'

'What would happen if you let it out?'

Miranda tried to imagine. Suddenly, the energy inside her seemed huge, a tidal wave. 'God, I feel like a pressure cooker about to explode!'

'You're allowed to explode,' said Rosa. 'That's what the group's for.'

'No, no, I can't. There'd be pieces of me everywhere, there'd be an awful mess.'

'You can let the pressure out without falling to pieces,' said Rosa.

'Maybe I'll do it later.'

'You'll do it when you're ready,' said Rosa.

Back home afterwards, Miranda could still feel the energy simmering inside her and wondered whether she would be able to sleep. But sleep came quickly, and with it a vivid dream. She and her mother were living in a country house, and Miranda was shouting at her mother that she must go, they must not live together anymore! She went outside into a huge garden where Rosa opened a gate which sent a flood of water rushing downhill, filling a large pool. Miranda yelled to the people in the garden to get out of the way or they would drown. Then she saw that some of them were already in the expanding pool, swimming and splashing and laughing, and she longed to join them in the rushing, tumbling flood.

*

Spring came early, a particularly beautiful spring. The trees outside Miranda's window shone with a luminous green that she found astonishing, as though she had never seen spring leaves before. The bulbs in her window-box suddenly became miniature daffodils standing to attention. Rollo sat on the windowsill yattering at the nesting blackbirds; fortunately his portliness precluded any hope of attaining his predatory ambitions.

As spring progressed Miranda indexed and typed; she meditated, she went to her groups and lectures – but nothing eventful happened. She wrote a story about a suicidal woman which Jocasta criticised with her usual asperity but which prompted from Flaxman the comment: 'You have a very odd mind, Miranda.' Coming from Flaxman this was a kind of compliment.

She took her hurting teeth to a dentist who referred her to a dental hospital, where she had to make many visits learning to floss properly before they would treat her. What with these visits and her work and the Support Group and the Circle, she was busy enough. But still nothing happened, nothing to really change things, and still the pressure cooker bubbled inside her, and sometimes after the Support Group or meditating she could sense energy rising within her, darting through her system like a shoal of tiny electric fish. And still she did not know how to let it out.

She dreamed she found her wardrobe full of her mother's clothes, and threw them out of the window. She dreamed she was moving and had to rearrange all her furniture. She dreamed she was walking down a long, dark corridor, and at the end there was a man she did not know, who reached out and held her gently to him.

She consulted *I Ching*, which told her: *It is not well to strive upward, it is well to remain below. The bird meets with misfortune through flying.*

But she wanted to fly – oh, how she wanted to fly.

4

ENCOUNTERS

Over Easter there was a break in Miranda's groups and classes, and the index she was working on was both complex and boring. When, oh when, was something exciting going to happen, where were all the good things Cassie had forecast? She was nowhere nearer discovering her purpose; on the contrary, her life seemed to have come to a halt. So she was not only surprised but quite pleased when Julian telephoned to invite her to lunch on the Sunday after Easter.

By bedsitter standards, Julian's wasn't bad. It was light and airy with a view of treetops, but curiously bare and impersonal. The chief sign of Julian's habitation was the desk strewn with papers covered in his black handwriting, in the midst of which sat an overflowing ashtray. Julian's own appearance shocked Miranda: in the two weeks since she had last seen him he had grown even thinner; he looked quite fragile in fact. 'You've lost weight!' she exclaimed.

'Oh, please don't you start! My mother spent the whole of Easter telling me to eat, and my father kept on about me being on the dole. They don't understand. I've got to get the novel finished.'

'How's it going?'

'Terribly slowly...' He uttered a deep sigh.

'I've brought the book I said I'd lend you.' It was a book about reincarnation, a subject that fascinated them both.

'Oh, thanks, it looks interesting.' As he took it Miranda observed that his hands were trembling and the cuff of his sweater was unravelling.

'Would you like some white wine?' he asked. 'It's only plonk, I'm afraid. The dole doesn't run to fine wines.'

Despite the exigencies of the dole, he had cooked a rather good, if eye-wateringly hot, prawn curry. During its consumption, Julian launched into a peroration about his parents, who had recently retired. He was hazy about what they had retired from – Miranda had somehow gleaned the impression that they had owned a newsagent's and that Julian was ashamed of the fact.

'They're not old,' he said. 'They could be doing something with their retirement, but they just spend their time watching television. They don't have any interests. It's such a waste of their lives.'

It flashed through Miranda's mind that what was really bothering Julian was the sense that he was wasting his own life. As lunch progressed, it dawned on her that he was seriously depressed; over mugs of Nescafé, he admitted as much. 'I just don't know where I'm going anymore. I only know I've got to finish the novel, but God knows if it will ever get published.'

'Oh, I'm sure it will. Jocasta thinks so, doesn't she? Did you go and see her about it?'

'Yes, she went over quite a lot of it with me. But I didn't agree with everything she said. Anyway, I don't know if she knows anything about publishing.'

Miranda said, 'It must get lonely, writing on your own all day.'

'It can do. There's the Circle, and I do see friends – Fergus lives quite near, we sometimes meet for a drink – but… maybe I have too much time to think. I start thinking about my life and it seems to be going nowhere.' He flashed her a small smile. 'And don't tell me to think positive.'

'I wasn't going to,' said Miranda, who had been about to suggest something of the sort.

He heaved a heavy sigh. 'I don't know why I'm such a mess, I didn't have a traumatic childhood. Maybe I should be analysed or something. But I can't afford that.'

Miranda said cautiously, 'You could try One-to-One counselling. It does help.'

'That's what you do in your Support Group, isn't it? Isn't that the same as analysis?'

'Not a bit. For one thing, you take it in turns to listen to each other, so there's no expert sitting there judging you. And it's absolutely not about analysing, it's about getting stuff out of your system. Emotional Release, they call it – ER for short. There's rather a lot of jargon, I'm afraid. We could try it, if you like.'

'I've got to do something!' said Julian. 'Well, OK, then.' The alacrity with which he agreed made Miranda wonder if this had been the real purpose of his invitation.

'All right, let's give it a go. Just a short session, to see how you get on.'

Miranda outlined the principles of One-to-Ones, explaining that if Julian wanted to laugh or cry that was perfectly OK, since these were forms of ER. Julian looked anxious. 'Or you can just talk,' said Miranda quickly.

One-to-One counselling involved sitting opposite each other, holding hands and maintaining eye contact. As they arranged themselves on two upright wooden chairs, Miranda realised that she and Julian had never actually touched before.

'Right,' she said, taking his hands. 'You start by telling me something good in your life.'

Julian thought long and hard. Finally he came up with, 'Well, you're here.'

That was nice. 'Good. Now tell me what's bothering you.'

Julian had no trouble telling Miranda what was bothering him, at length and much as before. He was a failure, he was nearly forty and his life was going nowhere, and he couldn't see the novel ever getting published. Emotional Release, however, was not immediately forthcoming.

'I'm no good at this,' Julian said, after ten minutes of critical self-analysis. 'I can't let go.'

'Try contradicting that,' said Miranda. This usually worked when people were stuck. 'Say the opposite.'

'I can let go?' he said tentatively. 'I can let go... no I can't!'

'You're doing fine. Try it again.'

'I can let go, I can let go, I can let go...'

He was beginning to sound more convinced. 'I can let go! Oh, this feels odd. I can let go! Oh, I can see what you're talking about, now. I can let go... goodness, this is weird!' He began to laugh.

By the end of his session, Julian was quite flushed. 'I do feel better, actually,' he admitted.

Miranda felt a sense of accomplishment. 'You see, it does work! Now it's your turn to listen to me.'

Julian's worried look returned.

'It's all right, all you have to do is listen. The key is to give me your full attention.'

They took hands once more. *Better keep it light*, thought Miranda, *Julian might not be able to cope with too much emotion.* Her positive opening statement was that she had enjoyed Julian's curry; then she turned to her problems with

Daphne. As she spoke, she mentally gave Julian full credit for attentive listening; during their pub chats he would have been incapable of not interrupting.

Meanwhile, her hands in Julian's, his large, dark eyes fixed on hers, Miranda's own attention was wandering. She had always thought his eyes his best feature: now she saw that they were not grey but hazel, the irises rimmed with black. She began to feel almost hypnotised, sucked in by Julian's earnest gaze.

She was also, she suddenly realised, becoming distinctly stirred. She didn't want to go on talking, she wanted to fling herself at Julian. This was embarrassing. It never happened during One-to-Ones with the men in the Support Group. Moreover, she sensed that Julian too, was stirred. She struggled on lamely talking about Daphne, hypnotised by Julian's steady gaze. By the end of ten minutes the atmosphere between them was electric.

They released each other's hands. Miranda thanked Julian for being a good listener. Julian said he'd like to try it again sometime. Neither of them referred to the almost tangible current now flowing between them, and when Miranda said she had better be going, Julian made no attempt to stop her.

She arrived home in a state of confusion. She had never felt a moment's lust for Julian before, what had come over her? She wished she was one of those women like Jocasta who could leap happily into bed with anyone she fancied, without all the complications that followed such events in her own life. But Julian wasn't the leaping type; he was in fact much more vulnerable than she had realised. What she had taken for self-sufficiency was a screen for massive self-doubt. As well as wanting to bed him, she wanted to put comforting arms round him and make him feel better.

'Damn, damn, damn!' she said to Rollo, flinging her jacket on the sofa. He looked up, startled, from a half-washed paw.

'It's all right for you,' she said. 'You're well out of it.'

Whereas she was a sex-starved woman approaching thirty-five, fancying a little boy lost of nearly forty. 'Damn, damn, damn, damn, damn!'

Rollo returned to a close scrutiny of the areas between his toes.

*

Miranda arrived at the next Circle evening at the last minute, to avoid the possible embarrassment of sitting near Julian. Jocasta devoted the first hour to outlining her plans for producing an anthology of her students' best writing. Several short story and poetry magazines were circulating at the time, usually self-published; Jocasta thought the Circle's work quite good enough to be saleable. Contributions must be in by August, and volunteers were needed to form an editorial committee. Across the room Miranda glanced at Julian's pale face; his eyes were firmly fixed on Jocasta.

In the bar afterwards Jocasta came up to Miranda and said amiably, 'I do hope you'll write something for the anthology – an article, maybe? Julian says you're interested in fringy things. Maybe you could write something on – I don't know – alternative medicine?'

Miranda's annoyance at learning that Julian had been talking about her to Jocasta was mingled with pleasure that Jocasta actually wanted her to write something. 'I'll think about it,' she said.

'Good, you do that.' Jocasta rubbed a hand over her creamy forehead. 'I picked the wrong evening for this meeting. Do you ever feel awful?'

Miranda was puzzled. 'Depressed, do you mean?'

'I'm never depressed,' said Jocasta. 'But I get very tired sometimes, I have so many demands to meet. Do you know anything about homeopathy – is it any good for cystitis, d'you know? Maybe you could write something about homeopathy? Anyway, how is your writing? You haven't brought anything in for a while.'

'Well, no. I've rather lost confidence.' Miranda didn't dare say that her loss of confidence was largely Jocasta's doing.

'But you must keep going!' Jocasta trilled. 'You have a voice, and you have a lot of perception. You must keep taking notes, lots and lots of notes.'

'Oh, yes, I am taking notes,' said Miranda.

'Anyway,' Jocasta drew herself together in a gesture indicating that the audience was over, 'I look forward to an article from you soon. About a thousand words.'

Praise from Jocasta was a novelty. Perhaps she didn't realise how harsh she could be. Living at top speed, she never had time to pause and let people in.

Fiona hailed her. 'Hi – how was your lunch with Julian?'

Over Fiona's shoulder Miranda could see Julian talking earnestly with Fergus. In the next alcove sat Flaxman, deeply and apparently none-too-happily engaged with Sharon, a recent recruit to the Circle. A friend of Jocasta's, she was a plump, motherly woman; as a pair she and Flaxman looked peculiarly ill-assorted.

To Fiona she replied, 'He's awfully depressed, actually, he got me to do a counselling session with him.'

'Oh.' Fiona sounded disappointed. 'Counselling? I have been wondering about you two; I thought you might have something going. I mean, he's attractive and intelligent, and he seems to like you.'

'You think he's attractive?'

'Well, yes – don't you? He has a sort of feline allure, don't you think? Those Byronic good looks. And that lovely public school voice.'

'Grammar school, actually.'

'Really? Anyway, you two always seem very pally.'

'I think he just needs someone to listen to his problems.' Behind Fiona, Julian seemed to be avoiding her eye as intently as she was avoiding his.

'I don't know.' Fiona looked around the crowded bar. 'This place is seething with testosterone – but where does one find a decent man?'

To which Miranda had no answer.

*

A week later Miranda was prevented from going to the Circle by a last-minute visitation from Daphne, accompanied this time by a wheelchair as well as crutches. Once again, she was staying with Margery. Miranda already had a heavy workload; even Clive was making more demands on her than usual. But Daphne had told her on the phone that her illness was taking it out of her: this was not the moment to let her down. Miranda tried to get an appointment for her with Cassie, but Cassie was away at a psychic fair.

It was a horrible week: Daphne was at her most abrupt and autocratic. She barked commands at Miranda: 'I want this typed this evening. I'd like you here at nine tomorrow.' She would come out with an idea, rephrase it, and flap her hands about saying, 'What's the word I want – you know what I mean,' and then complain, on reading Miranda's typescript, that that was not what she'd meant at all.

Miranda told herself Daphne was stressed, in constant discomfort, frustrated by a body that refused to function, and she was dashing round London doing group interviews and meeting clients, having to be helped up and down steps. On several days she returned exhausted to the Finchley flat at five in the evening to start dictating to Miranda. How could Miranda complain of fatigue? Daphne was genuinely suffering, confronting much greater challenges than any she had to face. All the same, grumbled a small inner voice, just how far was one supposed to make allowances?

Perhaps that was Daphne's spiritual purpose – to provide Miranda with the opportunity to give without counting the cost. But she did count the cost; her price was a barrowload of resentment.

Back in the haven of her flat, she stomped round fiercely, Emotionally Releasing her pent-up frustration by yelling at the absent Daphne. Rollo hid under a chair. Miranda was almost as angry with herself as with Daphne. It was all very well enacting psychodramas at the Support Group and ranting at some poor person standing in for Daphne. Faced with the actual Daphne, she just couldn't do it.

*

It was almost June. Nearly half the year had passed and Miranda seemed to have achieved nothing. She tried making a list of goals, as recommended by the Support Group: they were much as before. She wanted to be happy, to be a better person, to make a bit more money. And underneath all that she wanted – so badly that she could hardly bear to write it down – she wanted to love and be loved.

'Perhaps I should do a Jocasta,' she said to Fiona in the Pig and Apple. 'Just seduce all and sundry and to hell with it.'

'Don't you dare!' said Fiona. 'That wouldn't be you at all. Actually, I'm fed up with hearing about Jocasta's little conquests – last week she insisted on telling me all about them, all sort of little-girlish and giggly. Apparently her live-in lover walked out last year and she's celebrating her new-found freedom by collecting as many scalps as possible. I honestly wouldn't emulate her, somebody would be bound to get hurt and it would most likely be you.'

'Did I miss much last week – apart from Jocasta's conquests?'

'Actually, no. Everyone was being very silly and childish. Fergus arrived in a top hat which he kept on throughout, and Flaxman was being more than usually pretentious.'

'I rather like Flaxman,' said Miranda.

Walking on Hampstead Heath last weekend she had bumped into Flaxman on his way to visit Sharon. 'She must be very sad,' he said in his lilting voice, with its hint of West Country. 'She's written to me saying she doesn't want to see me anymore and I've no idea what I'm supposed to have done. So I'm going to see her to try to clear things up.'

What on earth could he have been up to? 'I didn't know you were together,' she said.

Flaxman shrugged. 'Jocasta thought we'd get on. I fear she was mistaken.'

Watching him stride away, cloak swinging from his broad shoulders, she thought, *goodness but he's gorgeous… stop it, Miranda!* The Knight of Cups had better turn up soon before she made a complete fool of herself and accidentally jumped on someone totally unsuitable.

As for Julian, they had met for another One-to-One session during which he continued to be obsessively self-analytical and Miranda determinedly ignored the annoying twinge in her loins. She was now sure that she had imagined that any attraction between them was mutual. At least

Julian admitted to having got something out of the session. Miranda wished she were better able to help him.

*

'This evening,' announced Al, 'we are going to work on Reclaiming Your Power.'

Al took his role as Support Group focaliser very, very seriously, and he regularly brought up the subject of power. Some members of the group shared his enthusiasm, particularly a Marxist couple who kept trying to turn unjudgmental listening sessions into political debates. Miranda wondered whether Al actually approved of this, or was simply not powerful enough to stop them. She hated these discussions; in her opinion politics divided people, whereas the Support Group was supposed to unify them. But she was beginning to realise that there was a catch-22 in the Support Group ethos: if you didn't like what was going on, it was not the group's fault: it simply proved that you needed to do more work on yourself.

On this occasion she found the courage to respond, 'But I don't want power.'

Al beamed at her encouragingly, and said, 'What does power mean to you Miranda?'

'It's that great Monty Python foot coming down out of the sky,' she said. Power was Daphne, power was her mother, power was Jocasta pulling everyone's work to pieces.

Al said, 'I hear you, Miranda. But that's the abuse of power. Power to me means – like children, you know!' He waved his arms around in a bouncy sort of way, the wings of his cheesecloth shirt flapping round his wrists. 'Children are oppressed, you'd agree? We've all been oppressed as children by people who were bigger and stronger than us and abused that power. That's why it's important now to re-empower ourselves.'

He turned back to the group and asked each member to say what they thought power was. Miranda was relieved to learn that some people found it just as scary as she did. When they had all done, one of the older women looked at Miranda earnestly and said, 'Thank you for bringing that up, Miranda. You are a very powerful woman!'

Miranda, not feeling in the least powerful, burst into tears, and the whole group hugged her.

On her return home, the phone was ringing. It was Daphne, a new Daphne, small-voiced and chastened. 'I've rung to apologise for being so shitty the other week,' she said without preamble. 'Actually, I was a bit out of my depth with the client.' It emerged that the information she had so exhaustively acquired and Miranda so painstakingly written up was not what the client had actually asked for. 'I'm very annoyed with myself. I should have listened better at the briefing.'

'I suppose it's a useful learning experience,' said Miranda trying to be positive, while fearing she sounded like Al. Daphne, however, took it well.

'That's true, I suppose. Sometimes I need to be brought down a bit, I do know that. And I've rung you because I knew you wouldn't give me any bullshit about it all being quite all right really.'

Was that really how Daphne saw her? A no-bullshit person? Perhaps she was stronger than she had thought. After ringing off, Miranda picked up Rollo and swung him in her arms as she danced round the room, chanting, 'I am a powerful woman!'

PART 2

SUMMER: FLOWERING

1

JULIAN HAS
A LITTLE PROBLEM

At the beginning of June there was a particularly strange evening at the Circle. Fergus read a story into which he had incorporated a love scene in a wood, lifted straight from Julian's novel. In Fergus's version the lovers were being watched by a peeping Tom, who was being watched by a policeman, who was being watched by Julian. It was original and witty; Jocasta bestowed on Fergus unusually high praise, and suggested that everyone should try writing each other's stories.

Halfway through the evening Flaxman walked out without a word, disappearing for longer than it normally takes to go to the loo. Afterwards in the bar he was talking very loudly. He marched up to Jocasta and said, 'I like making love with words.' Then he turned to Miranda and announced, 'I've been to psychiatrists, you know, and they all told me I was mad. But I've got a lovely psychiatrist now, he gives me lovely drugs.'

'Oh, good,' said Miranda, definitively crossing Flaxman off her list of potential Knights.

'Sharon won't see me anymore,' he went on. 'Jocasta says she's suicidal.'

Jocasta, standing nearby, swung round. 'Don't tell her I said that!'

As Flaxman teetered off, Jocasta remarked to Miranda, 'I don't mind people taking drugs but I wish they wouldn't do it here. Sharon is actually being completely paranoid, she says she doesn't want anything more to do with me or Flaxman or the Circle. But please, if you see her, you absolutely mustn't say I was talking about her.'

'I'm not likely to see Sharon,' said Miranda, wondering why Jocasta was repeating things she didn't want repeated. Whereupon Jocasta began repeating something applicable to Miranda herself. She prefaced this by gripping Miranda's upper arm with an unexpectedly cold hand. 'Look, I've been wanting to talk to you. Let's find a corner.'

They found a corner. Miranda seated herself with a sense of foreboding.

'It's about Julian,' said Jocasta. 'Now, listen, I don't want to manipulate you. The thing is, he's been confiding in me. He really feels very strongly attracted to you. He hasn't said anything because he's scared of rejection. But he really is suffering.'

'Oh.' Miranda was stunned, both by this information and by the fact that Julian had chosen to confide in Jocasta, of all people.

'I'm not manipulating you, honestly. But he's so unhappy, I do think it's up to you to make it clear where you stand.'

During their One-to-One Miranda had mentioned that she hated being manipulated; she really must remind Julian that One-to-Ones were supposed to be confidential.

'The thing is,' Jocasta went on, 'even if you don't want a full-scale affair, you two could have a jolly good friendship.'

'I thought we had a perfectly good friendship.'

'But he's so attracted to you, it's in the way.'

Miranda said, 'I had no idea.'

Jocasta was wearing a scarlet, Indian cotton dress with a deep V-neck through which two small but bouncy breasts were peeking at Miranda; between them hung a heavy bronze-looking pendant. Miranda had seen it before at a distance. Now she found her gaze almost magnetically drawn to it. It consisted of a five-pointed star within a circle with a zigzag line running diagonally across it, and in the centre a blood-red gem. Miranda couldn't take her eyes off it. It seemed to have a power of its own.

Suddenly aware that she was staring at Jocasta's décolletage, Miranda dragged her gaze away.

'He feels a lot for you,' Jocasta insisted. 'And he's so talented,' she added, as a final selling point. 'Well, good luck.' She rose abruptly and wove her way through the crowd to the other end of the pub.

Miranda remained where she was, simultaneously moved and annoyed. Julian had given her no indication of his feelings – and this was none of Jocasta's business. Anyway, why did the ball have to be in Miranda's court? When Julian himself joined her a moment later, bringing her a drink, she decided not to mention the conversation. Instead she asked, 'What did you think of Fergus's story? Did you mind?'

'No, I was flattered. It was clever,' he said. 'Very Magritte, mirrors beyond mirrors. Perhaps I'll put Fergus in that scene.'

'Would he fit into the plot?'

'Oh, I'm not bothered about plot, that'll take care of itself.'

Miranda thought that if she were ever to write a novel, she would want a rough idea of the storyline, but Julian seemed to be relying on his subconscious to come up with it. Jocasta's words ran through her head while Julian moved on to a monologue about Magritte, reality and illusion, and the general arbitrariness of existence; it was all very theoretical and impersonal, why couldn't he be real for once?

At closing time they walked together to the tube. Despite her annoyance there was something very erotic about knowing that Julian wanted her. Damn Jocasta! Perhaps she should invite him home with her – no, no, she couldn't. Instead, she invited him to lunch the following Sunday.

*

Miranda did a lot of thinking before that lunch. She wished Julian were not so clearly vulnerable. What she really wanted was someone who would simply take her hand and lead her to bed saying, 'Come on, let's play,' as Daniel had done before Miranda's kisses had turned him into a toad. Other people managed to be friends and just enjoy going to bed together; she feared that with Julian it would not be that simple. But the sexual pull was growing stronger by the minute.

On Sunday Julian arrived looking unusually smart in a cream linen jacket Miranda hadn't seen before, bearing a new section of the novel for her to type, and a record of Mendelssohn's Violin Concerto which she had once told him she loved. She was touched, particularly in view of his financial state – but he reassured her that he had won some money on a horse the day before. 'I'm lucky that way,' he added.

It was a sunny June day, and after lunch they took the North London Line to Hampstead Heath. On Parliament Hill they stopped to gaze at the London skyline and the trees of Highgate shimmering in the heat. Miranda sat and then lay down on the already drying grass; Julian lay down beside her. She placed her hand two inches away from his hand. Why didn't he take it?

Suddenly he said, 'I asked the *I Ching* about you.'

'Did you, indeed? What did it say?'

'Inner Truth.'

'Hmm.' How perceptive of *I Ching*. 'What exactly did you ask it?'

'Oh – I wanted to know something about your character.'

He was clearly not going to expand on this, so she said: 'As a matter of fact, I asked *I Ching* about you.'

Julian frowned. 'Oh, I don't know if I like that.'

'You did it to me!'

'Yes, well. What did it say?

'It wasn't very clear.' This was actually not true. *I Ching's* answer had been all about restraint and controlling one's animal passions, and conflict. Not exactly auspicious.

She decided to take the bull by the horns. 'I'll be honest about why I asked,' she said. 'Did you know Jocasta has been talking to me about you?'

'What d'you mean?'

'The other night in the pub she came up to me and said… well, that you felt something for me… is it true?'

Watching Julian's handsome profile out of the corner of her eye, she saw him go pink, white, and pink again. He sat up, grass in his hair. 'I should never have said anything to her! God, I said I couldn't trust her!'

So why confide in her? she wondered. She said: 'I think she was trying to be helpful. Did she get it wrong?'

'No.' There was a long pause while he stared at his knees. At last, he addressed the horizon. 'I am, er, very attracted to you. But I thought… I was afraid if I said anything, you might be brusque with me.'

'Brusque?' echoed Miranda, brusquely.

'I thought you might reject me.'

'What makes you think I'd reject you?' she said, more gently.

'You're so … self-sufficient, you don't seem to need anyone.'

'That's what I've always thought about you.' She leaned on an elbow and gazed into his worried, beautiful eyes. 'Of course I need someone,' she heard herself say.

Even after this declaration, the conversation turned to matters metaphysical. It wasn't until they were halfway back to the train station that their hands took each other with no apparent decision on the part of their owners.

When they got back to her flat Miranda made two mugs of tea which remained undrunk since, again apparently without conscious decision on either part, they were suddenly on the sofa bed hugging, then kissing, violently. Miranda was astonished at the intensity of it. She was beginning to melt into a jelly when Julian suddenly leapt up and said, 'I'm sorry, I can't! I think I'd better go!'

'What's the matter?'

'It's not you – it's me. Sorry, sorry, I must go.'

Bewildered, Miranda accompanied him to the tube, hoping he might be a little more self-explanatory, but Julian said he felt too overcome to talk; he would explain it all another time. Miranda retraced her steps resolving to tick Julian off her list, but rather fearing she wouldn't. His kisses were still on her mouth. Goodness, but she did want him – she was astonished how much.

*

After the following Friday's Circle, Miranda tentatively invited Julian to come back with her.

'I'd like that,' he said.

Given the Circle's propensity for gossip, they decided not to leave together. Miranda particularly did not want

Jocasta noticing. Julian left well before closing time, and Miranda waited several minutes before joining him outside the underground. The mood of conspiracy added to the already heady atmosphere enveloping them both.

On the train, she tucked her arm into his. 'Promise me you won't say anything to Jocasta.'

'I don't intend to, it's none of her business… though I suppose it might be difficult if she asks me direct.'

'Are you likely to be talking to her, then?'

'The thing is, she's offered to let me play her piano. I can't refuse an offer like that. But I don't particularly want to talk to her.'

In her flat, Miranda drew the curtains against the summer night. She turned and looked at him. What was it about him? He stood there doing nothing, with all the power of a super-magnet. She held out her hand. 'Come on,' she said. 'Let's play.'

The game they played started enjoyably if hesitantly, but twenty minutes in, Julian pulled away from her. 'I can't, I can't, oh, I'm sorry, I'm sorry!'

'What is it, Julian?' She stroked his dark hair, which had taken on a wild life of its own. Her chief fear had been that he might be impotent. That had happened to Daniel during their final doomed phase, and she had coped with it badly. She had never felt so unwanted. Trying to talk about it had made matters worse; he accused her of being predatory and insatiable.

However, from the moves of the game so far, it was tangibly clear that impotence was not Julian's problem. He said, 'I haven't been able to have a full relationship since … well, I had an affair two years ago, and the last time we … well, something went wrong. She wasn't very sympathetic. I suppose I was on my way out, anyway. She was an odd girl.

An actress. Very ambitious. I was too scared to try again for ages, and then when I did, I couldn't.'

Miranda was mystified. 'But what exactly went wrong?'

He looked away, red with embarrassment. 'Well, it hurt, you see.'

Miranda didn't see. 'Well, getting hurt is a risk you take.'

'No, I don't mean emotionally. I mean ... it ... hurt.' Julian could clearly take no more questioning.

'Come here,' said Miranda. 'I shan't hurt you.'

Gradually, matters – and Julian – became a little clearer. She decided to ignore the problem for the time being. The options still available to them were still extremely enjoyable. And there was no harm in taking things slowly.

Over breakfast, he said, 'I'm sorry it wasn't, you know, the whole thing.'

'Honestly, don't worry about it. You were lovely.'

He looked like a four-year-old receiving a gold star. 'You're being awfully nice about it. I was afraid you'd despise me. But I do want it, I want you. I'll have to do something about it. Maybe I should get myself circumcised.'

*

Circumcision was probably unnecessary, said Miranda's nice woman doctor when she went to get a prescription for the pill and was emboldened to mention Julian's problem. 'If he was all right in the past, it's probably just anxiety. As he gets more relaxed I'm sure he'll be fine.' And she went on to suggest gentler and more erotic ways than surgery of negotiating an over-tight foreskin.

Over the next few Friday nights Miranda began putting these suggestions into practice. By the beginning of July, although they had still not played a full match, their games were becoming increasingly pleasurable. Miranda would never have wittingly cast herself in the role of sex therapist but she was enjoying it. So, evidently, was Julian, as well as grateful for her patience.

Miranda in fact appreciated the lack of haste, the chance for their bodies to get to know each other. For someone who looked so insubstantial, Julian was surprisingly physical. Julian the intellectual, Julian the remote, was demonstrating a very different side of himself – a tactile, sensual and caring side. He was remarkably sensitive to Miranda's needs. Daniel had never touched her like this, with such tenderness and skill. It was a long time since she had felt truly female, she realised. She was not in love with him, but she was beginning to feel for him – in addition to pure lust – a kind of tenderness that was new in her dealings with men.

*

Friday nights began to extend into full Saturdays. They walked, they talked, they cooked meals together, they teased each other as they had never done before. Julian shared with her his passion for music, and introduced her to a deeper way of listening. He told her he was considering learning to meditate, and listened without the usual counters of 'yes, but' when Miranda explained the theory of positive thinking as expounded by Warren. 'If you put out positive energy, positive things come back to you.' It made a certain sense, he said, with furrowed brow.

Between Fridays, Miranda was as busy as ever. After another morning at the dental hospital she was at last put on a waiting list for an operation. She wrote an article on her dance class for Jocasta, who received it with surprising enthusiasm. She attended her groups and lectures. She finished her heavy index and the publishers praised her work and immediately commissioned another, for a slightly higher fee. And she had an increasing amount of work to do for Clive, who seemed to be taking on more than was healthy for a one-man operation.

She was glad to be busy. During the week Julian was occupied with his novel, and in any case she was determined not to let any relationship become her whole existence, as it had with Daniel. Nor did she want to be Julian's whole existence. He could be heavily intense at times, and his occasional dark moods were hard to deal with. Of course, he had never actually said that he loved her; even so she felt a little guilty that she couldn't be more committed.

She decided to ring Cassie for advice. After her session with her Cassie had said, 'Ring me any time, dear. And I don't say that to everyone!' Now was the time. She also wanted to make an appointment with her for Daphne, who would soon be descending on her again.

'I'll do my best to help her,' said Cassie. 'And I'm glad you've met someone, dear. I said you would. It'll do you good.'

'But I'm not in love with him, and he is so thin-skinned. I don't want to hurt him.'

'Well, it's early days yet. He's a grown man, he's responsible for himself. Just go with the flow.'

*

Really, Miranda decided a week or so later, things were going rather well. For once she wasn't dreading Daphne's forthcoming arrival – though Julian protested when she had to cancel their next Friday night.

'That'll be a whole week without you!' He sounded tragic. It was flattering, of course, but wasn't he overreacting?

'We can meet on Sunday. But I'd better warn you – I'm going to be away for a week in July. I'm going on a meditation course in the country.' Guru Chakrao was coming over from India, and the Fellowship newsletter had announced that his personal presence would advance meditators' spiritual development by leaps and bounds. 'I booked it ages ago. I didn't know this was going to happen – us, I mean.'

'No, I suppose not. I'll miss you.'

*

When Daphne arrived, her schedule was already full, and Miranda had to cancel the provisional appointment she had made for her with Cassie. Cassie said: 'Get her to ring me. There are things I have to tell her.'

Daphne was sufficiently curious to telephone Cassie a day or so later while Miranda enjoyed a liberated walk round the block. Although Daphne was being pleasanter than sometimes, Miranda was already wondering whether she would have any energy left for Julian by the weekend. When she got back, Daphne was sitting in her wheelchair in Margery's living room, looking relaxed for the first time that week.

'What a fascinating woman!' she said. 'She gave me healing down the telephone – I could feel it, like warm water going through me. Amazing. I feel all smoothed out.'

Miranda was pleased. 'Did she say anything interesting?'

'Oh, she really made me think. She said I've been trying to fight my body, when I should be listening to it. She said when it feels bad it's because I'm meant to be resting and going inwards. Actually, it's just what my consultant keeps saying – he keeps telling me I mustn't force myself, and I haven't wanted to listen. But I think I've got the message now.'

'Wow,' said Miranda.

Daphne frowned. 'She said – don't laugh – she said I have a strong spiritual streak which I've been denying, and that when you have a physically limiting illness, there is a purpose. It's meant to make you stop and think.'

Miranda said bluntly, 'It doesn't seem to have succeeded so far.'

Daphne laughed. 'Cassie says it will in the end. My body will simply give up.'

'Oh, Daphne!'

They looked at each other across the small room, silent for a moment. Then Daphne put on her glasses and said, 'We've still got this report to finish. Shall we get on with it?'

2
MIRANDA HAS
SEVERAL PROBLEMS

As July approached, Julian seemed resigned to Miranda's forthcoming departure. What neither of them reckoned on, however, was that one's week's separation would turn into three. A few days before the meditation course, Clive's wife telephoned in a frantic state. Clive had been rushed to hospital with a heart attack – would Miranda hold the fort at his office full-time for a few days? She had no option but to agree. Then, just as she was about to leave for Clive's house, Daphne called.

'I've got to come to London again the week after next, and Margery will be away for the first three days. It's an awful bore, but could you come and stay with me at her flat? I suppose I could manage alone but… I'm not on terribly good form at the moment.' That probably meant that she was quite unwell. Again, Miranda could not refuse.

Since Clive had been seriously overworking recently his heart attack was not totally surprising. But it was a shock; he was not yet fifty, and far more relaxed than Daphne. When Miranda visited him in the intensive care unit his normally rosy face was deathly white, but he hailed her as heartily as a man could while wired up to a multiplicity of tubes and machinery.

'I actually died for three minutes,' he told her with some pride. 'And I can tell you for a fact there's no life after death.'

Miranda doubted whether three minutes were enough to be so certain, but this was hardly the time for a metaphysical discussion. She was just glad he was alive now. She left with a lengthy list of instructions including phoning Clive's clients to say that he had a virus, all issued behind the back of a nurse who fluttered round the room like an anxious chicken, telling Miranda not to tire him.

By Friday evening she had barely enough time to pack a few clothes and organise Rollo's feeding, watering and stroking with the schoolteacher who lived in the garden flat below hers. Cursing Julian's phoneless state, she managed to catch Fiona just as she was leaving for the Circle, and asked her to give him a message.

'Yes, of course, I'll get him to call you. How's it going with you two?'

'Oh, fine, really. We're taking things slowly.'

Fiona had of course said 'I told you so' when Miranda confessed that she and Julian were sort of together, and would she please not mention it to Jocasta. She made no mention of Julian's problem; Fiona had recently remarked, 'You know, I feel sorry for men, being led about by that little thing all day.' Miranda didn't want Julian's not-so-little thing belittled; she was getting quite fond of it.

'By the way,' added Fiona, 'Jocasta's putting on a potluck midsummer lunch for the Circle at her place on Sunday week, can you come?'

'Probably not. That's when Daphne's arriving.' Miranda felt disappointed. She had never seen Jocasta's house, a privilege usually reserved for specially selected members of the Circle.

'Oh, shame. I was going to ask you to bring your notebook so we could inspect Jocasta's wastepaper baskets together!'

Julian rang that night from the phone box outside the Pig and Apple, and Miranda explained that she wouldn't be available for three weeks. There was a long silence.

'Julian?'

'I'm here.'

'I'm really sorry. I wasn't expecting Daphne back so soon.'

'Do you have to stay with her?'

'I can't not. She can't really manage on her own.'

'You might have let me know earlier.'

'I'm really sorry, truly. I didn't know myself and there was no way to contact you.'

He sighed. 'I expect I'll survive. I'll miss you, though. It's my birthday on Wednesday week, you know.'

'Oh, Julian, I didn't – oh dear, maybe we could meet for lunch?'

*

On the train journey to Kent, Miranda realised how much she was banking on the meditation course. She was longing to see Guru Chakrao in person: an enlightened being who had the answers to all those questions about the meaning of life. Perhaps she would at last learn how to live, she told herself; she was still trying to get the hang of it.

The course was being held in an old manor house converted into an adult education college; it was surrounded by green lawns and leafy woodland. The moment she arrived and breathed in the country air, Miranda started to unwind. Here, she thought, she could stock up her reserves of energy before being incarcerated with Daphne in Margery's claustrophobic flat.

The course participants gathered after tea in the once-elegant drawing room, where pink plastic chairs contrasted with the Adam fireplace and ceiling. Miranda took stock of her fellow meditators. They were mainly youngish professionals, interspersed with a sprinkling of hippies; some she had met before at Warren's lectures.

The room fell silent as Warren, accompanied by two blonde young women in saris, stepped on to a small dais draped with swathes of red and gold velvet. Warren beamed at the assembled company gesturing to them to welcome the Guru. As they all rose with hands together in greeting, a small, dapper man in a Savile Row suit stepped on to the dais. He looked slowly round at his audience, a broad smile on his brown face. *He looks almost too human to be a spiritual master*, thought Miranda. But his opening words were reassuring.

'Humanity,' he began, 'is everywhere suffering from a lack of love. With all our wonderful technological progress, we have neglected the poor heart of humanity, of nature, of the planet itself. And our hearts weep, nature weeps, the very planet weeps. But we have the solution: when we meditate, we open ourselves to spiritual love, and the healing process begins.'

His voice was beautiful, almost hypnotic. As he continued, Miranda drifted in and out of his talk, forgetting the chair digging into her thighs. This was what she had come to hear. His words reverberated through her whole being and resonated deep inside her, like music, like a cleansing stream, like Cassie's healing... Finally, the Guru raised his arms in a blessing that embraced them all, and concluded:

'I am here to heal the human heart.'

Oh, yes, thought Miranda, *please heal mine.* And she thought of Clive whose good-natured heart had collapsed under all the pressure he put on it, and of Daphne, whose heart must be hurting deep down beneath her controlling outer self. And she thought of Julian whose heart often seemed full of some secret hurt, and wished he had been here to share this moment.

Guru Chakrao sat down and said, 'Now I will answer questions.'

Recalling Julian's many objections to self-development, Miranda impulsively raised a hand.

'Yes, my child?'

She composed her question carefully. 'Guru Chakrao, do people have to be – er – neurotic to be creative, and if so, does meditating put an end to creativity?'

'That,' said Guru Chakrao, beaming, 'is a very beautiful question.'

All heads turned to see who had asked the beautiful question, and Miranda felt herself blushing. Guru Chakrao briefly studied the ceiling, before turning his gaze back on her.

'Artistic activity may be a way of healing neurosis, but it is also a means of striving for perfection. So an artist who becomes a fully integrated human being does not cease to be an artist. But he no longer creates, he reflects.'

That was the answer to give Julian, thought Miranda, scribbling in her notebook. A beautiful answer.

The meeting was followed by an unimaginative vegetarian supper. Miranda found herself seated next to Charles, a balding businessman; opposite them were a film editor whose name she didn't catch, and Olga, a Danish yoga teacher, who commented disparagingly on the whiteness of the rice and the bread. They were all favourably impressed by Guru Chakrao and they all agreed that meditating made life simultaneously easier and more difficult.

Charles remarked, 'It's exactly like Warren says. Things I've been sweeping under the carpet for twenty years have been popping up and refusing to lie down. I'm hoping to deal with some of them this week.' There was a murmur of agreement from the others. Miranda wondered what particular piece of dirt was going to pop up from under her own carpet.

*

Miranda's week was becoming a pleasant blur of meals and conversation, meditation in groups and alone, talks by Guru Chakrao, and peaceful walks in the surrounding woods. At the evening discussions people reported all kinds of interesting breakthroughs; Olga let it be known that while meditating she had had a vision of purple blossoms. Miranda experienced nothing so interesting, but once or twice she felt herself floating in a timeless space in which there was no thought, no anxiety, just lightness and peace.

Three days in, Daphne climbed into her head and wouldn't leave. Even after her talk with Cassie, Miranda couldn't believe Daphne would ever change. She found herself dreading the following week, cringing in advance at the irritations and above all the fatigue that Daphne always left in her wake. She was unable to return to that inner peaceful place; Daphne was marching around in her psyche demanding attention.

That evening, Miranda asked another question. She tried to make it general. 'Guru Chakrao, how can one deal with people who drain others of energy?'

The Guru looked at her, the whites of his eyes very white, the irises almost black. He seemed to be looking right through her. He said: 'People don't drain you. You give them too much. Continue to meditate. When you draw on the energies of the universe, no one can drain you.'

'But what should I — '

He flashed her a short smile of dismissal and turned to the next questioner.

Miranda felt distinctly short-changed. She had been hoping for some practical tips on managing Daphne. Anyway, he was wrong; she didn't give too much, she knew she never gave enough.

Next morning when she tried to meditate painful thoughts kept bubbling up and this time, something clicked. She remembered the child she had been, trying and trying to please her mother, to deserve love, to earn approval, and never succeeding, never giving enough, always in the wrong, however hard she tried to please. This was how it was with Daphne; it was like climbing a glass mountain. And she resented it, and felt she was a horrible person for resenting it. Unable to sit still any longer, she went outside and walked through the quietness of the gardens to the edge of the woods. Once among the sheltering trees, her tears began to flow. In this state, she bumped into Warren.

'Ah, the meditation's working, I see,' he said gently. 'Come and have a chat after lunch.'

Warren's office was peaceful. On the sunlit lawn outside sprawled a colourfully dressed group of hippies, one of them playing a sitar rather badly. Warren listened while Miranda let everything flood out, from her childhood onwards. Tears poured out of her from a seemingly bottomless hot spring. When she finally came to a sobbing halt, Warren said:

'These things do surface during this kind of week. I know it's painful, but it's really good, it's part of the healing process. Wounds come to the surface when they're ready to be healed. Just let the pain flow through you, don't block it; you can only let go of it by feeling it. And letting go will create a space that can be filled with divine love, and then you'll find that you can give freely to others without being drained.'

Miranda nodded. Warren was giving her hope.

He went on, 'You'd feel a lot better if you could forgive your mother.'

Miranda's tears instantly dried. 'That… would be difficult.'

'Maybe the time isn't right yet. But if you could heal your relationship with her, all your other relationships would be a lot easier.'

As she left he enfolded her in a huge, comforting Australian hug. What a kind man he was, she thought. But as for forgiving her mother – surely that would mean condoning her behaviour, letting her back into her life, to stamp all over her again – no, she couldn't, she couldn't.

She reminded herself that the hole where mother love should have been could be filled with divine love. Was there really such a thing? When she was a child, God was a remote figure whose approval could only be earned by being very, very, impossibly good, whereas Miranda knew herself to be irretrievably bad – her mother made that quite clear. But maybe she had got it wrong; maybe God was actually on her side, maybe He, She or It had been pouring out love all this time, only something had got in the way.

*

Miranda arrived home late on the Friday. On Saturday she did her laundry and shopping, telephoned Clive's wife and learned that he was a great deal better, checked on Rollo's welfare, and cooked a lentil loaf to take with her – Daphne had several times expressed approval of health foods, though Miranda had never actually seen her eat any.

Early on Sunday morning she was at Margery's flat in time for Daphne's arrival, full of good intentions about drawing on divine energies. She helped Daphne unpack, made up beds for them both, and produced the lentil loaf.

Daphne stared at it coldly and said, 'Actually, I'm going out to lunch.' Her London lover had rematerialised (how did she do it?) and was taking her out for the rest of the day. This liberated Miranda to go to Primrose Hill to pick up a tape dictated by Clive from his hospital bed, type most of it during the afternoon, and return to Margery's flat in time to help Daphne to bed.

On Monday Miranda helped Daphne get up at six-thirty to prepare for a client meeting, after which she dashed home to finish Clive's report, delivered it on the way back, picked up a pizza for lunch, and spent the afternoon working with Daphne.

At five-thirty, Daphne yawned and stretched and said, 'I'd like to go to the theatre tonight. Have you got a newspaper?'

Miranda stared at her. 'Oh, Daphne, it's so late – why didn't you ask before?'

Daphne gave her a severe look over her glasses. 'The trouble with you, Miranda,' she said, 'is that you don't like moving fast.'

Miranda quelled a strong temptation to slap Daphne and started telephoning theatres. For Daphne's choice of plays there were either no tickets or no wheelchair facilities. They ended up eating the despised lentil loaf while Daphne complained about the unhelpfulness of the social services.

That night Miranda lay down in Margery's soggy spare bed in a state of total tension. Divine love had gone out of the window hours ago. She was so tired she felt sick. No, she didn't give too much, she thought; she felt so resentful that she wasn't giving anything at all.

By Tuesday morning Miranda could hardly wait for Margery's return. She was already exhausted. Daphne, by contrast, was feeling stronger. 'Order me a cab,' she commanded after breakfast. She was going shopping for designer clothes, essential for business, she said.

As the driver helped her and her wheelchair into the cab, Miranda said, 'Do remember what Cassie said about taking it easy!'

Daphne said sharply, 'I can't afford to!' and snapped at the driver: 'Harvey Nichols.'

*

Miranda met Julian on his birthday for lunch in a pub off Soho Square. Meeting again after the gap, Miranda felt quite shy and Julian seemed ill at ease. He pecked her on the cheek and muttered, 'How are you?' in a tone indicating that a full answer was not required.

Miranda handed him the birthday card she had somehow found time to buy. 'I'm terribly sorry, I haven't been able to get you a present.' Her head and shoulders were aching. She added ineptly, 'Still, it's the thought that counts.'

'Oh, it doesn't matter,' he said, as though he thought it did.

'I'll pay for lunch,' said Miranda.

They ordered scampi in baskets and two glasses of house white wine.

'Did you go to Jocasta's get-together?' Miranda asked.

'Yes. I played her piano, it's quite a good one. Needs tuning, though.'

'Does she play?'

'No, I think an ex-lover left it behind… I really don't know what to make of her, you know. She was very odd with Fergus, sort of flirting with him and then putting him down. But she was encouraging about my novel; she offered to go through it with me over the summer break.'

'That's nice of her.'

'I don't think she's nice.' Julian picked up a chip and looked at it critically.

'Well, it's generous of her to give free tuition on top of all her other commitments.' Jocasta's main source of income was freelance editorial work which kept her quite busy. 'I don't know how she finds the time.'

'She makes the time,' he said pointedly.

'Is that a dig at me?'

He clasped his hands together, the knuckles white, and muttered, 'I am finding the gaps in our relationship very hard to take.'

'Look I didn't plan Clive's heart attack, or Daphne coming.'

'I hate that woman!'

'Well, I'm sorry!' said Miranda crossly. 'I'd much rather not work for her, but she is ill – and I do have a living to earn.'

She went home feeling let down. What she really needed was a man who would draw her to his broad chest and say, 'You work so hard, you need some rest, let me take care of you!' Did such a being exist?

She recalled the 'tricky woman disrupting things' from Cassie's tarot reading; it had to be Daphne. But as for the Knight of Cups, however strong the attraction between them, a knight in shining armour Julian was not.

*

At the end of the next Circle evening Julian approached Miranda, looking tense and drawn. 'I want to talk to you alone,' he said. 'Can we go to a different pub?'

'Sure.' Mystified, she followed him to a pub round the corner.

There he handed her an envelope addressed to her. 'I was going to post this,' he said, 'but I wanted to be there when you read it.'

It was a farewell letter. It began: *I knew when we started that you had no real feelings for me. I had hoped that in time you might come to love me, but it is obviously hopeless.*

There followed a list of all the ways in which Miranda had hurt his feelings, and a catalogue of her character defects which included obsession with personal growth, over-consciousness of money, her frequent belittling of Julian, her total lack of sensitivity on his birthday, and her constant busyness. It was clear that he came last on her list of priorities. *I had hoped never to say this,* continued the handwriting from which she had so often typed, *but it is best that we end our relationship now, it is causing me too much pain.*

Miranda didn't know whether to scream, hit him or hug him. She heard herself say at a distance that she would be sorry to lose a friend and hoped they could still talk when they met at the Circle.

It wasn't until she got home that she began to feel extremely angry. Had all that physical closeness meant nothing? Not to mention all that typing? Did she really belittle him? She had been trying to encourage him, as a person and as a writer; clearly she'd been doing it wrong. She could recall several occasions when Julian had taken offence at something she'd said, but she had never meant to hurt his feelings. It was as if he leaped on the slightest opportunity of having his feelings hurt and hugged it to him. As for being money conscious, if he had some money himself, if he had a telephone, if he had a car, their whole relationship would be a lot easier.

I had hoped that in time you might come to love me. He had never said he loved her. *Damn him*, thought Miranda, as she removed Rollo from her pillow and got into bed. He doesn't love me: all that demandingness, that isn't love. She felt sad at not being loved, and suddenly wished Julian were in bed with her.

3

CHILDE ROLAND MAKES IT

Childe Roland to the dark tower came...
Robert Browning

The following week was horrible, and not just because of Julian's letter. Miranda was finally given a date in October for a dental operation to clear an infection, which would involve drilling through the bone above her front teeth; she was dreading it. In addition, she was indexing a deeply depressing book about South Africa, full of injustice and torture and little children living in drainpipes. She felt bad about being paid for it, as if she were somehow colluding in the oppression. When Daphne phoned to say she was coming to London at the end of the month, Miranda wondered how she would cope.

The peace she had found in Kent now seemed like a mirage. Her sleep was disturbed by anxiety dreams. In two or three she was caught in some kind of struggle with a man and a woman; the details were a blur. But one dream was very vivid, almost filmlike: in it she was the child slave of two Ancient Egyptian magicians, cowering in an underground room where her masters drew on her energy to practise their dark arts. She awoke feeling terrified. She wondered if it could possibly be a past-life memory; she was becoming more and more convinced that the difficulties of her current life were payback for wrongs she had done in previous lives.

Going over the dream afterwards, she realised with a start that one of the magicians had worn a pendant just like Jocasta's… had she really dreamed that, or had her imagination added it afterwards?

She felt very alone. Julian was obviously a lost cause. To be so hypersensitive he must have been wounded somewhere deep inside, somewhere that neither their One-to-Ones nor their intimacy had managed to touch. If, as propounded by Warren, no relationship occurs by accident, perhaps she had been allotted the spiritual task of helping Julian to reach his potential? If so, she had clearly failed.

*

Writing groups can be strange places: sometimes thoughts and ideas seem to fly across the room from one person's head into another's. At the final Circle evening before the summer break, the first story to be read was about circumcision. Miranda dared not look at Julian, who was seated well away from her, studiously pencilling notes. To judge from the story, circumcision would not be a comfortable or even wise procedure. In Julian's case she was sure it was unnecessary, but now she would never know.

Julian read next; he had brought a reworked section of his novel which he had already read once at the Circle. Its faults paralleled those of its author – beautiful but elusive, gloomy and repetitive. After he had finished, the praise he must have been craving was not forthcoming.

Jocasta came down on him unusually heavily, pointing out that both the female characters were referred to as 'the girl', which was not only confusing but sexist. Miranda asked whether either of 'the girls' was going to develop, or were they simply sex objects? Judy wondered why he kept rereading the early parts of the novel instead of moving on, and Fiona wanted to know what it was actually about? With each criticism Julian's shoulders drooped lower.

In the pub afterwards Miranda joined Judy and Fiona. At the other end of the bar Julian and Jocasta were in a serious-faced huddle.

'Poor Julian,' said Judy. 'He looks really beaten up.'

'He's too sensitive,' remarked Miranda, trying to harden her heart.

'I thought you wanted a sensitive man,' said Fiona.

'I want someone who's sensitive to me,' said Miranda. 'Julian's so sensitive you have to think three times before you open your mouth.'

'Oh dear,' said Judy. 'I thought you two were getting on so well.'

'So did I,' said Miranda ruefully.

At that point Jocasta came by on her way out; at the door a new young man awaited her. As she passed she mouthed at Miranda, 'Very low!', nodding in Julian's direction.

Reluctantly but inevitably, Miranda walked over to Julian. 'Would you like to talk?'

'There's a seat over there,' he said, leading her to a pew at the back of the pub. There Julian unburdened himself. Everyone had been completely insensitive about his work, even Jocasta. He was a failure, he always would be. The novel was not worth going on with.

Miranda resisted the urge to shake him. 'It's probably because everyone knows you're a good writer; they come down harder because they expect a lot from you.'

After she had bought them both drinks he seemed

slightly cheered. Drawing a beer circle on the tabletop with his forefinger, he asked: 'So, are we still friends?'

'Your letter made me really cross,' said Miranda. 'You hate being criticised but you listed every criticism of me you could think of. You weren't even fair. I didn't want to be working for Daphne on your birthday! Anyone would think I did it to annoy you.'

He looked at her. 'I'm sorry,' he said. 'Perhaps I overreacted. I started feeling terribly pushed out. There are lots of good things I could have written about you.'

'Then why didn't you?'

'Perhaps I will next time.' For the first time that evening he produced a brief but sweet smile.

Somehow, this conversation became an unspoken agreement to pick up where they had left off. She was probably doing the wrong thing, thought Miranda. What was the pull of this hypersensitive man? When they got back to her flat, Miranda reminded herself of all the Support Group teachings about accepting people as they were, and her doctor's advice, and once they were ensconced in her sofa bed their embraces, if still incomplete, were extremely pleasant.

'When are you going to write something again?' asked Julian between takes.

'God knows, I hardly have time to keep notes at present.'

'I've started keeping a dream journal,' he said. 'Jocasta thought it would help with the novel.'

'Mmmm.' Not particularly wanting Jocasta in bed with them, Miranda began employing diversionary tactics.

'Oh, that feels nice. Mmmm. Keep doing that. I don't know why she was so hard on me this evening. Don't stop, that's lovely... she's always said it's got potential. Ooooh, mmmmm.'

'She once told me I had potential,' said Miranda. 'You could have knocked me down with a feather.'

'A feather,' he murmured, shifting position. 'A feather... allow me to... knock... you ... down with ... a feather.'

Jocasta vanished.

*

In the morning he showed her his dream journal, kept in a small black notebook, and read her some of his dreams. They sounded very like his novel. In one he was in an empty house full of empty rooms; then, in a ballroom he met a woman with whom he began dancing – at which point he became very bashful and refused to identify his dream partner. Miranda assumed it was herself.

When he went out to buy some cigarettes he left the book lying open at that page. Clearly Miranda was meant to read it, so she did. The woman in the dream was Jocasta. How very odd... of course, he had danced with her at Judy's party. And Jocasta's treatment of his writing was a little like a dance, two steps forward, one back, and a capricious skip here and there. All the same – bloody Jocasta, how dare she enter Julian's dreams?

*

As the summer progressed, things between them seemed to be going well again. During the Circle's August holiday they kept up their Friday-to-Sunday routine, which gave them both time and space during the week. Julian was writing steadily and was more relaxed and open. Miranda had no idea where they were heading, but at the moment their relationship felt right.

At the end of August Julian accompanied Miranda to a Support Group reunion at Liz's house in Richmond. Miranda was amazed not only that he agreed to go, but that once there he actually seemed to enjoy himself. It was a happy day; Miranda was glad to be back with the original group from the previous summer, free of Al and Marxists. Liz was warm and welcoming; it was sunny, and the group shared a picnic lunch in the small, rose-filled garden.

Julian was placed in a subgroup co-led by Rosa, who told Miranda confidentially, 'I like your Julian. He's rather nervous, but he's got real potential.' At one point Miranda overheard him loudly proclaiming from the next room: 'I am a powerful man!' *Perhaps he could be*, she thought, *if only he gave himself a chance.*

At the final gathering, Julian drifted towards Liz's piano. It was the first time Miranda had heard him play, and she was impressed. He played a couple of Chopin nocturnes, skilfully and with feeling, and they were received with enthusiastic applause.

As they waited at Richmond Station for the train home Julian began to kiss Miranda. Little butterfly kisses rained down on her face and neck, hundreds of tiny kisses, delicate as a shower of flower petals. He only stopped when the train arrived. Miranda thought, *Perhaps he really does love me.*

*

'You are being awfully generous,' said Julian, nuzzling her neck. 'I think you are the most generous person I know.'

Miranda glowed. It was a Sunday afternoon. They had spent most of the weekend in bed. Julian had not totally overcome his anxiety. Childe Roland had several times approached the Dark Tower and backed off at the last minute, but he was getting closer all the time. And Julian's activities, though incomplete, were a great deal more enjoyable than Daniel's in his fully functioning days – which Miranda now recalled as not unlike being run over by a small lorry.

Miranda said, 'I'm not being generous; you don't realise how much you are giving me.'

It was Julian's turn to glow.

Not that it was all roses. Julian's depression tended to return when least expected. The weekend after their sunny Saturday in Richmond, he announced that he felt totally empty. Since humanity was irredeemable, it seemed ridiculous for people to prance round being positive, and he didn't think he had any positivity in him anyway. He feared that if he lost what Miranda called his negativity there would be nothing left of him at all. Miranda tried to haul him out of this mood, pointing out all that was good in him, his creativity, his humour, his intelligence, his gentleness.

'Then why do you keep putting me down?' he said.

'When do I put you down?'

'Well, like… when I borrowed your camera at Liz's, you made it abundantly clear in front of everyone that you thought I was incapable of taking a photograph.'

'I was only showing you how the camera worked, for God's sake! Don't be so touchy!'

'You see? You're putting me down again! Rosa was lovely to me,' he added.

On the plus side, after some prompting from Miranda, he was being more thoughtful around the flat, emptying his ashtrays and helping her cook and wash up. One day, she showed him some of her writing notes; he read them with great care and said, 'Miranda, I'd really like you to write something of stature, not just bits and pieces.'

She shrugged. 'I never have time to get down to any proper writing.'

'Because you're always putting your talents at the disposal of people like Daphne.' *Julian could be right*, she thought. But she had her own secret fear: if she were free to exercise her talents, she might discover she had none. Meanwhile, she was due for another bout of Daphne. She hoped Julian would be more understanding this time.

*

Margery was on holiday and uncontactable, but Daphne had keys and was sure Margery wouldn't mind them using the flat; Miranda would, of course, have to stay with her there. Determined not to be caught out this time, she organised a minicab firm to be on tap for the full period and booked tickets for a well-reviewed production of Uncle Vanya, after ascertaining that the theatre could accommodate wheelchairs. She did an extra-long meditation before leaving for Margery's, and asked the powers that be to let her be a channel for divine love, and to get it right this time.

On the Monday evening, as Miranda scrambled eggs for their supper, Daphne launched into an account of the horrible holiday she had just spent in Wales with her Bristol chap.

'I've never felt so disabled in my life! He wanted to dash around visiting castles – absolutely exhausting – and then he expected nights of mad passion. And the last two days he'd booked us into this hotel which allegedly caters for disabled people: well, they put all the disabled people down one end of the dining room virtually screened off so no one had to look at us, it was perfectly humiliating!'

'Daphne, didn't you discuss this holiday with him before you went?'

'No, I wanted him to surprise me. Huh, he did!'

Miranda's sympathies veered towards the Bristol chap, who until recently had probably only experienced Daphne as a business dynamo and vibrant sexy woman. It seemed to be her peculiar gift to put people in impossible positions and then complain when they didn't come up to scratch.

'I don't suppose it'll last anyway,' Daphne continued. 'He's nearly fifty, too old to adapt to someone like me. But he's awfully good in bed.' She sighed.

'That does count,' commented Miranda, with the benefit of recent experience.

Daphne behaved tolerably until the evening of the theatre visit. It was not the best night for an outing; Daphne had to meet a client at nine the next morning. Her mind seemed only partly on Uncle Vanya; in the interval she remarked, 'You'll have to iron my shirt and skirt when we get back.'

Miranda tensed. She told herself that Daphne didn't mean to sound dictatorial; she was just being Daphne. But could she never say 'please'? And why on earth had she left it so late?

After the play, Daphne declared herself famished and insisted on going to a restaurant. Chicken Kiev and profiteroles at eleven at night were not what Miranda wanted. What she wanted was to go to bed because she was very, very tired. Daphne appeared not in the least tired. In the taxi home she exclaimed, 'Oh my God, I haven't written the conclusions for tomorrow's report. Why didn't you remind me? Oh, well, it's too late now, I suppose.'

Miranda heard herself make the expected offer. At one in the morning she found herself, muzzy with Pouilly Fuissé and fatigue, typing at Margery's kitchen table while Daphne dictated, corrected herself, changed her mind, and redictated.

Then, after helping her to bed, Miranda ironed Daphne's skirt and silk shirt.

*

Before leaving on the Thursday morning, Daphne asked Miranda to help her pack. As Miranda folded the beautiful, luxurious clothes, Daphne sat in her wheelchair going through her expenses.

'Honestly,' she complained, 'London is so expensive, and the accounts people are really niggly. Do you know, the minicab firm charged me for waiting time while I just popped into Harrods, I thought that was so mean.'

Miranda would usually have let that pass, but her whole body was buzzing with fatigue. From her mouth the words sprang out:

'Just as well I don't charge you waiting time.'

"What d'you mean?'

'Well, you pay me for my secretarial work, but not for the rest of the time I'm with you.'

Daphne swung her wheelchair round to face Miranda, her eyes and mouth a trinity of outraged Os. Then she burst into tears. 'I thought you were my friend! I thought you were doing it out of friendship!'

Oh, God, the guilt! It was shocking to see Daphne cry. But once Miranda had opened her mouth, she could not stop. All her resentment erupted, her feelings of being used and walked over and taken for granted poured out, all confused and jumbled. Then she, too, burst into tears.

'It's not about money!' she tried to explain. 'You just expect too much of me, I'm exhausted!'

Mascara streaked down Daphne's peach-skin cheeks; she wiped her face with a tissue. 'It's absolutely beastly of you to attack me like this when you know how ill I am.' Somewhere inside Miranda pity lurked. She tried to be rational.

'I'm not attacking you, but you don't seem to realise – you expect me to drop everything and come running – I do have a life, you know!'

'But I thought you were doing it out of friendship!' Daphne wailed again.

'Yes, of course, I'm sorry, I'm sorry, I'm just so tired—'

'You think I'm not tired? Have you any idea what it's like for me, trying to live a normal life when it's like climbing a mountain just to go to the loo?'

Shrill words bounced off the walls of the small bedroom. In the mirror above the mantelpiece Miranda could see their two faces reflected, both pink and blotched and ugly.

'You're spoiled, let me tell you!' shouted Daphne. 'With all your meditation and groups and self indulgence! Do you know what I think? I think you're jealous of me because I'm ill and you're well, and you haven't got half my energy!'

Miranda took a deep breath. She said slowly, 'I wish I did have half your energy. And I don't understand why you have to live this crazy existence. You heard what Cassie said, you should take it easy. You've got a psychology degree, why don't you do something less demanding?'

Her knuckles white as she gripped the arms of her wheelchair, Daphne spat at her: 'Because nobody would employ me!'

Miranda felt as if she'd been punched in the stomach. For a silent moment they stared at each other.

Then Daphne sat up straight, wiped her eyes and took her powder compact out of her calfskin handbag. She said, 'Well, I won't take this too seriously. You're obviously projecting. This is all to do with your mother, really.'

Miranda almost laughed. The objective fact was that

Daphne's approach to life was often very like her mother's. It would have been just like her mother to disclaim any responsibility for the row. On the rare occasions as a child when Miranda had tried to stand up for herself, the response would be: 'You must be unwell, to talk to your mother like that.' Never, never, never, 'Could I possibly be in the wrong?' Miranda could no more win a battle with Daphne than she could with her mother.

Somehow they finished packing in time for the minicab and Daphne paid Miranda. As the car departed, Miranda looked at the newly printed notes and wished she had the guts to tear them up. Instead, she spent one of them on a taxi home, where she hugged Rollo and burst into tears again. She wished she really could have been a friend to Daphne. During the row the superwoman mask had slipped and at moments Miranda felt she was with a real person, a person she might actually have liked.

Oh, why wasn't Julian on the phone? She posted him a hasty note to say she was at liberty again, and asking him to ring her. Then she telephoned Rosa to unburden her guilt. Rosa said crisply that it sounded as though Daphne had had it coming and she hoped Miranda hadn't apologised too much. Finally she asked: 'Does Daphne have anyone to phone when she gets home?'

'I don't think so,' said Miranda. Daphne had lovers, not friends.

*

Next day Miranda took herself to Hampstead Heath and swam among the ducks in the Ladies' Pond. Autumn was in the air. It was early September and already the water was icy, all the better to cleanse away the past few days.

As she opened her front door, the phone was ringing. It was Julian.

Miranda said, 'Can you come over? I badly need a hug.'

He came. He hugged her, a long, enfolding hug. 'It's been awful,' she said into his shoulder.

'Poor Miranda,' said Julian, smoothing her face. Then he began smoothing other bits of her.

'I can't, I'm too tired,' she said.

'You don't have to do anything.' He led her to the sofa bed where she flopped while he undressed her, stroking and smoothing as he went. 'Just a cuddle,' he said. 'Just a little cuddle.'

But to the surprise of them both, Childe Roland took over and on this occasion entered the Dark Tower and took a cautious look round.

In the evening, Miranda started ridding herself of Daphne's money. She took Julian out to a concert and an Italian restaurant. He protested slightly, but she pointed out that she needed a treat. 'You can take me out when the novel's a success,' she said.

When they came back, full of music and food and fondness for each other, Childe Roland not only entered the Dark Tower but comported himself like a parfait gentil knight for a surprisingly long time. *At last*, thought Miranda, as they fell asleep holding each other, finally she'd got something right.

PART 3

AUTUMN: FIREWORKS

1

INTIMACY AND ANXIETY

Three weeks later, Miranda was wondering why Julian wasn't happier. They were spending more time together, both in bed and out of it. Their first night of joyous fulfilment had extended itself into the entire weekend; since then Julian had taken to staying over until Monday morning. In bed, he was a new man. His confidence was growing; he was loving, masterful, inventive and apparently tireless. To Miranda, their physical relationship seemed near-miraculous. Before Daniel it seemed to her that the sexual freedom of the '60s, far from liberating women, simply put them under an obligation to be available. Refusal laid her open to accusations of frigidity; acquiescence usually left her feeling hollow. And Daniel had left her feeling totally undesirable. Julian was restoring a part of her that had for a long time been hurt and hidden.

In bed, he was generous with himself and with his words. 'You are beautiful,' he told her again and again, and she felt beautiful. 'You are kind,' he said, and she felt kind. She no longer worried about where they might be heading; the heights of the present moment carried them on a wave of shared pleasure which could take them where it would.

In daily life, however, their life together ran less smoothly. It was not easy to work in his presence; even when occupied with his writing, his busy back, curved over the kitchen table, seemed to demand attention. When she typed his manuscript, correcting any spelling or grammatical mistakes would be taken as criticism. In addition, there were times when he would be enveloped by a black despair, a loneliness, a sense that the whole world was against him, which Miranda found hard to handle. Neither of them could understand what was at the root of these moods. One-to-One sessions helped a little to release him from the blackness, but not from its mysterious source. The most traumatic childhood event he could recall was sitting in a high chair being made to eat an over-runny boiled egg.

'You really ought to join a group,' she told him. 'It's not a good idea to do One-to-Ones with people you see all the time.' But Julian did not want to join a group.

When Miranda's efforts to comfort him failed, she had to quell her own impatience. She tried to get him to see that he was reinforcing his gloom by constantly harping on it. People create their own reality, she said, quoting Warren; Julian was very creative, why couldn't he create a bit of happiness for himself? Her efforts were received with his usual yes-buts. Once or twice she snapped at him: his reaction was to turn quite white, and Miranda had to soothe and reassure him.

So she dared not tackle him about his invariably dumping his wet towel on the bathroom floor for her to pick up, or the way he flung his clothes about the room before flinging himself at her, or his failure to wash the grill pan after cooking his breakfast bacon. She was quite glad that he was on the dole since on Mondays he had to return to Parson's Green to sign on. Then, when they met again the following Friday there would be joy and sexual congress unconfined. If he could visit her only at night, she thought, like Eros visiting Psyche, everything would be perfect. Psyche didn't know when she was well off.

Julian's writing, however, was going well. He produced some poems which Miranda could honestly say were beautiful, and his novel took a new spurt forward – though Miranda still found it mystifying. He visited Jocasta a few times to work on it with her, and to play her piano. After one of these visits he told Miranda that although he found her comments helpful, he still didn't trust Jocasta.

'I don't understand,' said Miranda. 'What could she possibly do?'

'I don't know. It's just a feeling I have.'

*

By mid-September, Julian seemed happier. The black moods were less frequent; his face had softened, he smiled more often. Miranda knew that she looked different, too. 'I do you good, don't I?' he remarked one day. Hugging him, she agreed that he did.

When the Circle resumed for the autumn term Miranda feared that their state of physical intimacy would be obvious to everyone. In fact, the other Circle members were far too taken up with their own complex lives to notice, apart from Fiona and Judy, who were already in the picture – and the eagle-eyed Jocasta. Flitting past them during the first evening she cooed: 'I do so love it when people get together!'

'Yuk!' said Miranda to Julian after she'd gone.

He uttered a sort of embarrassed snort. Miranda assumed he had told Jocasta about them, despite her pleas for privacy.

On the way home, Julian said, 'She really does, of course.'

'Who does what?'

'Jocasta. She loves getting people together. Fergus was telling me – you remember Flaxman and that woman…?'

'Sharon?'

'Sharon. She used to be very friendly with Jocasta, and she was a single mother, and Jocasta sort of… set her up with Flaxman. Of course it only lasted about five minutes, he was quite wrong for her and he took drugs when her daughter was there. But Sharon was badly hurt. And then Jocasta tried to do something similar with Fergus and someone else, but he wasn't having anything to do with it.'

Miranda digested this. She and Julian had been 'sort of set up' by Jocasta, she reflected, with a creeping feeling of discomfort. All she said was, 'Good for Fergus.'

*

Miranda greeted her thirty-fifth birthday secure in the knowledge that at least one gap in her life had been filled. She decided to treat Julian and herself to a really good evening out, and booked seats for *The Magic Flute* at the Coliseum, with supper at her flat first.

Julian arrived very late, grumbling about a delay on the tube and bearing a very small box of chocolates. There was no time to eat the chicken casserole she had cooked with much care; they only just got into their seats by curtain up. Miranda was annoyed, and showed it. She wasn't sure she believed the tube story; there was something in Julian's manner that made her suspect him of deliberately sabotaging the occasion. Surely he couldn't be retaliating for her 'total lack of sensitivity' on his birthday?

By the end of the evening, saturated in Mozart, their moods had improved. Back in her flat they started eating the casserole, looked into each other's eyes, and were rapidly entwined. Their lovemaking was better than ever. Lying beside him afterwards, Miranda thought, *this isn't just sex.*

When we make love we are in fact making something called love.

His arm round her, her head nestled in his shoulder, he suddenly said, 'Oh, dear, I think I'm having to grow up. I know I've often played little boy lost because women tend to mother me. You don't let me get away with that, do you?'

'I don't want to mother you,' said Miranda. 'I want a grown-up man in my bed.'

'Yes, I had noticed,' he said. 'As a matter of fact, I think there is one, right here…'

'Oo-oh yes, so there is…'

They stayed in bed together all next morning. After lunch, Miranda left to work for Clive, who was now fully recovered. When she got back, Julian was gone, and all the washing up had been done.

*

The only black spot on the horizon was Miranda's imminent dental operation. The surgeon had warned her that her face might be painful for a few days. She began to feel sorry for herself in advance, not thinking positive at all.

It would be nice to recuperate somewhere afterwards… She thought of Sally, an old school friend who had recently moved to Suffolk with her husband and two sons. Though they had seen little of each other lately, Sally had phoned her at Christmas and said, 'If you ever want a break in the country, feel free to invite yourself.'

Now was the time. She phoned Sally who said she would love to have her for a weekend at the end of October. 'The boys'll be home for half-term,' she said. 'You won't mind that, will you? You'll be amazed how they've shot up.'

The Sunday before her operation, Julian was on particularly good form. Fiona had put a freelance editing job his way, and Jocasta had given him a contact who might also have some editorial work for him. 'If I could earn some money, I could get a proper flat,' he said. 'I'm tired of living like a teenager.'

He really was growing up, thought Miranda. She decided she wouldn't be overburdening him if she offloaded her anxieties. She said, 'Julian, you know I've got this dental operation on Wednesday. I'm really scared about it.'

'Oh, nobody likes dentists. You'll be all right.'

'Yes, but this is quite a big operation, it's going to take at least an hour. I'll probably be all swollen afterwards.'

'You'll be all right,' he repeated. 'It may not be as bad as you expect.'

This was not the response she would have liked. She had half hoped that he would offer to go with her, but he didn't, and she didn't like to ask. Although he seemed far less fragile than a few months before, she didn't want to lean on him too heavily in case he toppled over.

'It means I won't be able to come to the Circle on Friday,' she said. 'I'll have a mouth full of stitches. You will ring me, won't you?'

'Yes, of course.'

*

The evening before the operation she phoned Cassie for reassurance. 'Just tune into Spirit, dear,' Cassie said. 'You'll be fine. I'll be thinking of you.'

Miranda said, 'I think God was having an off day when he designed teeth.'

She did her best to tune in to Spirit, and arrived at the dental hospital feeling quite jaunty, telling herself this was going to be a challenging new experience.

It was horrible. She spent two hours holding herself rigid while the surgeon and a student drilled through bone. She thought it would never stop. She wished she could take her head off and leave it in the chair and go for a walk until they'd finished. But she was trapped in the chair with a road drill inside her brain. Now and again the surgeon asked if she was all right, and told her what a good girl she was, at which she could only roll her eyes.

She sat there with nothing to think about except her teeth, wishing she hadn't refused her mother's milk as a baby. She recalled someone at Liz's weekend declaring that tooth trouble was a symptom of unexpressed anger... could that be so? Miranda didn't want to express anger; her mother had expressed enough for the two of them. Anyway, when she did let it out, as she had with Daphne, the results were disastrous.

She arrived home feeling shaky and weak. The anaesthetic began to wear off and the pain started. She took some paracetamol and the antibiotics prescribed at the hospital. She peered at her face in the mirror and quickly looked away. Her upper lip was three times its normal size; she looked like a miserable Bugs Bunny.

Fiona and Julian both rang in the evening to ask how she was, and Miranda said she was fine, because that was what one says, and it was too painful to say more. Julian asked, 'Shall I see you at the weekend?'

'Oh, Julian,' she mumbled, 'I can't... I don't think I can see anyone for a bit.'

She knew he would not want to come over without making love, and making love was out of the question. Nor did she want him to see her like this. He thought her beautiful; she could not let him see this hideously distorted person.

*

During the following week all was silent from Parson's Green. Miranda couldn't understand it. Surely Julian could at least send her a card? She couldn't eat properly yet and was getting nervy. She was still working on the index of the book on South Africa; writing entries like 'Children: imprisonment of' did nothing to cheer her. She tried to think positive, but she didn't feel positive, she felt ugly and unloved and alone. Why didn't he phone? She decided to consult the Tarot, and there was the Tower exploding, with two unhappy-looking people falling out of it head first. This did nothing to allay her anxiety.

A week after the operation Miranda wrote a postcard to the silent Julian asking whether anything was wrong. There was no reply.

*

'You don't look well!' Fiona put a glass of cider in front of Miranda. She had asked Fiona to meet her early at the pub. They were not the only early arrivals. Fergus was already at the bar listening patiently to one of Trevor's lengthy autobiographical dissertations.

Miranda was still in pain; she still had stitches in her mouth and had not been able to eat properly for ten days. Anxiety sat in her stomach where food should have been. 'Actually,' she said, 'I feel awful. I haven't had a word from Julian; I can't understand it. I've been wondering if something's happened to him.'

'He was all right on Tuesday,' said Fiona. 'Jocasta asked some of us to her place – I must say, she can be very hospitable – and he was there, he seemed fine.'

'Then why on earth hasn't he been in touch? He knows I haven't been well.'

'Oh, you know what men are like about illness, when it's not their own.'

'He didn't say anything to you about me?'

'We didn't talk, actually, he was mostly playing the piano. Jocasta was nauseatingly fulsome in her praise. He is very good, I must say.'

'Yes,' said Miranda. An image of that sunny day in Richmond flashed past her.

Fergus was standing nearby. Over his shoulder, he remarked, 'He doesn't treat his girlfriends very well.'

What did he mean? The bar was filling up, and private conversation was becoming impossible. Before she could ask him, Jocasta came up to her, all smiles. 'Miranda! You weren't here last week.'

'I did tell you I wouldn't be coming. I had this dental operation.'

'Oh, yes, how are you?'

'Not very well, really.'

'You look all right,' observed Jocasta.

You can't see pain, thought Miranda, wishing she'd had time to say it before Jocasta swept off in her long, rainbow-coloured skirt.

And then, Julian appeared in the doorway. Miranda rose and marched over to him, aggression covering her hurt.

'Oh, hallo,' he said, with a nervous smile. 'How are you?'

'Pretty awful, actually. Didn't you get my card?'

'Yes, I, yes, I did, but I knew I'd be seeing you tonight, so I, er.'

'Julian, what's happened, why haven't you been in touch?'

'Afterwards, we'll talk afterwards, OK? There's someone I've got to…' And he scuttered off to break into a conversation between Fergus and Trevor.

As the group began to troop upstairs, Miranda saw Julian talking to Jocasta, his eyes flashing in her direction and away again. She sat frozen through the evening's readings, noting that Julian had placed himself where she could hardly see him. Afterwards, she bought herself a cider and joined Fiona in one of the pews at the back of the pub. Fiona began criticising someone's story; Miranda heard not a word.

Suddenly Jocasta materialised out of nowhere and was leaning over her, her silky red hair hanging over her almost touching Miranda's face. Looking up at her, Miranda thought, *But she really is …*

Jocasta said conspiratorially, 'Julian's coming over, he's terribly contrite. Don't tell him I've spoken to you.' And she was gone.

'Why can't that woman leave us alone?' Miranda asked.

Fiona said, 'Here's Julian, I'll leave you to it. Let me get you another drink.'

And there was Julian. He sat down opposite her, looking not so much contrite as defensive. He said, 'I got your card. Sorry, I didn't have time to ring, well, I haven't been near a phone. You're all right now, aren't you?'

Miranda tried to keep calm. 'No, I'm not. Look, Julian, I've been ill. That was major surgery. You could have found a phone if you'd wanted to. To see how I was.'

'I did phone. You said you were all right.'

'That was ten days ago! Of course I said I was all right, I didn't want to worry you. I meant I was all right like… like people say they're all right when they've survived a car crash. Anyway, it hurt to talk. It still does.'

'I didn't know.'

'I did tell you beforehand how scared I was. Look, Julian, can't you see how hurtful it was for me not to hear from you all that time?'

He lit a cigarette with slightly trembling fingers. 'I don't see why. You've never minded before. I mean, there've been gaps before. I mean, in July, when you wouldn't see me for three weeks, you weren't worried about how I felt then.'

'For heaven's sake, you knew I couldn't see you! Anyway this is different. We weren't even sleeping together then.'

'Yes, we were!'

'Not... properly.'

Fiona placed in front of her a glass of cider, gave her a thumbs up behind Julian's back, and left with a show of discretion. Miranda gulped down a third of the glass. She was feeling extremely peculiar. She ploughed on:

'And this time I was ill. I needed... I needed... 'She couldn't finish.

'Then why did you say you didn't want to see me?'

'I never said that! I said I couldn't see anyone!'

'You didn't want to see me and it was just like July all over again, and I simply couldn't stand it in July, that was three weeks, it was awful!'

'But that was July! This is now, it's quite different!'

'You have no idea how difficult it was for me... '

'Why are you going on about July?'

The exchange continued to veer towards Julian's damaged feelings in July and away from Miranda's currently wounded feelings, whose reality Julian seemed unable to grasp. It was as if the last three months of loving intimacy had never happened.

Miranda drained her glass. Her mouth hurt. She had had no food since a lunch of soup, and she had drunk three glasses of cider. Her attempts to be calm were suddenly and violently superseded by boiling rage. As Julian returned for the umpteenth time to July, she yelled at him: 'Me, me, me, ME! That's all you think about!'

Edward, an elderly and inoffensive man who never uttered a word in the Circle, popped up from the other side of the pew partition, his balding brow furrowed with concern. 'What is wrong? Oh, dear me, what is wrong? Please don't fight!'

And at innocent Edward Miranda yelled even more loudly the words she had failed to yell at Jocasta: 'Mind your own fucking business!'

There was a sudden hush in the buzz of the pub, and every head turned towards Miranda, like marionettes on a single string. Edward popped down as suddenly as he had popped up.

Miranda was aghast. She hated scenes, particularly public ones, and here she was creating one. She, who never got angry, was screeching like a fishwife. She took a deep breath. She said to Julian, 'Look, I really am feeling ill. I am going home. Come with me if you want to.'

'All right,' he said, to her astonishment. As they walked away from the pub she said, 'God, I wish Jocasta would keep out of things.'

'What do you mean?'

'I just wish she'd leave us alone. She doesn't respect anyone's privacy, even her own. Fiona told me she was really bored with hearing about her silly little conquests. I shouldn't let her bother me.'

But Jocasta's hair and the heavy pendant hanging over Miranda's face, Jocasta's slightly blurred features hovering over her, had made a peculiar impact. The thought that had half-formulated in her muzzy mind completed itself: *But she really is a witch!*

2

THE TOWER STRUCK BY LIGHTNING

They spent the night barely touching, and the next day they were very careful with each other. Neither referred to their row. Seeing that Miranda was in genuine physical pain, Julian was thoughtful and tender. After breakfast he said, 'You know, I don't think I really realised before that other people have real feelings.'

Miranda stared at him. Sometimes Julian seemed more like a teenager than a grown man. 'Well, that should help with your novel,' she said.

The following weekend, however, their relationship had mysteriously deteriorated. On the Saturday, Julian by turn criticised Miranda and took offence at perceived criticisms of himself. He niggled about where they should go for a walk; in the end they didn't go out at all. Then he complained that he felt ill because he had had no exercise. At supper he suddenly didn't like mushrooms; he had never not liked mushrooms before. But he stayed, and they went to bed, and there they met as fully and wholeheartedly as ever. After an hour or so they both felt a great deal better.

At midnight on Sunday they were lying holding each other when Miranda brought up a subject that had been bothering her. At the Circle on Friday Jocasta had very obviously been avoiding her. Miranda assumed she was displeased at her – she went hot all over whenever she thought of the scene she'd created. She asked, 'Has Jocasta said anything to you about that row we had in the pub?'

Julian enacted the mumble of someone half asleep, which he wasn't.

Miranda went on, 'She can't seem to keep her hands out of other people's business.' *Jocasta's hair swooping over her face.*

'She has her good points,' said Julian, abandoning his pretence of drowsiness. 'She's been helping me a lot with the novel.'

'She likes you. I've sometimes wondered – has she ever made a pass at you?'

Julian emitted a nervous giggle.

Hang on, thought Miranda. *That is a guilty giggle.* 'Oh!' she teased. 'More than a pass!'

Julian emitted an embarrassed laugh.

For a second, Miranda also thought it funny. Since Jocasta seemed to be reaping her way through the entire male population of the Circle, it seemed inevitable and unimportant that sooner or later her scythe would arrive at Julian. She, too, laughed. Then her brain started working. Given Julian's professed distrust of Jocasta and the fact that it was only a few weeks since he had got his sexual act together... 'When was this?'

Julian said blithely, 'But you knew!'

Miranda felt as though she had swallowed a bucket of ice. She finally understood. Jocasta had not only bedded him; she had chosen to bed him the week of Miranda's operation. And Julian had co-operated.

'You mean... while I was ill?'

'But you knew! I thought that was why you were so angry! I thought Fiona had told you.'

'Does Fiona know?'

'You said she was fed up with hearing about Jocasta's conquests – I thought Jocasta must have told her—'

Miranda sat up. 'You bastard. You absolute bastard! How could you do that?'

'But why should you mind? You've never been committed to me. Look, it just happened. I was a bit down after the Circle that Friday and Jocasta asked what was wrong, and I said you were too busy to see me—'

'I was in too much pain to see anybody!' She was shouting again.

'I don't see why you should be so upset. You don't love me, you think I'm worthless—'

'What are you talking about?'

'You're always diminishing me!' He raised himself on an elbow and said furiously, 'You keep trying to change me, and I don't want to be changed. I just want to be myself.'

'I've only been trying to help.'

'I don't want to be helped!'

Managing to bite back the words 'after all I've done for you!' Miranda said coldly, 'Well you gave me every impression that you did.'

'I was happy as I was.'

'You were not happy! You were always moaning.'

'There you go again.' He hissed at her, 'You keep telling me what's wrong with me and telling me to be different. You're always going on about accepting people as they are, and you don't accept me as I am.' He sat up and shouted, 'You make me unconfident!'

The part of Miranda that was a good growth movement student applauded Julian's new-found ability to express his feelings. The rest of her was outraged. She got out of bed and said, with all the superiority she could muster, 'I have been trying and trying to lift you up. And you drag me down!'

Julian muttered something and lay down again with his head under the duvet. Miranda went over to the window and stared through a gap in the curtains at the autumn trees glowing sickly yellow in the light of the street lamps. Julian and Jocasta – the betrayal! This wasn't happening, she was having a nightmare. Rollo rose from his armchair with a pink yawn and rubbed himself round her ankles. She picked him up and cuddled him for comfort, and the insensitive creature started purring. She buried her face in his fur, carried him back to the armchair and curled up in it, clutching the cat and shaking.

*

In the morning they both looked and felt dreadful. Julian, with set jaw, cooked himself breakfast (*her* eggs, *her* bacon) while Miranda looked on disbelievingly. When, in icy silence, he had eaten and Miranda had had a cup of coffee and a cigarette, Julian said, 'I can't stand this. We had better stop seeing each other.'

'Fine by me,' said Miranda.

Pale and trembling, he put on his shabby navy blue coat. Miranda watched him, feeling surprisingly strong; she realised that she felt quite good, only slightly concerned that she didn't feel bad. At the door he said, 'Well, goodbye, Miranda,' in a dramatic tone.

Miranda said, 'Don't sound so tragic, it isn't, really.' She went up to him and put her hands on his stiff shoulders. 'I know you're feeling awful now, but you'll be all right.'

'I'll send you the ten pounds I owe you when I get it.'

'I suppose we can still say hallo to each other at the Circle,' she said.

He said, 'If you come, of course I'll speak to you. I don't know if you'll want to come anymore.' And he left.

When Miranda found the grill pan awash as usual with bacon fat she felt a little flip of fury. 'Good riddance,' she said to Rollo.

She laid out her tarot cards, hoping for some reassurance. There was the Knight of Cups, riding like Lancelot, tirra-lirra by the river, and there the smugly enthroned Queen of Wands, the powerful magical lady with her wand and her black cat. Cassie's interfering woman was never Daphne, she had been Jocasta all along. And there was the heart pierced by swords, and there the Tower exploding with two people flying out of it, anguish on their faces. It didn't help. She consulted *I Ching*, which told her: *Shock comes, and after shock, laughing words.* It was right about shock, but she couldn't envisage many laughing words in the near future.

As she made another cup of coffee, she began to blame herself. Jocasta had just been being Jocasta, engaging in an excessively ill-timed one-night stand. She wasn't worth thinking about – apart from the ironic realisation that without Miranda's ministrations Julian would never have been capable of slipping so lightly between Jocasta's sheets. No, the rift was clearly all down to Miranda's ineptitude. She had been trying to change Julian, she had made him feel unwanted.

She rang Fiona to tell her that she and Julian had broken up. It was evident from Fiona's response that this was one amour that Jocasta had not confided in her. Without going into full details, Miranda remarked that it seemed to be compulsory for male members of the Circle to go to bed with Jocasta. Fiona said, 'That woman is a mischief-maker. I should try not to let it get to you.'

After she had rung off, Miranda sat still by the phone. No, it was not all her fault! Julian would never have thought of bedding Jocasta if she hadn't made the first move. She had a sudden image of Jocasta as an exotic bird of prey swooping on baby-bird Julian and carrying him off to be gobbled at leisure.

Recalling his white, drawn face, she rang Cassie and asked for some healing. 'I had the most fearful row with Julian,' she explained. Out of some kind of loyalty, she didn't mention Jocasta. 'I've been trying to help him and I've just made things worse. I knew he was sensitive – but I didn't realise how sensitive...'

Cassie's voice was reassuringly brisk. 'Yes, I'm picking him up – oh, hang on a mo, I've got Giovanni here, my spirit artist, we're drawing a picture ... oh, yes, a lovely picture of you two together. There's a very strong link between you, very strong. I think you've known each other before.'

'In a past life, d'you mean?'

'In at least one, I'd say. When you're on a spiritual path stuff often comes up from previous lives... it'll be all right. Giovanni's drawing your eyes very big to show you're seeing clearly. I think he'll come back to you, lovey.'

For a moment Miranda felt buoyed up. Then she said, 'Cassie, he hates me. I wanted to help, but I'm afraid I've harmed him.' Cassie said gently, 'You can't have harmed him, you acted out of love. No real hurt ever comes out of love.'

That was when Miranda began to cry.

*

Her check-up at the dental hospital was not reassuring. The consultant tutted that she was not healing as fast as she should; her teeth shouldn't still be hurting. As she came through her front door her heart was weighing a ton. Into her mind came the story of the Goose-Girl, the princess who has lost everything, and whose horse's head has been nailed above the gateway. As she drives her geese through the gate she asks:

'Oh Falada, Falada, what do you there?'

And Falada replies, 'If your mother only knew, her heart would surely break in two.'

No it wouldn't, thought Miranda. *If her mother only knew, she'd probably say, 'Well, what else did you expect?'*

But her heart now spoke to another mother, a mother she wished she had had, whose heart would surely break in two if she knew how she was hurting, who would take her in her arms and gently rock her and tell her everything would be all right. Where was that mother? And since she had never known her, why did Miranda miss her so?'

She again rang Cassie, the most motherly person she knew, and this time told her the whole story.

Cassie said, 'Oh, these men! I'm glad I've given them up – give me cats any time. I'd forget him if I were you. I still think you had dealings in a past life. There's something that still needs working out.'

'The thing is— I'm sure he's been badly hurt at some time.'

There was a pause. 'That's not what I'm getting, dear. I think he's been thoroughly spoiled. Listen, my love, you're in shock, and I'm not surprised. We're sending you healing.'

Miranda felt the cool, calming current coming through the phone, soothing her pain and her nerves. She said, 'Cassie, I've got to ask – you see things coming, did you see this coming?'

Cassie said: 'It's like this. For one thing, people have

free will, there's always choices. He could have said no. And then, if I was allowed to warn people about every difficulty, they'd try to avoid going through things they need to go through. Nasty things often happen for a purpose.'

Miranda said, 'I suppose there's a purpose in this, but it's hard to see what. It's all so horrible. I've been wondering whether to confront Jocasta.'

'Don't have anything to do with her, is my advice. Well, it's Spirit's advice, too. Don't drag yourself down to her level. What you've got to do, my love, is learn to rise above it all, fly above it like a bird. You can do it. If you really want to help him, example's better than words, you know. We'll be with you, dear.'

'Will you send him some healing, too?' The image of Julian's ashen face was still with her. 'Yes, dear, though I must say we'll have to bore a hole in his head to get through. He's not seeing straight at the moment. And you need a change of scene – are you going away somewhere?'

'Yes, just for the weekend. To a friend in Suffolk.' Thank goodness she had arranged that weekend with Sally, she really needed it.

'That'll do you good, dear. You enjoy it.'

When she meditated that evening, Miranda tried sending healing light to Julian, and a strong sense of healing came into her own body, almost as if Cassie were in the room with her. Julian's cry, 'You make me unconfident!' rang in her head. Poor Julian: whatever Cassie thought, someone must have made him unconfident a long time ago.

*

On Friday she knew she had to go to the Circle. Going would be less painful than staying at home fantasising about what was happening there; even so, she felt sick and shaky at the prospect. She telephoned Rosa and asked for an emergency One-to-One. Rosa came over at lunchtime and let her cry and rage, and hugged her and held her, while her tears flowed like scalding water.

*

Fiona met her at the Pig and Apple in a state of righteous indignation. 'God, you look terrible!' she said. 'I have spoken to Jocasta. I told her she really must stop interfering with her students' private lives. She had the grace to look slightly embarrassed.'

When they assembled upstairs Julian was not there. Jocasta, looking her usual cool self, announced: 'I've decided to try out some automatic writing. Just write for ten minutes with no intellectual input, allow the words to flow on to the paper. It's a good way to get in touch with the subconscious, to contact your real feelings.'

Miranda whispered to Fiona, 'She's taking a bit of a risk, asking me to contact my real feelings!'

She put her biro to paper. A word came out: 'Anxiety'. As she paused for the next word to arrive, Julian walked in, looking wan, and Jocasta had to whisper instructions to him. Miranda watched their heads so close together, his misleadingly noble profile almost touching Jocasta's chestnut tresses. She wrote: *I am hurting, I am hurting.* Then she scribbled heavily over the words, in case anyone saw them.

She left early to pack for her journey to Suffolk next morning, and organised Rollo's care with her downstairs neighbour. She was looking forward to a weekend of peace and fresh air and green fields. As she was packing, Fiona rang.

'I wanted to tell you – I managed to corner Julian, but I couldn't get much sense out of him. He kept going on about how you'd belittled him and made him lose confidence. I said, what about Miranda's feelings and Miranda's confidence, but he didn't seem able to take in a thing I said. He said he just wants to live quietly and not be changed. What have you been doing to him, Miranda dear?'

'Just trying to make him more confident,' said Miranda sadly.

'Yes, well, I said I thought you were very fond of him and obviously he matters to you, and he did slightly hear that. I expect he'll come back to you. If you want him after all this. Leave him alone for a bit, and he'll start missing you.'

'Yes. Maybe. Thanks for trying.'

'You deserve to be happy,' said Fiona. 'It's a pity men can be such turds.'

3

A BONFIRE

Ducks can't count. Sally and Harold's garden sloped down to a stream, from which semi-wild ducks waddled up every morning to be fed. At intervals, Sally told Miranda, Harold would shoot one for Sunday lunch; the survivors still came back for breakfast next morning. Sally felt mildly guilty about this, but enjoyed consuming the ducks. 'It's silly not to eat them,' she said. 'They're always getting bread from me. It's natural, it's the food chain.'

Sally was one of the few friends Miranda had made at boarding school, an alien environment in which she had been not only guilty of being brainy and bad at games but was generally considered rather odd. Sally was both clever and good at games, and Miranda had appreciated her friendship. They shared an enjoyment of writers like Oscar Wilde, M. R. James and H.G. Wells, together with a desire to leave school and live adult lives as soon as possible, and although their paths had since diverged they had kept in touch over the years.

Sally had married Harold, then a law student, when she was only twenty. Miranda cried at the wedding; marrying seemed such a terrible thing to do. Primed by her mother, she thought of it as the death of love. But it suited Sally; she and Harold were easy together. Their two sons were good-looking, confident teenagers. Sally had consciously made a career of being a wife and mother, and did both well. Harold had recently joined a legal practice in Ipswich, and they had settled comfortably into a modern house in the outlying countryside.

When Miranda got off the train Sally was there to greet her, looking every inch the country wife. She had always been fair and rosy-cheeked; now she looked even fairer and rosier, and her body had filled out. But she frowned with concern at Miranda's appearance. 'You don't look well, my dear, are you all right?'

Miranda had decided to leave the Julian-Jocasta business behind. Hiding her emotions behind the smile of the good guest she explained that she was still suffering the after-effects of dentistry, which was true. During the night her mouth had been so painful that the explosion with Julian had been temporarily superseded by the fantasy of losing all her teeth.

Plucking a recently murdered duck for Sunday lunch, Sally remarked, 'I hate doing this. It'll look better with its head off. Now, where did I put the chopper?'

'Oh, yuck.' Miranda retreated to the living room and returned when the banging from the kitchen had ceased. Headless and featherless, the duck now resembled a limp soft toy.

Sally said, 'I haven't taken the entrails out yet, that really makes me want to be vegetarian. I'll do it later,' she added quickly, seeing Miranda's expression. 'I do hope you can eat all right?'

'More or less. I've been looking forward to someone else's cooking,' said Miranda.

'Good. There's rabbit stew in the oven for lunch today. Hope that's OK.'

'It smells delicious.'

Only the night before, Miranda had been sitting in the semi-darkness of the Circle. Now she had been swept into another, brighter world. Through Sally's kitchen window she could see the stream and the gently bobbing ducks, beyond the stream an unkempt meadow, where Harold and the boys were building a bonfire for a fireworks party that evening, and beyond that a height covered by woodland. It was peaceful, it was safe. Her body began to lose some of its tension.

Killing things, Sally was explaining, was part of country life. 'We have a permanent problem with mice here, so every few months we cure them.'

'Cure them? Of being mice?'

'Treat them, put things down for them, deal with them, make them be dead.'

'Oh. Oh dear… are the boys enjoying Suffolk?'

There was plenty to talk about other than Miranda's sore heart. Though there was a nasty moment when they entered the sitting room before lunch, and Sally said, 'Let me introduce you to Julian.' Propped on the sofa was a plastic male torso wearing a painted jacket and bow tie. Miranda hoped Sally didn't notice her jump. 'What on earth is it?' she asked.

Sally said, 'Isn't he silly? My brother got him in America. He called him Julian after a wimp he knew at school.'

Harold explained. 'It's what American women put beside them on the front seat when they're driving alone, so that nasty men don't force them off the road and do unspeakable things to them.'

'You're such a chauvinist, Harold,' said Sally amiably.

A blown-up plastic man with a silly smile and no arms or legs, and sticking plaster on his nose where a visiting child had bitten him. That was Julian.

'Why don't we use him as the guy?' suggested Bevan, the younger boy.

'He'd explode, stupid,' said his older brother, Tony. In fact a rather unpleasantly lifelike guy was already sitting in the garden, awaiting transportation to the bonfire.

'We're having Guy Fawkes early,' explained Sally. 'The boys'll be back at school on the fifth of November.'

'Have you explained to Miranda about the Martians?' asked Harold, handing Miranda a glass of sherry.

'Martians?'

'That's what Harold calls them,' Sally explained. 'They're the Martins, actually, they're all completely mad, but they're our nearest neighbours and they keep inviting us for drinks so we can't not ask them to the bonfire party. They live in a sort of crumbling gothic mansion up the road. There's Bunty, she's in her seventies, and her son Roger, who's a bit dim. He's a sort of farmer.'

'Roger is not dim, he is insane,' said Harold.

'He really is, actually,' said Sally. 'One day he had two tractors stuck in the stream. First one got stuck and he took the other to get it out and that got stuck too. He spent the whole day trying to get two tractors out of the stream.'

'His wife is even dimmer,' said Harold. 'Davina. She's tranquillised up to the gills. They've got a little boy, poor kid.'

'I would have thought country people were mentally healthy,' said Miranda.

'Don't you believe it,' said Harold. 'What are we offering them tonight?'

'Drinks when they arrive at six, then bonfire, then mulled wine, soup, sausages, cheese, French bread.'

'Better be ready early, then. Bunty always arrives early. Anyone else coming?'

'Jenny and John. They're our neighbours on the other side. They're normal,' Sally reassured Miranda.

*

Concerning the Martians, they had not exaggerated. Bunty, arriving early as forecast, was over six feet tall, with a perfect witch's face incorporating a beaky, corrugated nose and a mouth revealing acres of gum inhabited by the occasional tooth. 'The others are coming,' she said cheerily. 'I couldn't be bothered to wait.'

She plonked herself heavily on the sofa beside Miranda, the plastic Julian having been banished to the downstairs loo. 'Who have we here, who have we here, wha'?' she asked.

Miranda introduced herself, and Bunty launched without preamble into an account of how she had taken up painting late in life. 'I was always good at art, in those days it wasn't encouraged, but I kept on painting. Then I got married and had Roger and I had to stop, but I do a lot now. You'll have to come and see my work – how long are you staying?'

Jenny and John arrived next, a bland youngish couple, and the adults sat around with drinks and snacks while the boys added to the already enormous bonfire pile. Sally handed out Martinis, on which blue flowers elegantly floated. Bunty took hers with enthusiasm. 'Flowers!' she cried.

'It's borage from the garden,' said Sally. 'Borage is for courage.' *Oh, good*, thought Miranda, *just what I need.*

'I must show you my herb garden,' Sally said to her. 'I'm getting to be quite an expert.'

Lastly came Davina and Roger, with little Robin. Roger was almost perfectly square; Davina had a round, flat face with a double chin, resembling a squashed bun. She sat very still as though her head might fall off if she moved. Two-year-old Robin was very fair and very pretty; he ran about tweeting like a little bird, commenting on everything he came across. After a round of drinks had been downed and Bunty's glass replenished, Sally said, 'Let's show Robin the guy.' She took his small hand and led the way into the garden, followed by the rest of the party.

'Mickey Mouse!' exclaimed Robin at the sight of the guy. To Miranda's eye the guy looked a great deal more sinister than Mickey Mouse, but the little boy trotted up to it and shook a stuffed glove. 'Do you do?' he said politely.

Harold brought another tray of drinks out on to the darkening lawn.

'No more, thank you,' Bunty burbled. 'If I have any more I shall be too happy.'

'Can one be too happy?' Harold asked.

'Oh, I suppose not,' she said in a surprised voice.

Drinks drunk, darkness fallen, Harold armed everyone with torches to make their way to the bonfire field. Bevan and Tony took the lead, carrying the guy ceremonially across the footbridge across the stream. Harold placed his torch under his nose and unexpectedly pranced round the garden chanting, 'I am the Dong with the luminous nose!'

He led the way across the narrow footbridge. 'Right folks, let's go. Come on, Bunty, we'll do it American style, side by side.'

'Bunty's doing fine,' said Bunty, leaning heavily on Harold, her feet splaying as they stepped unsteadily on the wooden slats.

'This bridge is really too narrow,' Sally said to Miranda. 'Harold's mother fell in the stream in the summer. Luckily it's not very deep. Come on, Robin, I'll carry you across.'

The boys had already lit the bonfire, which was blazing nicely. 'The fy…yer!' trilled Robin, his face full of awe. Tony was roasting marshmallows on twigs and running round the fire proffering them to the guests. The flames began to roar and soar, and Robin gave a scream of fear.

'Look, Robin, pretty!' said his father crossly.

Robin shrieked, 'Pretteee!' with terror in his voice. *He will be very confused later on,* Miranda thought anxiously; forever more 'pretty' would mean violent and scary and the ritual immolation of Mickey Mouse.

Roger said impatiently, 'Come on, you're a big boy now.' He picked the child up and carried him closer to the flames.

'Down!' screamed Robin. 'Down!'

'What does that man think he's doing?' exclaimed Sally, and headed towards them.

Davina, close by, just stood there. Sally said, 'Put him down, Roger!'

Robin screamed again. Miranda thought, *I can't bear this!*

It was Bunty who went to the rescue. 'It's all right, Granny's here!' And she took the child firmly from Roger's arms and carried him away from the fire. Sally and Jenny clustered round him uttering soothing noises. As the fireworks were lit, Bunty continued to hold Robin close, smoothing the back of his head with a large, wrinkled hand.

Colours burst against the blackness, explosions filled the sky, fountains of fire, sparks spraying upwards like luminous sperm. The flames finally reached the guy which toppled downwards, looking for a moment horrifically human. Fine grey ash began to fall.

'We'll all be covered in dust, it's falling on our heads,' said Jenny, retreating.

'So it is,' said Sally. 'We'll have ash on our heads, for repentance.'

An explosion happens, echoed Miranda's thoughts, *and we will all have ashes on our heads for repentance.*

*

Witches were not all wicked, Miranda told herself, lying comfortably in bed that night. Sally had become a sort of white witch, with her duck-plucking and her herbs. Bunty, on her way back from the bonfire, had held her torch beneath her witch's face, turning it into a grotesque mask, and crying, 'Look at Granny!' Robin, oddly, was not frightened, and laughed with pleasure. Bunty was clearly a good witch.

Miranda winced at the recollection of Robin being taught to be afraid. What would become of all that bright vulnerability, in the hands of those parents? Who, she wondered, had taught Julian to be afraid? Once, he had turned to her in the night and said, 'I'm so frightened, Miranda,' in a small voice, and she had given him a hug, but he didn't say what he was frightened of. Life, perhaps.

Now she saw clearly what she had done. Julian was right: she had been trying to make him what he was not. She had wanted to heal his wounds, and instead she had opened them up. She had wanted a strong man and berated the little boy. She would have let Robin cry out his fear, but when Julian succumbed to self-pity she tried to hush him. She had tried to cure him him of being a little boy. He really hadn't understood that he had hurt her, or even that he could. He had felt unwanted, and Jocasta had seized the chance to add another notch to her broomstick and lure him to her gingerbread house – how could he resist?

*

On the Sunday morning Miranda woke depressed, but was careful not to show it. From an early age she had had plenty of practice in not showing what she felt. She lay in bed, feeling the weight in her stomach and listening to household noises. Her bedroom was on the ground floor; she could hear people in the kitchen chivvying each other without malice. This must be what a happy family sounded like.

'Tony, you must have a bath this morning, you wouldn't have one last night.'

'I did have one!'

'Oh, that was you? Is that why the floor was covered in water?'

Why couldn't she deal so lightly with Julian's soggy towels? Why couldn't he, come to that?

After breakfast Sally invited Miranda to help her pick spinach from the garden. Roses were still blooming. A black cat stalked along the bank of the stream, escorted by a flotilla of ducks. Bevan's voice came from the other side of the garden: 'Oh, Dad, you are stupid! Surely you know what parsley looks like!'

As she pulled up spinach, Julian continued to filter in and out of her mind. Had she really belittled him so much? She thought of the times when she had tried to pull him out of a depression or persuade him to join a group; the times when she had corrected his grammar or suggested a change to a poem, or expressed irritation about the mess he left around the flat. She would have done better to keep her mouth shut – he took all her comments so seriously! But, oh, Julian, it was all very well accepting someone totally and unjudgmentally in a One-to-One but surely no one could do that twenty-four hours a day?

She helped Sally prepare Sunday lunch, duck and all, while Harold took the boys to church. While they washed spinach and peeled potatoes, Sally asked about her life. Miranda told her about the South Africa index, Clive's coronary, her difficulties with Daphne, and her dental operation, successfully editing Julian out. The only person she had told the whole story to was Rosa, though Fiona had quickly got the picture. Perhaps Miranda was still obeying her mother's commandment: 'Thou shalt not speak to others about family problems'. The commandment immediately following this was: 'Thou shalt not show thy pain'.

There was an element of shame, too, in her reticence. Sally would never have let a Julian into her life in the first place. She had married a solid man with a solid profession – the kind of man Miranda never met. She was happy with her countrified life, Sally said, as they waited for the menfolk to return from church. 'Though I try and improve my mind from time to time. I've been reading *The Gulag Archipelago* for months.'

'Are you enjoying it?'

'Not really, it's very heavy going.'

'Then why are you reading it?' asked Tony, coming in. 'Gosh, that duck smells good.'

'Because it's good for me!' said his mother. 'I want to make sure my mind doesn't deteriorate totally as I descend into middle age.'

'We're not middle-aged!' protested Miranda.

'We're past thirty-five, technically that's middle-aged isn't it? According to the Bible, our allotted span is four score years and ten. At least we don't look middle-aged. Well, you don't. Do I?'

'Not in the least.'

Sally was so strong, thought Miranda, sipping a sherry while her hostess put the final touches to lunch. She considered the other powerful women in her life: Daphne, Jocasta, both technically middle-aged, both youthful. They seemed like characters from different plays; she couldn't imagine them in the same room as Sally. She couldn't imagine Julian here either. Once, he had said that he might like to get married some day, but as he was addressing the ceiling at the time Miranda didn't assume this had anything to do with her. In Sally's world, husbands had good incomes, they commuted to panelled offices, sent their sons to public school and skilfully carved roast ducks they had shot themselves. Miranda couldn't imagine Julian doing any of these things; he would never fit in here. She found it a little strange that she fitted in here herself, but she seemed to. She wondered whose play she was in.

After lunch she and Sally went for a walk, leaving Harold chopping logs in the garage. 'It's good for him to do something physical,' said Sally. 'Gets things out of his system.'

'How do you get things out of your system?' Miranda asked.

'I don't think I have much lingering in my system.' Sally sounded surprised.

'You're always so equable.'

'Am I? Perhaps it's to do with having had a totally cabbage-like childhood. I do get ratty at times, but I come straight out with it, and then it's gone.'

'You didn't seem to mind yesterday when Harold said your rabbit stew tasted like soap. Which it didn't, by the way.'

'I really didn't mind. Perhaps it did taste like soap to Harold.'

'I'd have thrown it at him!' said Miranda. 'Well, I'd have wanted to.'

'Oh, I must tell him that! He just said it, it wasn't malicious.'

Miranda was impressed. Why couldn't she be like that with Julian? Sally went on:

'I had to learn with Harold, though. When we were first married, he did sometimes say things that were hurtful, and we did have some rows – Harold always said I was overreacting. Then one day I sat down and thought about it, and I realised I could either be hurt and suffer, or decide not to be hurt. Because the important thing was our marriage, not winning points. You have to compromise.'

Miranda had always thought of compromise as weakness; to compromise from strength was a new notion.

Sally went on, 'I mean, nothing's perfect. I married Harold because I loved him, and you can't force people to be what they're not.'

'Maybe that's why I'm not married,' said Miranda. 'Perhaps I want too much.'

*

When Sally saw her off at the station on Monday morning, laden with spinach, borage and sage, Miranda was feeling a great deal better. Perhaps things were not that terrible; people could have rows and get over them. She and Julian had only been lovers in the full sense for a few weeks; it couldn't be over yet. She straightened her shoulders. She had borage for courage. She would not let the witch get the better of her.

PART 4

NOVEMBER: BATTLING WITH THE WITCH

1

OUTER DARKNESS

Sporting a newly grown ponytail, Al addressed the Support Group assembled for the autumn term. 'For the next six weeks we shall be focussing on the oppressive social factors that prevent us from being the fully developed, beautiful human beings we really are – factors like classism, sexism, racism, ageism, and so on. Ultimately, the plan is to form subgroups for those of us who are oppressed in specific ways – women, men, older people, the working class, racial groups...'

But this was not what she'd come for! Al had told Miranda on the phone that this was to be an advanced group doing in-depth work, his tone implying that she was privileged to join it. She had been looking forward to offloading her still-swirling emotions to an all-accepting audience, but this no longer seemed the place to do it in. Miranda looked round at the twenty-odd people forming the opening circle. Rosa was there, but several of the faces fixed raptly on Al were new. Three of them belonged to a trio of dungareed women from a Camden Town squat. They looked strong and fierce and scary.

Al had clearly rehearsed his speech with care. 'We are going to start by looking at the stresses caused by classism. Since we all come from different backgrounds, we must be very sensitive to each other, and be aware not only when we are oppressed but also when we act as the oppressor. We will be aiming to liberate ourselves from the lies society has imposed on us, to de-victimise ourselves, and be proud of our backgrounds, whatever they are.'

When Al asked for feedback, one of the Camden women expressed her enthusiasm by punching the air with a revolutionary fist. Miranda quailed: this was nothing like the we-are-all-loving people of Liz's reunion. When it was her turn to speak, she found herself shaking. She summoned what courage she had, and said, 'I thought the Support Group was supposed to bring people together, and this just sounds like dividing us. I don't agree about social issues causing everything, to me the cause of most people's problems is lack of love.'

Rosa, who was next, said she agreed with Miranda, and that as a Jew she had no desire to ghettoise herself by joining a Jewish subgroup. A couple of over-fifties protested that focussing on ageism would make them feel even older. Everyone else seemed thrilled at the prospect of exploring their social oppression.

As the evening unfolded Miranda felt increasingly under attack. Criticising other members was against Support Group rules. But when Sal, Kate and Rosie from Camden began releasing their emotions about the oppression inflicted on them by snotty schoolteachers, chauvinist doctors and patronising politicians, it was clear that members of the middle class were equated with the enemy and that their very presence in the group was deeply oppressive. Miranda began to feel totally unacceptable. How could she be proud of her background, which was obviously not only a personal disaster but a political and social one as well?

She noticed that Al had not suggested forming a middle class subgroup, though if anyone was oppressed by the middle classes it was people like herself who had been brought up in them. For middle-class values, albeit as filtered through her mother's somewhat individual consciousness, seemed to consist of a set of contradictory precepts, guaranteed to keep one immobilised. Miranda began listing them in her head:

Always speak the truth/never say what you really mean.
Stand up for yourself/don't answer back.
Show some initiative/do as you're told.
It is women's social duty to get married/marriage is slavery for women.
Men are there to look after women/men are useless at everything.
And the ultimate commandment:
Above all, what counts is appearances. You are to be judged on your marital status, your income, and the shine on your bathroom taps. The state of your heart and soul is irrelevant, not to say indecent.

*

It was a horrible evening. Miranda felt smaller and smaller in the presence of these proudly non-middle-class women, with their self-confidence and their Social Science degrees and their politics of power-to-the-people-except-people-with-BBC-accents. By the time she got home she felt very oppressed indeed.

As she cycled home, the streets were suddenly darkened by a power cut, and she had to wobble her way through eerie blackness. She recalled Cassie's warning about 'dark forces'; they felt very present. Once indoors, she seized Rollo for comfort and collapsed into a state of fear. She was scared of the Support Group, scared by the continuing pain in her teeth, scared of going back to the Circle on Friday, and scared that no one would ever love her, that she would be unloved, unaccepted, a half-person cast into the outer darkness for ever and ever and ever.

*

'The problem with men,' said Jocasta, 'is that they are quite unable to get their sexuality and their feelings together.'

'I know what you mean,' said Miranda, not knowing what she meant or why Jocasta should be saying this to her, of all people. She looked round the pub for escape. Jocasta had been psychologising all evening, opening with the proclamation: 'It's important for writers to work on their personal self-development as well as their writing.'

What, Miranda wondered, had inspired that, and what did Julian make of it? But Julian was studiously pretending she was invisible.

'So many men in this group,' Jocasta went on, looking round the pub. 'And I don't fancy a single one of them. They're all so immature!'

Under the circumstances, this statement sounded surreal. It had been a surreal evening; there had been another power cut, and after candles had been supplied and lit, Jocasta commanded everyone to recount a recent dream. 'Dreams are our contact with the subconscious, with our creativity,' she announced. Miranda wondered what she had been reading that week.

In the flickering candlelight, drawing out the secret contents of the group's minds, Jocasta seemed surrounded by an aura of occult power. To Miranda's heightened sensitivity it was as if she was demanding access to their very souls.

Miranda was careful to produce a boring and meaningless dream.

Now Jocasta was asking: 'Why haven't you brought anything to read lately?'

'I haven't written anything lately,' said Miranda.

'Oh, you have, I know you have!' exclaimed Jocasta almost flirtatiously. 'Bring something soon. I want strong women writers in this group.'

She sailed off, leaving Miranda with her mouth open.

'What was all that about?' enquired Fiona, joining her.

'I'm not quite sure. She said she wants me to write a story. And she may have been trying to tell me she's not interested in Julian.'

'She probably isn't,' said Fiona. 'I shouldn't worry about it too much. Julian is by no means the only person she has tampered with.'

'Oh?' In Fiona's dry presence Miranda began to feel more normal.

'You must promise not to tell anyone,' Fiona went on. 'The other evening I became the recipient of confidences from Fergus. He had a mini-fling with Jocasta just after her long-term man left—'

'But she must be a good fifteen years older than him!'

'He likes older women, apparently.'

Miranda wished she'd known that before. Fergus seemed so much more easy-going than Julian.

'Then almost immediately another of her old flames, Richard, had a bust-up with his girlfriend and went to Jocasta for comfort, and Fergus was unceremoniously dumped. Then when Richard went back to his girlfriend, Jocasta started going through her entire backlist. Comes the evening when you weren't here, and a group of people including Jocasta, Fergus and Julian went on to someone's flat after the Circle. Jocasta flirted with Fergus all evening and he felt like a puppy-dog expecting a biscuit. Then, at going home time, it was Julian who got bundled into her taxi. Fergus felt a bit deprived of his biscuit, but he feels he's well out of it now. And he also said... I wonder if I should tell you...'

'Go on.'

'Well, according to Fergus she'd had her eye on Julian for ages, well before you joined the Circle.'

Miranda's glass seemed to be travelling away from her at the end of a tunnel.

'Are you all right?' asked Fiona. 'You look a bit green.'

'I feel a bit unreal. If she wanted him, why on earth did she shove him at me?'

'Perverse, isn't it. Maybe she just said it to keep Fergus up to the mark.'

'I wish I understood what was going on. I thought it was just a one-night stand, but he's still avoiding me.'

'Fergus doesn't think it'll last. But he likes Julian, he's a bit worried about him. And you, by the way. What I'd like to know is what the great attraction is – she does seem to inspire very strong feelings in people. It can't be just sexual availability.'

'She's probably very good at sex,' said Miranda. 'With all that experience.' Jocasta must be possessed of secrets of the bedroom she could not begin to imagine.

'But she's not obviously sexy. It's strange...'

'And why does she have to play around with people's emotions?' Miranda thought of Flaxman and Sharon, and the unhappiness Jocasta's interference had created.

'Power,' said Fiona. 'It must be. She can't possibly fancy all the men she sleeps with. As if she didn't have enough power, sitting there judging everyone's writing, and dabbling with their psyches.'

'I really think she's a kind of witch,' said Miranda. 'Circe, turning all the men into pigs!'

Fiona laughed, and then frowned. 'You know what she sometimes makes me think of – a big red spider, sitting in the middle of a web.'

This image entered Miranda's head and stayed there. She remembered Warren saying that if you dwell on a thought you give it power. She really shouldn't give power to the thought of Jocasta as a spider in a web, but now it was impossible not to.

'Anyway,' said Fiona. 'Are you coming to Judy's play-reading tomorrow?'

Judy had recently met an agent who was interested in her nearly finished play. Jocasta insisted it needed more work before being submitted to anyone, and had arranged for it to be read in full the following Saturday afternoon.

'Yes, Judy's asked me to read a part. Are you going?'

'Yes. Julian is too, I think. Maybe you'll get a chance to talk. Listen, I'm sure this Jocasta business is just a flash in the pan. I mean, you had a real friendship with Julian. Bloody woman! You must be furious with her.'

'I don't seem to be. Just tired, really.'

It was at this moment that, glancing towards the door, she saw Jocasta and Julian leaving the pub together. They were unmistakably enclosed within a single bubble.

*

'Look, lovey,' said Cassie, 'if he's carrying on with this woman, are you sure you want him back?'

It was a good question. 'I seem to.'

'Personally I'd give him the boot,' Cassie said. 'But I'm not you, dear.'

She had phoned Cassie the moment she got home. 'Oh, Cassie,' she wailed. 'Why do they want to hurt me?'

'I don't suppose they do,' Cassie said. 'They're not thinking about you at all. Don't be hurt, keep your end up. It seems to me like the opposition's been at work. Now listen, my love, Spirit is telling me you've got to keep your heart high, keep resentment out of this and work on a ray of love, and that way you won't give the opposition any power.'

'I'll try.'

'We'll be helping you. It'll all work out in the end, my duck, but it's got to be in Spirit's way, not your way. Just keep working on the love ray. Think of gold light round your heart.'

Miranda was feeling calmer. She even had a sense of a misty gold and silver star in her chest.

'Now have a hot milky drink and go to bed, and we'll send you healing for a good night's sleep,' said Cassie.

*

On Saturday afternoon Miranda arrived at Judy's flat in St John's Wood, dosed with Bach flower remedies and trying to think healing thoughts. Jocasta was already there, drinking coffee with Judy in Judy's pristine Peter Jones kitchen. She greeted Miranda with a sweet smile.

'Oh, Miranda, good, I wanted a word with you.'

Miranda didn't want a word with her, but curiosity drew her after Jocasta into the garden, where a weak autumn sun was playing on some desperately surviving roses. Jocasta looked distinctly black around the eyes, like someone who had not slept much the previous night. She immediately resumed their earlier conversation. 'When are you going to bring a new story?'

Miranda said, 'I haven't had time to write – I've a lot on my plate.'

'Can't you give up some of your commitments?'

'One of them has just given me up,' said Miranda sourly.

'What's that?'

'Julian.' *Julian, you silly, grasping bitch.*

'Oh, no!' exclaimed Jocasta. 'That's not over, he can't stop talking about you. He's been in love with you for ages, he told me months ago, and he said it was hopeless because you weren't in love with him and he had no hopes of any long-term happiness.'

'But he... but I...?' Why was Jocasta telling her this? 'Look Julian's never actually said he loved me. His idea of a love letter is to write me a list of all my defects! But I did think we were getting on well, he hasn't given it a chance.'

'Perhaps he thought he hadn't a chance,' said Jocasta. This was weird. She was talking like a cosy aunt, not like someone who had clearly spent the previous night with the man under discussion. She went on, 'He's so insecure, poor baby. If only you'd try living together—'

'But I don't want to live with him!'

'I know.' Jocasta oozed empathy. 'You're like me! When you've been deeply, deeply hurt, you're afraid of making another commitment.'

'It's not that. I mean, we'd only just got our relationship off the ground, I didn't want to rush into anything...' Why was she having this conversation? Jocasta was standing very close to her, and Miranda stepped back. 'Look,' she said, 'my relationship with Julian, if there still is one, is very delicate and needs a lot of space.'

'Oh, I do understand!' Jocasta said. 'Fiona told me I must stop interfering between you and Julian, and I'm not, really I'm not, I just want to help. There is so little love in the world after all.'

So what were you doing last night?

Miranda said, 'Anyway, he won't even look at me, let alone speak to me.'

'He's so scared of rejection,' said Jocasta. 'And perhaps he feels guilty?'

'Quite possibly.'

'What about, d'you know?'

Miranda couldn't believe this. She stared at the withering roses and said. 'I really don't want to talk about it. It's cold, I'm going in.'

By now the rest of the group had gathered in Judy's sitting room, including Fiona, Fergus, Flaxman, and two or three people Miranda didn't know very well. Julian sat huddled in the depths of a chintz armchair, as black around the eyes as Jocasta. When Miranda appeared in the doorway he buried his nose in Judy's manuscript.

Judy's play was about an adulterous woman who neglects her daughter. Judy had cast Miranda as the neurotic mother and Fiona as the put-upon child, Flaxman was reading the lover and another man the husband. Oddly, Julian, the only experienced actor in the group, had been allotted the stage directions which he read with a tremor in his voice.

At the climax of the play Judy had written an impassioned argument between the mother and her unsatisfactory husband. Miranda flung herself into the part, pouring into it all her own rage and hurt. As she heard her voice rise accusingly, she could hear beneath it the echo of her attack on Julian that dreadful evening in the pub. God, was that what she'd sounded like? No wonder he was too scared to speak to her. But that wasn't her, Miranda the timid, Miranda the gentle! It wasn't her voice. It was, she realised even as it emerged from her mouth, the voice of her mother.

Afterwards she sat and let the discussion of the play flow over her, only slightly aware that it was not so much a group discussion as a one-woman critique of every flaw Jocasta could find in Judy's writing. Following a tea break (Earl Grey accompanied by an exotic selection of biscuits), Julian read another section of his novel. Watching him across the room she thought how good-looking he was, and what a beautiful voice he had, and wished he didn't look so in need of a hug. She tried to send him love, visualising a golden light which at moments felt as though it were truly reaching him.

'The girl,' commented Jocasta as Julian came to a hesitant halt. 'The characterisation is still not sharp enough. When are you going to give her a name? Is she based on someone you know?'

How did she do it, how did she dare? Julian mumbled an ambivalent assent; Miranda had the impression that Jocasta thought it was herself. It struck her now as eerie that the novel's hero was pursuing by turns two sisters, one good, the other morally flawed, particularly since Julian had created this trio well before Miranda had joined the Circle.

By now, everyone was tired and the group's comments deteriorated into a nit-picking argument about Julian's use of passive and active verbs. Jocasta rose and began gathering her flock to go to a fireworks party. Fiona said she had to dash off, and did so, throwing Miranda a sympathetic glance and, 'I'll call you!' Lengthy deliberations were held about which three members of Jocasta's group were to be favoured with a lift in the only car. Rather than witness Julian being scooped up again, Miranda went to the loo.

As she returned to the hall, she nearly bumped into Jocasta, who said in a pseudo-whisper, 'He's in the kitchen with Judy. Why don't you go and have a word?' And she turned to usher her party out of the front door, minus Julian.

Julian emerged from the kitchen, and they were face to face. 'Are you going to the tube?' asked Miranda.

'Yes.'

So there they were together in the street. Miranda asked Julian how he was; Julian replied that he was tired, and fed up with being penniless. He made some intelligent comments about Judy's play, and some emotional ones about the response to his novel. 'I think I'll drop it and start something else,' he said.

'No, don't do that. It's very good, honestly.'

At the foot of the underground steps they separated, Miranda to go north, Julian south. He said, 'Well, see you,' as he disappeared.

He was like a frightened deer, thought Miranda; she would have to woo him back with gentle words and sugarlumps.

*

Miranda returned home to the opium of an evening's television with Rollo purring on her lap; she was exhausted but oddly light-hearted. Perhaps letting off steam in Judy's play-reading had provided her with the emotional release she had been prevented from expressing in the Support Group. But as she lay down to sleep, she was suddenly wide awake, all comfort gone, hearing again the sound of her mother's voice in her own. It was the carping, complaining, always critical voice that had sent Miranda's father abroad and destroyed Miranda's courage, that had silenced her because there was no answering it, and even silence was wrong, because silence was sulking, silence was insolence, and it would go on and on, that angry voice, telling Miranda she was wrong, always wrong, wrong in every way, wrong to exist...

She had thought she was growing and changing, but all the groups, all the meditation, had only been plugging the gaps. All this time, that voice had been nagging away beneath the surface, telling her she was no good, never would be any good. And now it had burst out, pursuing her like a whirlwind, a word-wind, threatening to engulf her.

*

She finally managed to sleep, but at three in the morning she awoke suddenly from a vivid dream. She was dancing in a circle of people dressed in long garments; it was night, and they were in a forest clearing surrounded by blackthorn bushes and lit by a bright full moon. There were about a dozen dancers but three stood out, herself, a man and another woman. As they circled, faster and faster, the twigs and thorns caught at her cloak and her hair, and scratched her forehead. When she woke, there was still a tight band of pain across her brow.

The dream lingered into her waking consciousness the next day. It had been so real, it was more like a memory than a dream. It felt important to remember who had been leading the dance, but since it was a circle dance, it was impossible to tell.

2

TELLING STORIES

'Cassie? I'm sorry to bother you…'

'You're not bothering me, my love. I'm just waiting for a client. What can I do for you?'

'I wanted to ask… I had a dream last night… it seemed terribly real. I was wondering about past lives…'

There was a pause while Cassie tuned in to her sources. Then she said, 'They're telling me you have something to learn about power. It could be you misused power in a previous life, and that's why you're afraid of using it now.'

'Could we… could I have been involved in witchcraft?'

'Oh, most of us have, dearie, people like you and me. I've been burned at the stake at least once! Thank goodness times have changed. There's my doorbell, better go.' She rang off before Miranda could ask what she meant by 'people like you and me'. She was nothing like Cassie, surely?

*

November continued gloomy, with rain-filled skies and fearsome gales and further power cuts. Miranda brooded. More and more she wanted Julian back. She couldn't understand why. He was weak, he was immature, he had behaved appallingly. Why was she so drawn to him? Perhaps she just wanted to defeat Jocasta.

But it was more than that. She wanted the chance to try again, to get things right this time, to love him differently – she now allowed herself to use the word love – and for him to love her, even if it was only temporary, flawed love. And he would come back to her, not just because Cassie had said so, but because she, Miranda, knew it in her bones. For once in her life, she was not going to give up.

The following Friday she woke with a churning stomach at the prospect of going to the Circle that evening, of again seeing Julian and Jocasta floating together through the pub door. But she had to go, she had to keep going. As she drew back her curtains, the day was clear for once: morning light danced on the golden leaves outside and on the borage fading now in its vase on her windowsill. She must keep her face to the sun. Julian's fling with Jocasta wouldn't last. She would go to the Circle, behave normally, show that she was still his friend.

The telephone rang: it was Daphne, phoning, Miranda assumed, to confirm her visit the following week. But her voice sounded odd.

'I've been very ill,' she said. 'Really ill, I'm just out of hospital. They wanted me to stay longer, but I decided I'd rather be ill at home. It was the worst attack I've had, for a time I was just in a red haze of pain, I couldn't communicate with anyone.'

'Oh, Daphne, that sounds awful.'

'It was so awful I couldn't even realise how awful it was till it was over. The pain just took over. They offered me morphine but I refused, I was far enough out of it anyway. The psychiatrist was wonderful, one day he just came and hugged me for an hour.'

There was a sympathetic pain in Miranda's middle. 'How are you now?'

'Very weak still. Not so much pain.' Then she said, sadly, 'You know, Miranda, I've never felt beaten before, but now I feel… oh, not beaten, but not in control any more.'

'That doesn't sound like you.'

'It's certainly a new experience,' Daphne said philosophically. 'Anyway, I've left this call till the last minute, because I'm still hoping to get to London next week.'

'Daphne, you can't, you're crazy!'

Daphne giggled huskily. 'Possibly,' she said. She added, 'Are your teeth quite better now?'

'Not really, they're still hurting. The consultant thinks they'll settle down, but it doesn't feel right in there, somehow.'

'Poor you. I hope you'll feel better soon.'

God, Daphne was brave, thought Miranda. And she felt sorry for her, and sad for her, and purely selfishly hoped Daphne would not come next week, because working for Daphne ill was even worse than working for Daphne well.

*

Jocasta launched the next Circle evening by announcing a meeting of the anthology committee; she was planning on publication just before Christmas. Miranda glanced over at Julian, and was jolted by a very odd sensation. For an instant, she felt she was looking at herself.

At the end of the evening, after much debate about who was going in her direction, Jocasta departed with a small flock and without Julian, who was deep in conversation with Fergus. As Fergus left, Miranda's eyes met Julian's. He said awkwardly, 'You look as if you need a drink,' and went to the bar.

With Julian at her side, a glass of wine in her hand, Miranda started talking. She told him she might have to miss the next Circle because Daphne could be coming. She told him about her trip to Suffolk and the bonfire. She tried to weave a web of words to keep him there. Finally, she asked: 'Are you on Jocasta's anthology committee?'

He looked at her directly and said, 'I'm on everything with Jocasta.'

Miranda's stomach plummeted. She said, 'Oh. I see.'

'You do see, don't you?' he said unhappily.

Outside, yet another gale had brewed up, and they walked to the tube through sheets of rain; it was like being at sea. Julian had no overcoat. He said, 'I expect I'll get pneumonia. I'll only have myself to blame.'

'True,' said Miranda.

'I've been reading a book about the effects of the mind on your health,' he went on.

'Then you'd better not tell yourself you'll get pneumonia.'

At the warm mouth of the tube they kissed each other on the cheeks. His felt smooth and soft. He said, 'I'll phone you.'

*

Daphne was not coming. 'My consultant's given me strict instructions not to move for at least a month, except to slide into the loo. He says if I'm to hope for a remission I mustn't overdo things.' She sounded weak.

'Who's looking after you?'

'My mother's staying with me.' It was the first time she had mentioned a mother; Miranda had always thought of Daphne as alone. 'And they've fixed up a couple of nurses to come and do necessary things. It's very humiliating. It was all right in hospital, but it's different in your own home.' She laughed. 'You know, I've spent two and a half years pretending I haven't got MS, and I've finally got to recognise that I have. I've decided to write about it, do something creative for a change. I'm really being impelled to tape my thoughts and feelings about the illness, I'll send you them to type. That way you won't lose out financially next week.'

'Honestly, Daphne, you mustn't worry about that.'

'I'm not worrying about it, I'm sure you can do with the money. Listen, I'll miss you next week. You're one of the few close friends I can really talk to.'

Miranda was moved. Daphne's claim to friendship no longer seemed like a fiction. She said, 'Would you like me to ask Cassie to send you some healing?'

'That would be kind. She's amazing that woman, she's a witch!'

How funny, thought Miranda, she'd never thought of Cassie as a witch. But of course she was – a good witch, a white witch. She said, 'I'll do that. Listen, do phone, any time. And please do what the consultant says.'

'Oh, I'm a good girl now, I'm doing what I'm told.'

There was something terribly sad about Daphne doing as she was told. But at least Miranda had been granted a bonus of space and time, a chance to slow down. She was so tired. She would walk on Hampstead Heath, maybe do some writing. Jocasta wanted another story, didn't she?

*

It was on Hampstead Heath on a blowy but sunny day that Miranda found a story writing itself in her head. It was about a child with a difficult mother, who used her adult power to denigrate the child's creativity. The child's response was to create a secret garden in the woods, with rocks and wild flowers, a garden only she knew about. No one would ever see it, and her mother would never destroy it. Miranda began writing as soon as she got home; the words flowed easily and satisfyingly on to the pages until it was complete.

Then, shaking slightly, she looked up Jocasta's telephone number. Jocasta was not going to squash her creative efforts this time. Jocasta had said she had a voice, she had perception, hadn't she? Then let them be heard.

The girlish voice that answered the phone was unruffled by the slightest hint of embarrassment. Miranda told her firmly that she wanted to read her story next Friday, right through to the end without interruption.

'Oh, I'm sure that'll be all right,' said Jocasta vaguely. 'Miranda, look, I'm glad you rang, I wanted to talk to you. About me and Julian.'

Miranda went cold. Jocasta steamed on. 'You see, I know that you know, and I want to clear the air. I do realise you've had a bad time.'

'Did Julian tell you that?'

'No, I saw it in your face at Judy's. I asked Julian about it. I hadn't realised that you knew about our little fling, you see. Julian should have told me.'

Miranda said, 'Jocasta, I really don't want to talk about this.'

'But I want you to know that any physical thing we had together was purely peripheral. We've known each other for ages — we were just two old friends going to bed together, you know how these things happen. It wasn't important, nothing like a grand passion — and believe me, I know what a grand passion is.'

Miranda could have asked: if it was purely peripheral, why does Julian seem to think otherwise? Why are you lying through your teeth? But Jocasta's air-clearing did not include hearing anything Miranda might have to say, and she would only have got tangled answers.

Mustering her dignity, she said, 'The timing was particularly bad from my point of view.'

Jocasta responded: 'If you were really ill, you shouldn't have told him you were all right.'

'I could hardly speak!'

'Julian is a good friend, and he's helping me with the anthology. But I know you mean a lot to him. And he's certainly not the great love of my life, nothing like Grant, now he was a grand passion – he moved to Wales, but he's coming to see me at Christmas, anything might happen.' Did Julian know that? Was Jocasta actually planning to hand Julian back to Miranda when she'd finished with him? Still she bulldozed on, unstoppable: 'So you really mustn't think I've been trying to take Julian away from you – it was just one of those things that happen between friends.'

'Was it,' said Miranda icily.

'Well, I'm awfully glad we've cleared the air. I look forward to hearing your story on Friday – maybe we can include it in the anthology.'

Lying awake that night, Miranda realised that she was very, very angry. Far from clearing the air, Jocasta had swept her broomstick across the sky, covering the sun with a trail of sticky cobwebs. What must it be like to be Jocasta? What went on in her head? How did she justify the damage she caused? Oh, she was a witch all right. Jocasta was the Snow Queen who had swept Kay off to her palace of ice, and Miranda was Gerda who would journey after him, braving bandits and the northern snows. Jocasta was the hag in her gingerbread house, fattening up Hansel in his cage. That night Miranda-Gretel shoved Jocasta in the oven, over and over again, and watched her roast.

Stricken with stage fright, Miranda had to wait to read her story while Flaxman read an unfinished, rather touching tale about a country childhood. Julian, Miranda noticed, looked pinched and withdrawn. What could Jocasta be doing to him?

It was a novel experience for Miranda to read a complete story to the Circle, uninterrupted. It was well received; it seemed to have touched some common nerve. Of course, everyone in the Circle except Julian claimed to have had an unhappy childhood. Jocasta said, quite mildly, 'Miranda could perhaps have given us more of the mother's point of view.'

Judy intervened. 'But the whole point was it was from the child's point of view – that's why it worked!'

'Mothers,' said Jocasta, 'come in for such a lot of flak. Why is it people who don't want children have them, and people who do want them can't? I'd have loved to be a mother.'

The pub that night was in a state of general drama. One of the younger men had broken up with his girlfriend, another with his boyfriend, and Trevor looked as though his marriage to himself was on the rocks. Judy was distraught because, despite continued interest from the agent, Jocasta still insisted that her play needed a complete rewrite. Miranda was commiserating with her when Flaxman appeared and loomed over her. He put a glass of wine into one of her hands and took hold of the other.

'You,' he said, gazing down at her, 'are an unusually complex woman. Not beautiful, but an interesting face, a nice attractive face. As a matter of fact, you are fourth on my roster of desirable women.'

'What makes you think you're anywhere on my roster?' retorted Miranda, retrieving her hand. (Fourth, indeed!) Their attention was distracted by a kerfuffle around Jocasta, who was gathering her acolytes to accompany her to a disco. Her clear voice rang across the pub chatter: 'Sometimes I feel just like a mother hen with all her little chickens!'

'God, she sounds stupid sometimes,' said Miranda.

Flaxman raised one eyebrow. 'That was very tart! You sound less than fond of Jocasta.'

It was a relief that he seemed to know nothing about Jocasta's skulduggery with Julian; Miranda had assumed that the entire Circle was aware of her ignominious plight. She said, 'She has, let's say, over-interfered with my private life.'

'She does that,' said Flaxman. Then light dawned over his handsome features. 'You don't mean Julian! Oh. Yes, I can see he would appeal to the darker side of her nature.' What could that mean? 'Tell me more.'

'I'd rather not,' said Miranda, once again disentangling her fingers from his. At this point Julian himself appeared, and Flaxman withdrew with a great show of discretion.

Julian said, only slightly hesitantly, 'I liked your story. You see, you can write!'

'Thank you. How are you?'

'Oh, rather fed up. The Social Security people are being difficult, I'm thinking of looking for a job.'

'That sounds a good idea. It would give you more of a routine, as well as the cash.' And self-respect, she didn't add.

'Except,' he went on, 'that Jocasta is supposed to be laying on some editing work for me.' He sighed heavily. 'Life is very complicated at the moment.' He looked towards the door through which Jocasta had lately ushered her chicks.

'Are you going to the tube?' Miranda started putting on her coat.

'Yes. Are you?'

They walked out together. Miranda said, 'Do you mind if I take your arm?'

He offered it.

Miranda said, 'It's stupid, but I've had an awful desire to touch you all evening.'

'I feel the same,' he said. There was an arm-linked pause, their feet sounding in unison on the wet pavement. 'I'm in an awful muddle,' he said eventually.

'I thought you weren't looking very happy.'

'Something hurtful happened today. I thought Jocasta had some feeling for me!' he said aggrievedly. 'Now, I don't know.'

Miranda said, 'So… it's out of the frying pan into the fire?'

'Something like that. I don't know what to do.' He turned to her. 'I have no courage, you see.'

Miranda said, 'If you want to talk about it—'

'There are things I can't talk about to you. I don't want to blame you, but—'

'I should bloody well think not!'

They had reached the tube station, and suddenly he was hugging her.

'Gosh, that feels good,' she said into his coat.

'Yes, it does.'

'I'd ask you back, but I suppose it would complicate things further.'

'Yes, don't ask me, because I'd probably come, and it would. Complicate things. I need to be clear.'

'Is there anyone else you can talk to?'

'I sometimes chat with Fergus… he had a run-in with her, you know.'

'I heard.' Fergus, though younger, was probably more

mature than Julian; evidently they saw each other as co-victims rather than rivals.

Julian said, diffidently, 'Can you give me any advice?'

Christ, what a question, under the circumstances – and she wasn't even sure what the circumstances were. 'You could try praying,' she suggested.

'Yes,' he said humbly. 'I'll try that.'

Miranda said, suddenly knowing it to be true, 'Them up there do want to help, you know.'

He said, 'Yes, I do believe that. I often think about my grandmother – maybe she's trying to help… You're being awfully nice!' he added with some amazement.

Miranda was also amazed, not at her niceness, but that she seemed for once to be coming out with the right words. She said, absolutely believing it, 'It'll all work out in the end.' Gerda would rescue Kay from the Snow Queen's icy clutches. 'Come and see me soon,' she added.

'Yes, I will.'

*

'Have some more,' said Fiona, spoon poised over the dish of chicken risotto. 'You've hardly eaten anything.'

'It was delicious, but I can't, I'm sorry,' said Miranda.

'Are your teeth still hurting?'

'A bit, but it's not that, I'm just not terribly hungry.' Ever since her exchange with Jocasta, Miranda had found it very hard to eat: she would put food into her mouth, but it refused to go down.

'I did like your story,' said Fiona. 'I'm glad she let you read all of it. She's never given your writing a chance.'

'I know. She's always saying she wants strong women writers in the Circle but she's much kinder to the men.'

Fiona said, 'Come to think of it, you've had some stories published, haven't you? I wonder if that's why she's always been so down on you. She's probably envious.'

'Only in women's mags,' said Miranda.

'Publication is publication,' said Fiona. 'Jocasta had one play put on in a fringe theatre ten years ago, and a couple of poems in obscure magazines, and nothing since. And look at the way she's treating Judy's play, it's really good but Jocasta won't admit it. Anyway, that's a good story, it brought tears to my eyes. Was it autobiographical, dare I ask?'

'Well, sort of. I suppose the mother was my mother.'

'Did she actually tell you she didn't want you?'

'Yes. Well, what she actually said was she never wanted a baby. I must have been about six.' Home for tea after school, white bread and margarine and honey. 'I can't remember what led up to it. She just came out with it, quite calmly.'

'Mine never said so,' said Fiona, 'but I must say she sometimes gave the impression I was the worst thing that ever happened to her. That's why I'm so careful to let Franny know I love her, even when I'm annoyed with her. God, these parents! You spend your life getting over them. It's not as if we asked to be born!'

'I don't know,' said Miranda. 'I sometimes wonder if I did. I can just imagine sitting up on a cloud, or wherever one sits, saying, "My turn, now," and zooming off to get born before anyone could stop me. And then realising it was all a horrible mistake. Someone on the meditation course said we choose our parents – God knows why I chose my mother, I must have done something appalling in a previous life.'

'You don't honestly believe in all that reincarnation stuff, do you?'

'It makes sense to me. There's a kind of justice to it. Maybe I did the dirty on my mother in another life.'

'D'you really believe if you do something bad in one life you get punished for it in the next?' Fiona's expression was sceptical. 'I once heard someone suggest that being born disabled is a punishment for living an evil past life – that's horrible!'

'No, I don't think it's a punishment.' Miranda drew on a recent talk on karma given by Warren. 'I think you have a choice. The idea is that when you die, you're taken through your life story and you can choose to make up for any harm you've done. Or sometimes people just want the experience of, say, being disabled, to progress spiritually. So maybe I did something beastly to Julian and Jocasta in some life or other and they're getting their own back in this one.' (An image of the circle dancers flashed across her inner vision.)

'You don't need past lives to explain Jocasta's behaviour,' said Fiona. 'Anyway, I think it's copping out, blaming everything on previous lives. It's this life you've got to live.'

'Yes, of course, but that could include clearing up messes from the past. Anyway one life isn't long enough to learn how to live! I mean, at school you get educated, but nobody teaches you how to live. So you – well I – have to go to groups and things just to learn how to be a human being.'

Fiona said, 'I'm not sure about all these groups. Why don't you have some proper therapy? That's what I did after my divorce. It didn't transform my life, but it helped me come to terms with a lot of stuff.'

'I can't afford proper therapy.' This was true. But Miranda also had an idea that a proper therapist would see right into her, might uncover something shameful. In groups, you could always hide when you needed to.

'It's all very well blaming parents,' Fiona went on. 'But they didn't know any better. My parents weren't ghastly, but it simply wasn't done to talk about feelings, anything emotional got shoved under the carpet. That's how they were brought up.'

'OK, but why did they have to make us feel so worthless? I see it all the time with people in the Support Group. And maybe my mother didn't know how to love me – but did she have to hate me?'

And did she have to make Miranda hate her? There came into her mind one of those memories she didn't want. Humiliatingly pinioned across her mother's knee, crying, 'I hate you, I hate you!' with every slap, and the curious note of triumph in her mother's voice as she said, 'I know you do!' and went on hitting, hitting, harder, longer.

That night Miranda awoke with a story running through her head – story? Dream? Memory? – so powerful she had to get up and write it down. Of course she had chosen, demanded to be born, against all advice. And what was all that urgency about? No wonder her life had never gone right; it was all her own fault. What was more, in her haste to get here, she had left half her luggage behind.

3

ASKING FOR SUPPORT

November turned moodily into December. Julian did not telephone. Miranda was finding it increasingly hard to eat. She had lost weight and her nerves were on edge. Her sleep was broken by vivid dreams, dreams of being lost, of seeking for something, someone, climbing a mountain and never reaching the top. In one, she was locked in a small room high in a tower, with no exit but a narrow window; she had the fleeting sense that there was a story behind this, but the feeling vanished before she could grasp it.

Her workload had lightened but she was still brooding over Julian. Despite their last moment of closeness nothing had changed. As far as she knew, he was still trapped in Jocasta's web, unhappily but not unwillingly. She couldn't understand why she wanted him so badly; her yearning for him was growing stronger the longer they were apart. And it was not just sexual longing; there was a link between them, as Cassie had said, and it had been broken before its time. There was something between them that still had to be played out.

*

Daphne phoned again, much better but very upset. She had recorded three tapes for Miranda to type and asked her

Bristol chap to post them. He had somehow forgotten, and now couldn't find them.

'He's trying to punish me because I won't give up everything and marry him. I don't think he's even doing it deliberately, it's unconscious. Oh, these men! They want complete commitment and they're not prepared to give it themselves,' she said furiously.

'You're so right,' said Miranda.

*

Thoughts of Julian were revolving in her mind as she waited at the dental hospital the following week. Her mouth felt odd; Cassie suspected she still had an infection. 'Spirit can't do dentistry, I'm afraid, but we'll send healing to guide the dentists looking after you.'

Cassie's people must have got through, because this time Miranda's complaints were taken seriously and a Top Man came to look at her and her x-rays. She had an abscess, he informed her; he would make an appointment for another apicectomy in two weeks' time. Oh, God, more drilling, more stitching, more antibiotics – she couldn't bear it! Seeing her expression, the Top Man said he was sorry, it was nobody's fault, just one of those things.

Miranda left feeling totally downcast. She had bitten the poisoned apple, and the poison was still in her mouth. It was nobody's fault, just one of those things. It was all very well trying to fly above it all like a bird; she felt she was floundering in a muddy pool.

Back home, she made yet another resolution to stop brooding about Julian. But her thoughts had a life of their own; in perpetual motion they chugged on and on, speculating, planning, imagining, longing. She must let go of him for her own sanity. But she didn't know how.

*

'Imagine him leaving,' Rosa instructed. 'Just let him go through the door and say "goodbye" very lightly.'

Miranda had decided to use the One-to-One slot at the Support Group to deal with her obsession, and be blowed to oppression and classism.

'Say goodbye,' urged Rosa.

The word would not come out of her mouth. Instead, she said, 'Why is it that the men who are nice to me I don't love, and the ones I do love aren't there when I need them?'

'Who else wasn't there when you needed them?' asked Rosa.

'No one, no one was there.'

'Was your father there when you needed him?'

'No, of course he wasn't!'

'Perhaps you need to do some work on your father,' said Rosa.

But how could Miranda work on a father she could barely recall? How could she work on someone who wasn't there?

*

It made sense, she thought, as she cycled home. Al had once talked to the Support Group about 'frozen needs' – how when a child's most important needs aren't met, they stay stuck in the personality, creating unrealistic demands that can never be satisfied. How did it go? 'We repeat over and over again our attempts to obtain love from the very people who cannot or will not give it. A frozen need,' Al had announced, 'can lead to addictions and eating disorders.'

Well, Miranda had both – a Julian addiction and an eating disorder. Perhaps it was a father disorder, not mother for once. It made sense in theory. Father hardly ever there, father doesn't stand up for child when he is there, father disappears. Poor father, shadowy father. Daughter chooses men who can't give her what she needs. Classic, really. Knowing this intellectually changed nothing, of course. But working on it could be worth a try.

The evening before the next Support Group meeting Miranda telephoned Al and asked if he would talk about dealing with frozen needs.

'Sure,' said Al. 'This relates to your own stuff, presumably?'

'Yes,' sighed Miranda.

'So you'd be prepared to work on it in the group?'

'Yes, of course,' said Miranda, filled with terror.

'OK, it's a deal. Could be useful. We'll start off with it tomorrow evening.'

*

They didn't start off with it. Al forgot. He opened the session by sharing with the group, at length, his own concerns, which were to do with his responsibility for preparing the group for the impending social revolution. He didn't mention frozen needs. He didn't even look at Miranda.

Miranda was stupefied with disbelief. She had come braced for self-exposure, and Al had promised! Here was yet another man failing her when she needed help. He was the focaliser, for God's sake, he had no right to let her down!

When they had divided into smaller groups and it was Miranda's turn to say how she felt her mind went blank. She looked at the faces around her; her group included Rosa, and two of the Camden women. All their eyes were on her. She said, 'I don't feel anything. I don't exist. I'm not here. Al said he would give me time and he just forgot. So there's absolutely no point in asking for what you need because you bloody well don't get it!'

She stood up. 'I'm going home. I don't like it here.'

From feeling nothing, she was suddenly engulfed by rage. 'I don't need this bloody group anyway!' she shouted. 'I'll go home and do it by myself!'

But instead of going to the door, she found herself running to one of the windows where she wrapped herself in the long, dusty curtain and screamed.

Her subgroup gathered round her and encouraged her to spit out her total and utter rage at being ignored and unsupported. She heard her voice howling and wondered where it was all coming from, and whether she would ever stop, because the rage boiled up and boiled up, pouring out from some inexhaustible volcanic source. She hurled her anger into the room; it crackled and leaped from wall to wall. The other groups stopped their activities to watch.

Eventually she stopped yelling and began to cry. Her group laid her on the floor and wrapped her in a blanket and hugged her and rocked her, and told her that she was heard, and that she was brilliant at expressing her needs and deserved to get them met. Somewhere behind them Al hovered ineffectually.

At the end of the evening she was empty, exhausted. 'You were very brave,' Rosa told her, giving her an extra hug as they left. 'Will you be all right going home?'

'I'm fine, honestly.' Miranda did feel fine. In a curious way she had rather enjoyed herself.

*

Later she lay on her bed hugging Rollo and remembering. She remembered exactly what it felt like to be a tiny baby, what it felt like to be very small, left alone, wanting someone to come, wanting comfort. At first the baby cries, but no one comes. It cries louder. Then it stops crying. The baby shuts up. The baby shuts down. It understands, without words, that it is worthless, because otherwise someone would come. There is no point in crying for love, why would anyone love it? Because there is clearly something very, very wrong with the baby.

*

In the morning she felt a great deal better. Gosh, but she'd told them, hadn't she! And she did get her needs met because even if Al had forgotten, everyone else had listened. Sal from Camden had been one of the warmest in her appreciations, had fetched the blanket they wrapped her in. They had cradled her pain and acknowledged her fury. Perhaps she was allowed to get her needs met.

The baby wasn't worthless, she saw now. The baby had been the usual perfect baby, ready to love and to be loved. There was nothing wrong with it at all. And now that she was no longer a baby, there must be better ways of getting her needs met than shouting and screaming. That had been her mother's way, it didn't have to be Miranda's.

In the post there was a cassette tape from Daphne, containing not the promised rumination on her illness but a talk she should have given at a conference in Rome, had she been well enough to go. It was accompanied by a note asking Miranda to type it up asap for the conference organisers. With it was a second, pathetic taped message. She was back in hospital; her sight had almost gone. She could just about read but couldn't write. They were giving her massive doses of cortisone.

How could she bear it? Miranda wondered sadly. When she sat down for her morning meditation she tried to send healing thoughts to Daphne but had no idea whether they were reaching her. In her meditation, too, she found herself looking at a steep, slippery stairway rising out of a muddy pond. She saw herself struggling to climb the steps until she was standing at the top, and the stone beneath her feet was solid and secure.

*

When she arrived at the pub that Friday she went the bar and bought a cheese sandwich. She had been unable to eat any lunch and was feeling rather woolly. At the other end of the bar Trevor was announcing to anyone who cared to listen that he had a surprise for everyone. For a moment she didn't realise that she was actually standing next to Julian. Flaxman, on her other side, twinkled a smile at her, clearly under the impression that they were back together.

Julian jumped when he saw her. 'Oh, hallo, er, Miranda.'

On a sudden inspiration, Miranda seized the moment. 'Julian, can I talk to you?'

'OK.'

They moved into a more private corner and sat down. Miranda took a small bite of sandwich. She had to chew and chew each mouthful before she could swallow it.

Julian lit a cigarette and asked, 'What did you want to talk to me about?'

'I need to ask you a favour – I need your help.'

He said surprisingly, 'Of course I'll help, if I can.'

She told him about the forthcoming dental operation. 'I'm just so scared of going through all that again – would you come with me?'

He looked taken aback but not, as Miranda had expected, alarmed. 'Yes, certainly, of course,' he said.

Miranda felt weak with relief. 'Thank you. Gosh. It's on Wednesday. Would you like to come to supper the evening before?'

'I'm not sure I can, there may be a meeting of the anthology committee.'

'You could say no to Jocasta for once.'

'Oh, Jocasta – I don't know if I'm persona grata with Jocasta. We had a really serious row two nights ago, we haven't spoken since. I went back home, it's the first time I've slept at home since...'

Miranda stared at him. Would the shocks never stop? 'You mean you're actually living with her?'

'I thought you understood that.'

'You never said you were living with her! God, if I'd known...'

If she'd known she would never have kept going to the Circle. She would certainly not have asked him to go with her to the hospital. 'I thought you were... well, seeing her regularly, I suppose.'

He shook his head. 'No, it's been... much more than that.'

'I don't understand how it even started, you never seemed to like her much.'

'Liking... doesn't come into it really. It's quite simple. When you were away that Friday, a bunch of us went on to

Trevor's flat – his decor is truly weird, incidentally, I must tell you sometime – and I was feeling pretty low. I really thought you didn't want to see me. Jocasta asked me how things were going between us, and I said, not very well.'

'But that wasn't true!'

Julian looked surprised. 'We were quarrelling a lot, you were really nasty to me on your birthday.'

'I thought you were nasty to me, actually. And we did make it up.' Miranda remembered that night very well. If he had been harbouring so much hurt, how come he had been so loving, so passionate?

'We seem to have been doing a lot of misunderstanding,' he said. 'Anyway, Jocasta invited me home with her. I just needed some comfort, I suppose, and she was offering it. Then, after you got so angry, I was very upset… I moved in with her that week.' He sighed. 'She seemed to have strong feelings for me, then.'

'But why the lies? She talked to me as if it was just a one-night stand. She even suggested I should have you to live with me.'

'But you never wanted that.'

'Well, we were still getting to know each other, and you know, you weren't always easy to live with – but I never realised you were so unhappy about it, I really didn't. It's sometimes hard to understand what's going on with you, Julian, because you don't say the most important things.'

'No, I probably wasn't clear.' He ran a forefinger round the rim of his glass.

'So if you were so unhappy about me, what did you expect to get from Jocasta?'

He just looked at her. The look said 'everything'.

'You don't want to marry her? You can't be serious! She's hardly the marrying sort.'

'I know what she's like, I know about her goings-on. But she… I… I can't let go of her. It'll probably end disastrously,' he went on gloomily. 'But it's as if I've got to wait for the worst to happen. It's like living through a film that I can't leave. It isn't finished yet.'

But that was how it was with her, thought Miranda. What on earth was going on between the three of them? She said: 'You know, there seems to have been an awful lot of not saying what we really felt. I wish we could start again from scratch.'

'I wish we could too.' He added, without recrimination, 'I was very angry with you when I left. I'm sorry.'

'I just wish I'd known you were so fond of Jocasta.'

'I wasn't fond of her, I'm not fond of her. It's just that there is something between us. I don't even know what it is. She's hard all the way through, I know that. And she plays games. But I still want to be with her.'

'You are going to get hurt.'

He gave her a straight look. 'Probably. You know, I'm actually more resilient than people think. And – it's ironic, really – living with her, I'm getting to see myself differently. Like, the things that used to irritate you about me are the things that also irritate her.' At which Miranda could only rejoice. Perhaps she could thank Jocasta for improving him; he did seem clearer, more direct. 'And vice versa,' he added. 'You both have this thing of being busy all the time.'

'So what is the attraction?'

'We have fun,' he said. 'She's very nice to be with when she isn't being nasty… but it's more than that, there's a link between us, I don't know what it is.'

The Snow Queen entertains Kay in her palace of ice, she gives him icy treats.

'And now…?'

'I don't know if she's speaking to me. There was a plan to go dancing with some people tonight. I don't know if that's on.'

'You're waiting for her to decide?'

'Yes.'

Miranda sat through the entire evening's readings without hearing a word. She was barely aware of Trevor's surprise, which was to read out a kinky version of Cinderella dressed in a lime-green satin evening gown. Jocasta was not delighted.

When everyone returned to the bar Julian joined her, his face flushed. 'I'm expected to go dancing.' He threw her a hunted look. 'I know I'm heading for disaster.'

Miranda said, 'I'm sure it'll work out all right.'

'I wish I had your confidence.'

'I'm sure you'll do the right thing.'

He said: 'I don't want to do the right thing. I just want what I want.'

Kay's heart has been pierced with a splinter of ice, it has not melted yet.

'And what you want is Jocasta?'

'Yes.'

Well, at least that was clear. Then he said, 'There is one thing I really miss about you, though.'

'Oh?'

'Sexually there's something we had, something very subtle I don't have with her.'

Oh, God, thought Miranda, suddenly weak-kneed. Serve her right for asking him to express himself clearly. Then he added, 'But things have improved a lot.'

She almost poured her drink over him. 'Julian, I really don't want to know that! That isn't fair, that isn't fair!' Had he meant that to hurt her, or was he just totally naive?

Unwilling to witness the departure of the dance party, she stood up. 'I'm terribly tired, I must go.'

He said, with genuine concern, 'You really aren't well, are you?'

'Not really. That's why I'm so dreading next Wednesday.'

'I will come,' he said, very seriously. 'I'll phone you on Monday.'

'Don't say you'll phone unless you mean it, you did that before, and it makes it very difficult because I can't phone you.'

'I will phone you on Monday evening at six.'

*

When she got home the only thing she knew for sure was that she could never go back to the Circle again. Julian didn't need rescuing at all, he was enjoying the witch's hold on him. Oh, but it hurt. How arrogant she had been, thinking it was her job to heal his pain, when she was so full of pain herself. She must find a way to let it go before it consumed her.

Rollo chose that moment to jump on to her lap and his purr vibrated into her guts. Why was it so much easier to share love with a cat than with a human being?

PART 5

INTERLUDE

1

A LETTER TO THE GURU

Waking in the small hours, Miranda indulged in an enjoyable fantasy in which she seduced Julian and then returned him to Jocasta with the message that it had been just two old friends going to bed together, purely peripheral... but in the morning she woke with a new set of fears. She should never have asked Julian to go with her. Even if he kept his word, afterwards he would trot straight back to Jocasta's lair. But she wanted him, how she wanted him: the longing for him possessed her all morning. This was getting out of hand; it couldn't be normal!

Suddenly she remembered a talk that Guru Chakrao had given on unfulfilled desires. She riffled through her notebook and found the page.

> *Desires are natural... Earthly desires reflect desire for unity with the absolute. Overwhelming desire arises from emotional scars that need to be healed... through meditation and self-examination.*
> *'If desire is disproportionate you may not get what you want until you have stopped desiring it.*

Did that mean she wouldn't get Julian back until she had stopped wanting him? That made no sense.

Then an idea hit her. On the meditation course someone

had mentioned writing to Guru Chakrao about a personal problem and receiving a very enlightening answer. Miranda would write to the Guru.

She began her letter in a fever of urgency; she told him she was obsessed; she knew that the most important kind of love was Divine Love, but in the meantime it was human love she wanted – she had never had that, did she have no right to be loved? Her letter covered several pages and she took it immediately to the post.

On her return she already felt more peaceful. As she opened her front door the telephone was ringing; it was Fiona, wanting to know the latest. 'I saw you confabulating with Julian in the pub,' she said. 'I've been hoping you two are sorting things out.'

'Oh, Fiona, I feel such a fool! He's been living with Jocasta all this time!'

'Living with her?' It took a lot to shock Fiona. 'Well, they've been concealing that well, I must say. Good God.'

'It's very peculiar, he's not really happy with her.'

'It can't possibly last,' said Fiona. 'You know, I've been thinking, in a way you can't blame Julian. I don't think many men would resist Jocasta pouncing on them and sweeping them up. And then, you didn't want him living with you, did you?'

'No, we never discussed it properly... but not really.'

'Well, maybe that's really important to him, he probably needs a sense of security. Not that Jocasta is the ultimate in security blankets. Listen, Miranda, do you really love him?'

'Yes. I do.'

'Have you ever told him so?'

'No.'

'Then how's the poor bloke supposed to know? It sounds like there's been a communications breakdown somewhere.

I mean, all right, he and Jocasta have behaved badly, but have you looked at what you were doing in all this?'

'Yes, I've been realising how unwanted I must have made him feel. But, Fiona, I am scared of involvement. And he's not that easy to live with. You know, I was really nervous about asking him to help me with the washing up!'

Fiona said, 'Well, if he's learned nothing from all this he'll have learned that women like help with the washing up.'

Miranda laughed. 'Anyway, the good thing is he's agreed to come with me to the dental hospital next week.'

'Has he, now? Good for him. Make the most of it. You'll be meeting outside the Circle, away from Jocasta's influence, you'll have a chance to talk properly.'

'Yes, yes, we will.'

'Good luck,' said Fiona. 'Keep me posted.'

Putting the receiver down Miranda thought, how strange – it was as if Fiona had supplied an instant answer to her letter to the Guru. 'Have you told him you love him?' 'No.' But she hadn't known herself. She had been too scared of love to love. When you love someone, you give them power over you.

When had she started loving him? There came into her mind a sunlit memory of that evening waiting at Richmond station, when Julian had covered her face with little kisses. Yes, that was when she started building him a nest in her heart. She had never let him know, because she hadn't let herself know.

*

Cassie was less positive about Miranda's news. She said, 'Well, I'm glad he's doing the right thing, but you must just take it day by day… I'm being told this is an opportunity for you to learn to be strong, whatever happens, whether you get him back or not.'

'It's terribly difficult, Cassie. I feel I'm hanging onto him in my head, that if I stop thinking about him I'm going to lose him.'

'Duckie, real love isn't about hanging on to people. Now listen, you have a strong psychic link with this man, and if you try to force things, he'll pick it up at some level. Let him be free to choose. Just send him love, and trust. Let the water hold you up, dear!'

That night, Miranda dreamed she was Sally, swimming in the sea with her younger son, who was still a toddler. The water was turbulent, but the waves held them up. The child signalled to her that he was tired; she swam towards him and he put his arms round her neck. Together they swam back to the shore.

*

Both Miranda and Julian arrived early at the dental hospital. Before setting out, Miranda had consulted *I Ching* which for the first time in weeks gave her an encouraging answer. *Renewed advance,* it said, and: *On your own day you will be believed.*

They were both nervous. They sat in the dingy waiting room, keeping their voices low among the other waiting patients.

'How are things with you?' she asked.

He shrugged. 'I'm sort of back with Jocasta, but not full-time. We both needed some space. And Grant's coming to stay over Christmas.'

'Grant's the one who lived with her before?'

'Yes, her "grand passion", she calls him when she wants to put me down. He lives in Wales now. I actually don't believe anything will come of it.'

Five minutes before her appointment, Miranda began literally to shake with fear, her heart pounding. She clutched Julian's hands; he clutched hers back. 'I'll be thinking of you,' he said.

It was nothing like as bad as the first time, and much speedier. On this occasion the dental surgeon was a woman, with two very young student observers. The surgeon warned her students that they might faint, and Miranda thought, *What about me?* In the event, no one fainted; although Miranda emerged pale and shaken. She was very grateful when Julian not only found a taxi to take them home in, but paid for it – he had been lucky with the horses again.

It felt strange walking into her flat with Julian for the first time since September. The cat woke up to see who was arriving, and Julian exclaimed, 'Hi, Rollo!' as if greeting an old friend. Rollo gave him a dubious yellow glance and began ostentatiously washing his privates.

Miranda made some coffee. They sat side by side on the sofa bed to drink it.

'Does it hurt?' asked Julian.

'Not yet, I'm still numb. But I seem to be able to talk. Thank God it's over. Is my face swollen?'

'Only a bit.'

She was still strung on wires. 'Oh, Julian, I need a hug.'

They hugged. Miranda burst into tears and Julian held her. This went on for quite a long time, until Miranda looked up at him and said, 'I've been wanting you to hold me for weeks and weeks and weeks.'

He said, 'I didn't know, I didn't think you cared about me.'

'I know you didn't, but I did, I do, I don't think I knew myself. Perhaps I was just too scared to show it.'

'But you always seemed so strong!'

'I was scared underneath. And then, when you went off with Jocasta – it was the most awful shock.'

'I'm sorry,' he said. 'I really didn't know. I didn't mean to hurt you. I didn't do it to hurt you.'

'I know that. I'm not trying to make you feel bad about it.'

They hugged some more.

Julian said, 'You've lost weight! You're quite thin.'

'Yes, I haven't been able to eat.' She squeezed his ribs. 'You've put on weight!'

'Stop it, you're tickling, stop it!'

Miranda didn't stop it. 'She's been fattening you up!' she exclaimed.

'Stop it, you're turning me on!'

'I know,' said Miranda. She began stroking the back of his neck. 'Did you tell her you were coming with me?'

'Yes.' He sat up straight and picked up his coffee mug. 'She said she thought I'd be all right.'

'She… what? She thought you'd be all right?' The woman was unbelievable. 'It's me that's had the operation, for God's sake. Why – were you frightened of coming with me?'

'I was a bit… apprehensive. I've been very confused about my feelings for you. Jocasta thought you looked quite well, perhaps she thought you were dramatising – she said, "I've seen Miranda being completely irrational!"'

'Irrational!' Miranda exploded. She supposed Jocasta was referring to the scene in the pub. 'I was upset! How dare she judge me – she has no idea what I've been through!'

'I don't think she has, actually. She was just trying to help – at the start, anyway.'

'Funny sort of help! If she'd really wanted to help she wouldn't have grabbed you.'

'I was very upset,' said Julian. 'I thought you wanted to get rid of me.'

'That's what I don't understand. We were going to bed together, it was wonderful, and you kept saying I was generous, wasn't I showing you how I felt?'

'I suppose I needed to be told.'

Miranda took a deep breath. 'Julian, the thing is, whatever we have, it may be just sex, I'm not sure—'

'I'm not sure either.'

'But it feels more than that,' she went on tentatively. 'I think I really love you.'

When she spoke the words, something curious happened. She felt her heart expanding in her chest, as if it had been held trapped and squashed in a box and now someone had taken the lid off.

Julian said nothing, but hugged her even more tightly. She wanted the hugging never to stop. But she needed to know more. 'Are you going back to her now?'

'We... it's not over yet.'

'Do you think it's over with us?'

He said, 'No, it isn't, is it? What are we going to do?'

They stared at each other, Babes in the Wood. Meeting his beautiful eyes, Miranda said, 'It's silly, but it feels somehow as if we were on the same side, sort of allies in tribulation.'

'We are on the same side,' he said. 'I am very entangled with Jocasta. But I feel a lot closer to you now. And, God, I am actually finding it very hard to restrain myself, if you want to know.'

'Me too. But it wouldn't be a good idea.'

'No.'

He stayed for some bread and cheese. Miranda couldn't eat; her mouth was still unthawing. Julian said, 'You need to rest. Shall I pull the bed out for you?'

'If you dare,' she said.

He made up the sofa bed, carefully, and sat in a chair well away from it. 'Can we meet again, when you're feeling better?'

'Yes, let's. What are you doing for Christmas?'

'Going to my dreaded parents, for as short a time as I can make it. And you?'

'I'll be going to my aunt and uncle in Surrey. Just a couple of nights, from Christmas Eve.'

'Why don't we meet for lunch the day before? On neutral territory?'

They hugged some more. Finally they pulled themselves apart. Julian sighed heavily. 'I can't think why we're being so good,' he said.

'I'm trying to be spiritual!' said Miranda, and then found herself convulsed with laughter, which hurt. 'Anyway, I need to lie down, alone.'

'Yes, you do. I'd better go – if you're sure you're all right? Do you need anything – aspirin or anything?'

'No, I've got painkillers, I'll be fine.'

As she watched him go down the front steps she could almost see the wave of love she sent after him, and for that moment she truly felt herself letting go. A moment later, when he was out of sight, she thought quite coolly, *well, that's no bad thing, to let him walk off wanting me.* It would be quite easy, she thought, to seduce him back from Jocasta, at least over Christmas while Jocasta was occupied with Grant.

She was instantly shocked at herself. She had thought everyone else in this curious dance manipulative, but never herself – Miranda the innocent, Miranda who didn't play games. Seducing Julian back would surely not be the right thing, the moral thing, the spiritual thing? Much better to wait till his infatuation with Jocasta had runs its course. But how long would that take? Miranda wanted him now.

*

When Rosa rang later that week to ask if they could meet for a One-to-One, Miranda leaped at the chance. Rosa wanted to sort out her feelings about the Support Group; like Miranda she was distressed by the recent focus on political revolution.

'If they wanted me to get in touch with my feelings about oppression, they've succeeded!' she announced towards the end of her session. 'I've had enough oppression in my life without feeling oppressed by the group.' She grinned. 'Well, I don't have to go back, do I? Nor do you.'

Miranda echoed, 'That's right, we're big girls now, we don't have to go back to school next term!' The relief was enormous.

'As a matter of fact,' said Rosa, 'I'm thinking of doing a professional counselling course. There's one in Manchester that might suit me. I'd have to move up there, of course.

'Oh, Rosa... I'd miss you. But you'd be a very good therapist.'

'Anyway, your turn now.'

Miranda began: 'I've still got this pain in my middle, emotional pain. I know I've got to let go of it – why am I scared of letting go of it?'

'What would happen if you did?'

Miranda tried to imagine. 'I might feel even more vulnerable without it.'

'Try to just see yourself letting go of it.'

Miranda closed her eyes and saw herself handing a parcel of pain, carefully wrapped in red tissue paper, to someone else. The someone took on features.

'Oh, what a witchy thought!' she exclaimed.

'What's the thought?'

'If I let go of the pain, I'll be giving it to Jocasta. I don't want to do that.' That's what they had all been doing – Jocasta, Julian, herself – passing their pain on, one to the other. Somewhere the buck had to stop.

'Who gave it to you in the first place?' Rosa asked.

'Oh, my mother, of course, my mother... she gave it to me when I was tiny.' She could almost see her mother dumping it in her cot. Then she opened her eyes. 'It's her pain, it's not mine at all! It's not my pain, Rosa! I don't have to have it, I don't need it!'

'Can you let go of it without passing it on?'

Another image came into Miranda's head: Lewis Carroll's Alice holding the Duchess's screaming, sneezing baby. 'I can just put it down and it'll turn into a pig and run off into the forest. It'll be much happier as a pig!'

She saw herself putting the baby-pig-pain down, and watched it trotting happily off, a little black pig with a curly tail. She breathed a great sigh. 'That really does feel better!'

*

They met the day before Christmas Eve at noon at the Festival Hall café; Julian was catching an afternoon train from Waterloo. He had had his hair cut, in honour of his parents, she supposed; neat in a suit and tie he looked like a stranger. They shared a smoked mackerel salad and two rolls; Miranda had recovered quickly from her dentistry but still found it hard to eat. They exchanged presents. Julian gave her a record of Tchaikovsky's Violin Concerto; she gave him a copy of Khalil Gibran's *The Prophet*.

'So, is Grant actually coming?' she asked.

'Oh, he's definitely coming, but only for a week. Jocasta's being very silly about it… it's all head games, though.'

'I've been thinking of ringing her up and asking her intentions!'

'You'd get a very woolly answer if you did.'

'Don't you mind – about Grant?'

He made a face. 'Oh, with Jocasta you get used to being one of a crowd. She's a law unto herself. Funny, it would be different if it was you.'

'And what about me? The thing is, if we did get together again—'

'Oh, I do want us to,' he said quickly. He looked at her out of his dark eyes and she looked away quickly before she was drawn into them, out of her depth. She stirred her cappuccino with concentration: the chocolatey froth on the surface took on the shape of a butterfly. Perhaps she could take up a new career reading cappuccino froth…

She looked up at him again. 'I don't want us all tangled up with Jocasta.'

'Miranda, I'm not really a very nice person. The trouble is, I want you both.'

'You realise, if we did get together again, she could use me as an excuse for chucking you out.'

'That would be contrary to everything she says – about sexual freedom and friendship and everything. She knows I still fancy you, more than ever, in fact.'

'You didn't tell her that?'

'She… got it out of me.'

'She must have loved that. What did she say?'

'Oh, she just smiled and said it was "overlap".' From his expression Miranda could tell she had said more. Julian leaned towards her, took her hand in his. Electricity ran up her arm. 'It's true, I do fancy you much more than her. You're so little and fragile...'

'Jocasta's little, too.'

'Jocasta's as tough as old boots... The trouble is,' he burst out, 'I really am in love with both of you! I used to think it was impossible to love two people at once. But I do, and it's bloody uncomfortable.'

'I'll tell you what I think,' said Miranda, suddenly confident. 'I think you're in love with me, but you've got yourself a cushy billet with her.'

'You could even be right. I told you I'm not a very nice person.'

They walked down to the river; the weather was mild and grey, not like Christmas at all. On the Embankment they kissed and cuddled like teenagers. Miranda said, 'Julian, all other considerations apart, what do you want to do?'

'I want to go to bed with you,' he said.

Oh, God. There was no choice now. 'When did you have in mind?'

'Now, this minute. But we don't want to get arrested and I do have a train to catch. Let's see, I'll be coming back the day after Boxing Day, that's Wednesday.'

'Come over on Thursday, come and stay over the New Year.'

'Oh, yes, that would be... tremendous, oh, yes.'

'Just for a few days, we'll see how it goes. But then, if you want to go back to Jocasta, I don't think I can share you.'

'It would be very difficult for me, too. Let's not plan beyond New Year.'

'That feels right, somehow,' said Miranda. 'It'll be like a sort of... exorcism.'

'What do you mean?'

She shook her head. 'I don't know.'

'It's going to keep me going through Christmas,' he said. 'God, it'll be like going to bed with a new person, it's been so long... oh,' he nuzzled his face into her neck. 'I do love you, I want you, I want you.'

It began to rain. They went into Waterloo station; Julian's train was already in. At the platform gate they hugged and kissed some more. The ticket collector said, 'Can I have one?' and Miranda blew him a kiss.

When she got home she had a sudden surge of anxiety. This was wrong; she shouldn't be grabbing him back like this. But why not? Hadn't she earned a right to some happiness? Aloud, she told herself: 'I don't want to do the right thing. I want what I want.'

2

BLISS

'You've changed, Miranda!' said her cousin James. 'What's happened to you?'

'Changed how?'

'You're more... bubbly. You always used to be so quiet.' Bubbly she was, she knew it, positively champagne-like; the prospect of the New Year lit up everything. 'It's like you're coming out of yourself,' James went on.

Miranda glanced up at him. They were taking a walk in the local park while Aunt Phyllis and Uncle Tom slept off Christmas lunch. She was having some difficulty keeping up with his long strides. Tall and lean, a year or two older than herself, James was something in the City. Until now, she had dismissed him as a buttoned-up public school type, a species she had never found it easy to talk to. Now he was turning out to be unexpectedly pleasant company – and he seemed genuinely pleased at the change in her.

She said, 'A lot's been happening to me this year. It hasn't all been nice, though.'

'You look great, younger, somehow.' He paused and looked down at her. 'You look as if you'd shed a load.'

'Do I? I think I'm in the process of shedding quite a lot. Fancy you noticing.'

He said, 'It's funny, we've known each other since childhood, but we don't really know each other.'

Miranda said, 'When we were small my mother was always saying how wonderful you were – that didn't endear you to me.' James had been constantly cited as an example of the perfect child: self-confident, charming, good-looking, cheerful, and male – everything that she had so signally failed to be.

'Sorry about that! I remember her being fairly consistently horrible to you. It was very uncomfortable to watch. I don't blame you for cutting off relations with her – nor does Ma, incidentally.'

'I have wondered, sometimes. She is her sister, after all.'

'Your mother bullied her, too, when they were young.'

'I wonder what made her like that,' said Miranda.

'Ma says she was born awful.'

'I don't believe people are born awful. Even Hitler had a horrible childhood.'

'But not everyone with a horrible childhood turns into Hitler.'

'I don't believe Mummy and Aunt Phyllis got much parental love.'

'I sometimes wonder why people have children at all,' said James.

He sighed, and Miranda found herself wondering about him. Why had he never married? He was attractive enough, eligible enough. Maybe he was gay? She couldn't imagine his very conventional parents coping with that.

James went on, 'Ma thinks your mother grabbed your father and married him because she was desperate to get married before Ma did. And being a nice, kind man, he let himself be grabbed. Recipe for disaster, really.'

'Yes,' said Miranda, thinking of men who let themselves be grabbed.

'I just about remember him,' said James. 'He was a nice man.'

'Was he? I don't remember him at all, really.' She would have liked to ask more, but James went on: 'Did you know your mother came over for a couple of weeks in the autumn? She came to see a consultant to fix up a hip operation, and I took her out to dinner.'

'That was nice of you. What's she like, now?'

James considered. 'Rather fat, drinks heavily, talks non-stop and loudly, and is always right about everything. Taking her out is quite exhausting.'

Miranda laughed. She really liked her cousin, she decided. She asked: 'What's this about a hip operation? Can't she have it in France?'

'Doesn't trust frog doctors. There is absolutely nothing to beat frog food, frog fags, frog booze and frog lovers, but frog medicine is highly suspect.'

They turned to the subject of James's life, which seemed very busy. Perhaps it was his working hours that kept him single. As they returned to the house for yet more food, James put his arm round her shoulders and gave her a squeeze. 'It's been nice getting to know you, cousin,' he said. 'Let's keep in touch.'

*

Julian was due at four o'clock on Thursday. By four-thirty, she knew he wasn't coming. At four-forty he arrived. By four forty-five they were in bed.

'I've been thinking of this all through Christmas,' he said, looking down at her.

'Me too… I was afraid something would happen, that Jocasta would summon you, or you'd have second thoughts…'

'No way. Nothing would have stopped me… mmm, oh, God, I've been looking forward to this.'

It was better than it had ever been. It was, as he had predicted, like going to bed with someone new, but someone who knew exactly where and how to touch and kiss and stroke, whose rhythms coincided effortlessly with her own. It was... extraordinary.

During a cigarette break, Julian said, 'It's so different with you. It's never really been easy with Jocasta.'

'What? Look, Julian, I don't want to know what it's like with Jocasta.'

'Fergus found it easier with his previous girlfriend, too.'

Wanting and not wanting to know, Miranda sat up. 'Did Fergus tell you that?'

'He hinted at it – but no, she told me, when I told her it was better with you.'

Miranda was staggered. 'You told her?'

'It was worrying me... and she's always asking questions about what one's thinking and feeling, it's easiest to tell her in the end.'

'I suppose she takes notes on it all. God, she must love me!'

'I think she's quite fond of you, actually.'

'She has a funny way of showing it... look, can we stop discussing Jocasta, it's making me very uncomfortable. I don't want Jocasta here!'

But he had brought her in, and she stayed, flitting around the room and swooping down at intervals to butt into their conversations. Once past the discomfort, Miranda had to admit to herself that she was extremely curious about Jocasta.

Scrambling eggs, some timeless time later, she asked: 'Does she know you're here?'

'No. There was no chance to tell her.'

'Won't she mind terribly?'

'How can she mind? I'm not supposed to mind about Grant. Anyway, she actually said to me, "You must see Miranda!"'

Once again, it crossed Miranda's mind that Jocasta might have had enough of Julian; perhaps she was returning him to her. 'You're doing more than seeing me,' she pointed out.

'Well, she needn't know.'

*

Jocasta was not easy to dismiss. Next morning, Julian told Miranda, 'Phew. I dreamed I was in bed with Jocasta and Grant came in and said, "What are you doing here?"'

'Not hard to interpret,' said Miranda. 'Why weren't you dreaming about me?' She caressed his shoulder.

'I don't need to, you're here. It's the first dream I've remembered for ages. I don't have dreams at Jocasta's, isn't that weird? It's been bothering me, because I need to dream, to write.'

'How odd... Julian, I simply don't understand. If sex isn't marvellous and she's so devious and she's even stopped you dreaming, what is the big attraction?'

He said slowly: 'Well, for one thing, living with her is fun. It's a bit like brother and sister, we play a lot. When she's not too busy.' Julian sat up and began putting on his socks. 'There is something else,' he said slowly, his back towards her. 'I'm a bit ashamed of this... she brings out something rather nasty in me at times. I've discovered with her that I've got a cruel streak. And that turns her on, for some reason. It worries me.' *The splinter of ice in Kay's heart...*

Miranda hesitated, then asked: 'And you still want to go back to her?'

He turned and looked at her directly and sadly. 'That's how things stand at the moment.'

'You don't look very happy about it.'

'I'm not very happy about it. I don't know what it is... it's different with you.'

He took his socks off again. 'You're so warm!' he said. *Warm enough to melt a splinter of ice?*

*

They spent four timeless days together, their existence a magic island floating on a horizonless sea. They walked on Hampstead Heath. They cooked meals for each other. They hugged a lot. They were tender with each other. They listened to music. They drank wine. They went to see *Annie Hall* and Miranda cried at the end when it was all over, grieving in advance for Julian's departure.

They never tired of making love. In bed, all Julian's power, all his masculinity, creativity even, blossomed and flowered. In the dark of the night he was her demon lover, Eros visiting Psyche, never showing his daytime face. But his daytime face had also changed. The wounded child was growing into a caring man. On the second morning, holding her in his arms, he said, 'But you're so thin! Oh, Miranda, I'm sorry, I'm so sorry I hurt you, I really am.' There were tears in his eyes.

She stroked his hair. 'It's all right. I'm all right now.'

*

'She's always talking about "relating",' he said. 'But I don't think she really knows what relating is. She's read every book on psychology humanly possible, and she's always trying to analyse people, but she's never had any therapy herself. I've told her she should get herself sorted out.'

Somehow, the conversation kept reverting to Jocasta. 'What did she say?' Miranda asked.

'She laughed. You see, she's not unhappy. She's as cold as ice.'

'Listen, Julian, can we not keep talking about Jocasta? I imagine you having exactly the same sort of conversation with her about me.'

'There's nothing bad I could say about you.'

'I don't want you saying anything about me. I can just imagine her asking you what I'm like in bed – and you telling her!'

'She is a voyeur,' he agreed. 'I know when I go back – if I go back – she'll say, "Tell me, tell me!"'

'Well kindly don't tell her! This is between you and me, nothing to do with her!'

*

They walked, they ate, they made love. Buying a newspaper, washing up, smoking a cigarette, cooking, all became erotic activities. And alongside eroticism, friendship grew in an entirely fresh way. They played, they laughed and teased each other. They forgot to look for each other's faults.

'I can't believe this, I can't believe it!' sighed Miranda, lying back after an hour or two of pleasure.

Julian said, 'You've changed so much – I can't believe how you've changed!'

'So have you! But I haven't changed really. I'm just letting myself out. Maybe it's because we're just in a little four-day box, it feels safe. Oh, Julian—' she flung her arms round him and held him tight, 'it's so good to get another chance!'

'I never thought we would,' he said. 'I suppose it's because you hung on... I don't deserve it.'

'Jocasta kept telling me it wasn't over, it was terribly confusing. How was I supposed to know you were living with her?'

'She was always saying, "I know you'll go back to Miranda," but I thought that was just to make me say I wouldn't. And when she talked about you, she kept saying you were irrational, and that... it frightened me, I guess. Particularly after you'd got so angry in the pub.'

'I probably was irrational that night. I was feeling really ill, and I was struggling to keep us together when I didn't know why things had gone wrong. It was horrible, Julian.'

He held her tenderly, he stroked her back between the shoulder blades. 'I'm sorry, I'm sorry. I didn't know.'

'Who's irrational, anyway? Pushing you at me with one hand and taking you away with the other. I can't think what goes on in her head.'

This time Julian said, 'That's enough of Jocasta. Let's play doctors and nurses.'

*

Over the four days they played doctors and nurses, and *Romeo and Juliet*, and the stranger in the opera box, and the sheikh and his captive, and the princess and her slave. They were wicked children playing forbidden games; they were Tristan and Isolde; they were Rapunzel and her prince escaping from the witch. They made love to Bach and Beethoven and the Beatles, to Tchaikovsky and Rimsky-Korsakov. They indulged themselves and each other without inhibition. They agreed that it had never, in both their lives, been like this with anyone else.

On Saturday morning, over toast and marmalade, Miranda said, 'Julian, you do realise, this isn't real life, we couldn't either of us keep this up in real life.'

'D'you think we'd get sated?'

'I suppose we might. I can't imagine ever being sated. What is it between us? I feel so… connected with you.'

'I know. It's the same with me.'

They stared at each other. It was almost unbearable. Julian seized her hand, still holding a slice of toast, and propelled her back to bed.

*

On New Year's Eve they stayed in. Miranda put on a long red dress she had hardly ever worn – formerly too tight, it now fitted her perfectly.

'You look stunning!' said Julian. 'You look like a new person.'

'I feel like a new person.'

She lit candles all around the room. Julian opened a bottle of wine. They raised their glasses to each other. Miranda said, 'I love you.' Once again she could physically feel her heart expanding, as though the casing that had cramped it for so long had cracked open a little further.

'I love you too,' said Julian. 'God, why is that so hard to say?'

'It is hard, isn't it? Listen,' she put her glass down and took his face between her hands. 'I love you, I love you.'

'I love you, Miranda.'

'And you are going back to Jocasta.'

His face tightened. She dropped her hands. He moved

away, and said, 'What is it about her, do you think? Why am I so in thrall to her?'

'What a question to ask me!'

'I can't understand it myself.'

'Is it because you have some power over her?'

'I wish it was!'

Miranda said, quite lightly, 'Well, I think she's a witch, she's cast a spell on you.'

He laughed and relaxed. 'She'd like to think she's a witch. If anyone's a witch, it's you!'

'Oh!' A kaleidoscope spun in her head. Surely Jocasta was the witch, the enchantress. 'A white witch, I hope.'

'No…' He closed his eyes. 'Some light colour, maybe silver.' Then he opened them. 'No – in that dress, you're a red witch, a scarlet witch.'

*

On their last day together reality began to impinge. Julian had to leave the next morning to sign on. Meanwhile Clive telephoned and asked Miranda if she would mind terribly typing an urgent document, he would pay double her usual rate. She couldn't refuse; although Julian had contributed to their feasting, she had spent more than usual on food.

Julian said, 'If you had a spare typewriter, I could do some work on the novel while you're typing.'

Miranda went to her wardrobe and produced her ancient manual typewriter from the top shelf. Julian looked distinctly taken aback. He flung himself on the bed and moaned, 'I'm so tired!'

Miranda said, 'You can give up your Dying Swan act right now, it doesn't impress me.'

The Julian of a few months before would have taken offence. This Julian laughed and sprang to his feet. 'Can you give me some typing paper?'

Clive's typing didn't take long. After he'd collected it and paid her cash, Julian and Miranda returned to bed. A couple of hours later, Julian said, 'Maybe it's as well I am going tomorrow. Much more of this, and I'd explode, or expire.'

'Me too. It's been so good it's almost unbearable.'

Then, in the evening, he suddenly became withdrawn, a little boy who didn't want to go back to school.

Their last act together was quite different from the rest of the weekend, rallentando, very gentle, very delicate. In the morning he looked at Miranda and said, 'I think these have been the happiest four days of my life.'

*

An hour after he had left, Fiona rang. 'I thought I'd better tell you, Jocasta rang me, to ask if I knew where Julian was. She'd been to his flat, would you believe, and he wasn't there. I suppose she thought I'd know if he was with you.'

'What did you say?'

'I said it was none of my business where Julian was, of course. But it was odd how upset she sounded.'

This didn't sound like the hard bitch Julian had been depicting, this woman frantically hunting for her lost lover. Nor did it sound as if she wanted rid of him. 'Oh dear,' said Miranda. 'Oh well, he'll be getting in touch with her soon. He's just left me to go back to her.'

'Oh, Miranda, honestly! How could he? You must feel terrible!'

'She seems to have got him on some sort of string. He didn't seem happy to go. Anyway, we had… we had a good time. I don't know why, but I feel OK about it. Today, anyway.'

All that day, it was as if Julian was still with her. His presence filled the flat. In bed that night, she could still feel the weight of his body on hers.

Later, she woke from a dream in which she had captured a witch, a strong, tall woman from whose hands she removed three swords shaped like pins. As she opened her eyes, she wondered – was she disarming the witch, or simply removing the pins from her waxen image?

Rollo jumped onto the bed; she sat up and stroked his velvet person. Julian was no longer there, his presence had become an absence. He must be back with her. Well, Miranda had got what she wanted: New Year together. What she had not expected was that for four and a half days she would be so perfectly, utterly happy.

PART 6

SPRING: RENEWAL

1

A NEW PAGE

New Year, a new blank page. No point in making resolutions – look what happened last year. But Miranda knew what she wanted. She wanted to be happy, now that she knew it was possible. At the back of her mind she knew that she should be searching for her purpose, the important whatever-it-was that she had been insisted on being born for. But at this moment, more than anything, she wanted some peace. She might even get it. This year there would be no more Support Group, no more Circle, no more Jocasta. Sadly, there would be no more Rosa, who was shortly moving to Manchester for her counselling course. And no more Julian…?

*

Two days after his departure he telephoned, his voice small and unhappy; no longer the fantasy lover – more Hansel back in the witch's cage. But he had not actually seen Jocasta, let alone moved back in.

'We had a long talk on the phone. Apparently Grant didn't come up to expectations, he was just using her as a hotel.'

'Poor old Jocasta,' said Miranda, almost meaning it.

'She guessed I'd seen you. She said, "How was it?" and I said, "Wonderful!"'

'Oh, Julian, you didn't!'

'Well, it was wonderful. She said, "I'm so glad."'

'Honestly, Julian, no woman wants to be told how wonderful her rival is!'

'Jocasta is not exactly an average woman. Anyway, I'm going to see her next weekend. I'll have to see how it goes. She hinted she had a fling with someone else over the New Year... listen, I'll phone you again when I've seen her, I promise.'

Of course he would move back in with Jocasta; she obviously gave him something that Miranda could not. Well, he had made her no promises. She could let him go.

*

The Guru Chakrao Fellowship marked the New Year with a Sunday gathering and Miranda decided to go, to get the year off to a good spiritual start. When she arrived at the centre in Kensington a group of devoted helpers, all young and female, were preparing a vegetarian lunch in the large basement kitchen. Sensing their comradeship, Miranda wondered why she hadn't become a devoted helper too.

It was a bright day, and the house was filled with flowers. At lunch she joined her acquaintances from the Kent course, including Olga the Danish yoga teacher, and balding Charles who was still, he confessed, retrieving rubbish from under his carpet. 'I must have done some pretty dire things in my last life,' he sighed, crumbling a granary bread roll.

Warren, sitting nearby, grinned at him. 'Keep meditating,' he said. 'You can help to heal your past lives while you're healing this one.'

Charles looked at him doubtfully. 'Surely past lives are past.'

Olga leaned forward, earnestness furrowing her already well-lined features. 'Oh, *no!*' she said. 'From what I have read lately, since there is no such thing as time, our past lives are happening concurrently with this one. Isn't that right?'

Smiling noncommittally, Warren said, 'There is a theory to that effect.'

Charles said, 'Forgive me, but that sounds like total rubbish.'

'It's all to do with quantum theory,' said Olga. 'It's very, very interesting. If you look at life from the quantum point of view, time simply doesn't exist. Our so-called past lives may be actually going on at the same time as this one, and influencing this one.'

'What do you think, Warren?' asked Charles, in a man-to-man voice.

Warren said cautiously, 'I certainly believe that the personalities we are in this life are not the whole of us. So I suppose it's possible that some aspects of ourselves are living out lives that in some way affect this one – either in the past or the present.'

Miranda felt a shiver go down her spine. This theory was exciting, and scary. Could it explain her pull towards Julian, and his towards Jocasta? Was something else going on, in another time or dimension, between the three of them? She thought again of her dream of the moonlit circle dance... now there flashed through her inner eye a brief image of circles, moving circles overlapping with other circles... Feeling slightly dizzy, she blinked and turned her attention to Warren. He was saying, 'It's best to avoid getting into too much speculation and mind-games. It's this life we're meant to be living. Past lives are only relevant when there's unfinished business that still needs dealing with.'

Olga looked put out. 'I have had some very interesting experiences,' she said meaningfully. 'I know what I know!' And she attacked her nut roast with severity.

*

Miranda came away from the get-together feeling nicely smoothed out. Meditating in a group lifted her on to a different plane, a peaceful plane in which Julian, work and dentistry receded, and the joy promised by Guru Chakrao became a real possibility. After lunch, Warren gave a talk on living in the present moment, following the flow, without anticipation or expectation. *Yes*, thought Miranda, *yes, that's how life should be lived, flowingly, without anxiety.* Warren made it sound so easy.

Over the next few days she made a real effort to live in the present, determined not to hanker after Julian, though he still hovered at the back of her mind like an unruly moth outside a lighted window. It was helpful that the book she was currently indexing engaged her near total interest. It concerned the possibility of travelling in future to other universes through black holes in space.

*

Julian rang again, upset and anxious. His weekend with Jocasta had not gone well; they had bickered and rowed. 'She won't make any commitment to me, she keeps harping on about Grant.'

Miranda was irritated by his aggrieved tone. 'You want commitment from her? So where does that leave me?'

'I want to go on seeing you. Everything's been on Jocasta's terms so far, it's time for me to lay down my terms.

Anyway, we've decided to give each other some space, while she thinks things over. I'll keep in touch, shall I?'

'If you want to.'

'Of course I want to.'

Apparently he was keeping her on as some kind of understudy. She decided not to care. She returned to her indexing and learned that if a spacecraft enters the gravity field of a black hole, time will slow down and the spacecraft will stretch ad infinitum, never to escape. But if a means can be devised of going through the black hole the spacecraft will break through into a totally new universe.

*

'Julian wasn't at the Circle last Friday,' said Fiona, as they ate baked potatoes in a small café near her office. Miranda had just given her an edited account of their New Year. 'Fergus asked me rather sweetly, "Has poor old Julian been given the push?" What's going on?'

'They're giving each other some space,' said Miranda wryly.

Fiona gave her an ironic look over her horn-rims. 'Anyway, you remember Fergus told me Jocasta was hankering after Julian ages ago? Well apparently, round about Easter, she said to Fergus, "I think I could love Julian."'

'Love!' Miranda was shaken. 'Good God!' The idea that Jocasta might love Julian – could, indeed, love anybody – had never crossed her mind. Desire, possessiveness, wish to control, all of that – but love?

'I suppose it puts a slightly different light on her behaviour,' said Fiona.

If she loves him, she'll certainly keep him, thought Miranda. Oh, what a muddle. If only she had known, she might not have hung on to him. But if she loved him, why on earth had Jocasta pushed him at Miranda?

*

They met for a cheap curry in Camden Town. It was nearly a month since their New Year idyll. Julian was nervous, but greeted Miranda with a huge, enthusiastic hug. 'You're still too thin,' he said. 'Are you eating enough?'

'Oh, yes, I'm all right now… I hear you didn't go to the Circle on Friday,' she said, as they seated themselves.

'My God, news gets around, doesn't it! It was quite an effort of will, actually. Jocasta sent me a note afterwards saying, *How do you like being the manipulator now?* I don't know what she meant – we'd agreed on a break.'

Gazing at his sensitive face framed against the gold and maroon flock wallpaper, all Miranda's love for him welled up. He seemed very confused, at one moment resenting Jocasta, the next talking of returning to her. 'Though I'm still very annoyed about her behaviour over the New Year – I told you she had it off with someone else, I don't even know who!'

'Well, why shouldn't she? Grant didn't come up to scratch, and then you go and tell her about your wonderful New Year with me.'

'She told me to see you – what did she expect? She wasn't nearly so nice about you as before. She said, "Oh, Miranda was just putting it on for your benefit."'

'She was hurt, for goodness sake.' Julian's naivety was sometimes staggering.

'She has no right to be, the way she carries on.'

'The way she carries on is very odd,' said Miranda, 'if she's not that keen on sex.'

'She isn't really. She always has to analyse the whole thing afterwards. We hardly touched each other when I saw her. She had cystitis and she was having trouble with her veins.'

Miranda was not totally sorry to learn that the Snow Queen had troublesome veins. She changed the subject. 'How's the novel?'

He sighed. 'It's been difficult to write over the past few weeks – you can imagine.' Then he covered Miranda's hand with his own. 'Miranda, let's go back to your flat this afternoon.'

His touch made her whole body tingle. But she said virtuously, 'You really must sort things out with Jocasta first.'

'But I want you.'

'I know. But I'm not going to share you with Jocasta.'

'Oh, Jocasta!' He frowned at the plastic chandelier. 'What is it about her? I wish I knew.' Then he looked back at Miranda. 'Actually, I think I'm getting bored with the Jocasta situation. I expect it'll fizzle out naturally.'

*

It fizzled out a great deal more speedily than Miranda expected. Fiona telephoned immediately after the next Circle to inform her that Jocasta had arrived at the pub accompanied by a totally new young man, one Kenneth, who had been at her side all evening. Julian had left early and alone.

'After he'd gone, Jocasta was prattling on about Julian quite nauseatingly,' Fiona reported. 'She said,' Fiona parodied Jocasta's voice in a babyish squeak, '"I'd like to have taken his dear little face and kissed him! You know how when you've had a relationship with someone you're still fond of them!" I could have slapped her, after all she's put you through.'

And Miranda had been concerned about Jocasta's feelings! Jocasta didn't give herself time to feel hurt, let alone worry about hurting other people. She was not a spider in a web, she was a frog leaping after the nearest fly, not caring what lily pad she landed on.

*

On Sunday morning Julian and Miranda were standing hand in hand on top of Parliament Hill, looking over the frosty green grass towards a London that in the hazy January light looked like a fairy-tale city.

Julian said cheerily, 'So, here we are. Just the two of us.'

The day before, he had phoned Miranda to say, flatly, 'It's over. She didn't even tell me herself. Fergus told me Jocasta had phoned him on some pretext, and when he asked about me she said, "Oh, that's over!" I was quaking when I went to the Circle. It was so peculiar – she behaved as if there'd never been anything between us.'

Under the circumstances, Miranda thought his sense of victimhood unjustified, but today he seemed to have overcome it. This probably had not a little to do with their reunion the previous night: it was still there, the magical connection between them that was somehow more than the sum of its parts; they were both still glowing with it.

'Is it just the two of us, really?' she asked, now. 'I don't know how you feel about her, now.'

'Nothing. Just a blank, really. I suppose I knew all along it wouldn't last…' Suddenly, Miranda's world seemed to slip sideways; her knees felt weak. 'What's the matter – you've gone quite white!' said Julian, in alarm.

'I feel terribly odd, sort of unreal, like in a dream.'

'Here, sit down.' He led her to a bench and put his arms

round her. 'It's all right, it isn't a dream, I'm here.'

Now Julian was the strong one, the caring shoulder. She clung to him to stop herself from floating down the side of Parliament Hill.

'I think it's… everything's been so upside down and I'd just got used to the idea of you being with Jocasta, and now you're not, and it's all too much!'

He held her and rocked her, making soothing noises.

'I'm scared!' she suddenly realised.

'What of?'

'That it'll all go wrong again, we'll quarrel again, you'll go off again…'

'I expect we will quarrel,' he said with unwonted realism. 'But it won't be like before. I want things to be different.' He held her some more, and she leaned on his shoulder. He said, 'By the way, I won £40 on a horse yesterday. Would you like to go to the opera?'

Miranda gazed at the London skyline and marvelled at Julian who could lose Jocasta on Friday and win £40 and herself on Saturday.

*

After supper that evening, Julian suddenly said: 'D'you know, if I'm honest, the worst thing about splitting up with Jocasta? I'm a bit ashamed to admit it.'

'You can tell me if you like,' said Miranda, fearful of what he might come out with.

'I felt such a fool at the Circle on Friday! I hate being made to look ridiculous.' Then, in a sudden burst of anger, 'My father was always belittling me, telling me I was a fool!'

Was this the clue to his touchiness, was this the pain he had kept buried? It had never come up during their One-to-One sessions. Miranda said carefully, 'So your childhood wasn't all that wonderful?'

'It was when I was small, I was really close to my mother. But my father... when I was little he was mostly away in the army. It was after he got back... I hardly knew him, and he was terribly keen on discipline and being manly – you know, "big boys don't cry", sort of thing.'

Miranda pictured an artistic small boy being told to behave like a man; she recalled little Robin at the bonfire. She thought, *but Julian and I are alike: his father, my mother, we are mirror images, we are brother and sister.* No wonder she wanted to heal his wounds. She stroked the back of his neck. 'You can get over that sort of thing,' she said. 'It's what's been imposed on you, it's not the real you.'

'You mean... by doing One-to-Ones and stuff?'

'Or just... seeing yourself differently, perhaps.'

He looked at her with a kind of admiration. 'You are actually quite wise, aren't you?'

'Am I? I need to remind myself of that, as much as you.'

He took both her hands. He said, 'Do you know, it seems almost a miracle that we're together again. It gives me a real sense of awe.'

And Miranda thought: *'but this could work! This could really work!'*

*

When she reported on their progress to Cassie, she was somewhat dismayed at the response. At first Cassie said, 'Well, I said he'd come back to you, and he has...'

'And you said he'd change, and he has.'

'Well, that's good, make the most of it. But I'm not sure this man is your ultimate destiny. Sometimes people come into our lives because we have something to learn, and then we have to move on. I wouldn't put all your eggs in the Julian basket, dear. The opposition hasn't finished with him yet.'

'Really? There's no sign of it at the moment.'

'That's when the scorpion strikes dear, just when it's at its quietest.'

Miranda digested this. Then she remembered something else she had wanted to ask. 'Cassie – about past lives…'

'I'm not an expert on that, dear, but sometimes things pop up during a reading.'

'Perhaps I should come and see you for a proper session.'

'Yes, come and see me. When you're ready.'

Something about her words sounded significant. Cassie didn't just mean 'when you have time'. Ready for what? Miranda wondered.

2

JOCASTA FEIGNS DEATH

Three weeks after renouncing the Circle for good they were back in the Pig and Apple. Judy had begged them both to come and read in her play; following its continued disparagement by Jocasta, she wanted a second opinion from the members of the Circle. Jocasta had reluctantly agreed only when Judy told her that her agent wanted to come along.

'You'll have to make sure Jocasta keeps her hands off him,' Miranda remarked.

'It's all right, he's gay,' said Judy. 'Do come. You read Marguerite so well. And Julian could read your lover this time. He's got such a lovely voice. It'll be all right now it's all over with Jocasta.'

'I don't know that I want to see Jocasta,' Julian had said at first. 'But I suppose it'll be all right if we go together.'

Over the last three weeks their lives had become intertwined as never before. They had had a long, sensible talk. They agreed to be honest with each other about their feelings. They agreed not to make any commitments as yet. Meanwhile the closeness they shared in bed now seemed to spill over into every corner of daily life. Doing things as ordinary as supermarket shopping together gave them both an extraordinary joy.

Julian was now spending four or five days a week with

Miranda, diligently writing while she indexed. Miranda had pointed out to him a competition for fantasy novels advertised in *The Guardian*. Following an afternoon's agonising about how hard it would be, how the strain would affect his health, and it probably wasn't a fantasy novel anyway, Julian had decided to finish it in time for the competition deadline. He had never been so decisive. Could it be the flower remedies Miranda had given him (Larch for lack of confidence, Walnut for letting go of old ties)? Could it be because they were together again? Or was he simply allowing himself to grow up at last?

Julian's explanation was simpler. 'It's the attraction of the gamble,' he said.

Miranda knew Julian's weaknesses; now she was getting to know his strengths, his capacity for kindness, his gentleness, his persistence with his writing. It was in bed, as always, that they were at their best together. There they met totally, not only in body and mind but at some other, deeper and more mysterious place, as if their souls were entwined as closely as their bodies. It seemed very possible, Miranda thought, that they really did know each other from some other time, some other life, or lives.

*

A week before Judy's play-reading, Julian developed a headache which lasted all day. He slept a lot and Miranda crept about, fearful of disturbing him. When she took him a cup of tea he said, 'Why am I so often ill when I come here? I can't understand it.'

'Do you think you're nervous about seeing Jocasta again?'

'I don't know, I won't know till I see her, I suppose.'

His headache was still there next morning.

'I had a horrible dream,' he told Miranda over breakfast. 'I was in a big house, and Jocasta was there, and then she went away and someone told me she was dead. I went and looked: she was lying on the floor and I realised she really was dead, she had killed herself, and I cried and cried, and the more I cried the more anguish I felt. Then you came in, and I woke up.'

'Oh, Julian... d'you think it was a farewell dream?'

'I don't know. She often talked about suicide.'

'Jocasta did?' Miranda gawped.

'She was just trying to impress me, she didn't mean it. Oh, God, I wish I didn't keep getting these headaches, I'll never get the book finished.'

An idea occurred to Miranda. 'We could try doing a One-to-One about them.'

'About my headaches? We could try, I suppose.'

They arranged themselves opposite each other, holding hands. Julian frowned, closed his eyes, opened them. 'I don't know how to get at it,' he said.

'Try being the headache.'

He closed his eyes again, and was silent for a good minute. Something in the atmosphere changed; Miranda felt a little scared. 'Can you tell me what's happening?'

Julian opened his eyes. 'It's... energy, wanting to get out. I can feel it swirling around in my middle. Oh! I know what it is, it's power, potential power.' He looked white, a little scared.

'What would happen if you let it out?' Miranda asked.

'It might overpower people, I have to keep it restrained.'

'Just let it be there... what's it doing now?'

'I can feel it coming up into my head... that's what's giving me the headaches, it must be!'

'Can you let it out, somehow?'

He pushed the air upwards with his hands, pushing the energy up and away from his head. 'Gosh, that actually does feel much clearer! Phew, thanks.'

She had to ask. 'Why do you have to keep your power restrained?'

'I don't know…' He closed his eyes and was silent for a moment. Then he said the one word: 'Atonement'. His face took on an anguished expression. After a long pause, he said, 'I did something I…' He opened his eyes again and shook his head like a dog shaking off water. 'I don't know what that was about. Maybe it was a dream. Let's drop it.'

*

On their arrival at the Pig and Apple, Jocasta greeted them gaily. 'Hallo, you two! How nice to see you.' She was wearing the curious pendant that so intrigued Miranda. It still reminded her of something – something not good. Recalling Cassie's words about the scorpion, she wondered why she had agreed to return to the Circle that evening. To test the fates, perhaps. Perhaps she was a gambler, too.

A moment later, Flaxman pounced on her with a detailed account of a commune he had visited in Wales, where he thought he might retreat and grow herbs. This enabled Jocasta to pin Julian briefly in a corner; through Flaxman's monologue and the general hubbub Miranda heard her saying something spiky about people who didn't say goodbye. Julian extricated himself as soon as he could, and headed for the bar.

Jocasta flitted off to meet Judy and her agent, Finn, a small man with a greying goatee. Fergus approached and took the opportunity to reassure Miranda. 'I don't think you need have any worries about Jocasta. She's completely taken up with her new man.'

'Where is the new man?' Miranda was curious about Julian's successor.

'He doesn't seem to be here tonight. Anyway, I think she's completely gone off Julian. He's actually come out as one of Jocasta's least scathed men,' he went on, with the wry smile of the once scathed. 'You know, he is really much stronger than people give him credit for. He was actually very clear about ending things with Jocasta.'

'Was he? But I thought...' At which point Julian returned with their drinks.

*

The evening's readings opened with Trevor reading a bleak short story about the death of a child, which Jocasta criticised for its lack of compassion. Trevor said that Jocasta had missed the tone of his story simply because it was unsentimental, and what was wrong with people dying? They did it all the time. This led to a discussion of death, during which Jocasta looked straight at Julian and said, 'There's a curious thing in Julian's novel – has anyone noticed? All the characters who die aren't actually dead at all, they're only feigning death.' Miranda hadn't noticed, and wondered how she had missed it.

She and Julian gave Judy's play their best. With Julian reading the part of her lover, his dark-velvet voice making the most of Judy's words, the experience was totally different from that fraught afternoon at Judy's flat. The general reception of both the play and their performances was enthusiastic; only Jocasta was unusually silent, while Finn's expression was inscrutable.

Afterwards, after buying Judy a drink and praising the play, Julian announced that he wanted to leave; he was very tired and his headache was threatening to return. As they made for the door, Jocasta's girlish voice raised itself above the chatter of the bar, and she swept towards them, digging into her tote bag. 'Oh, Julian, I nearly forgot – I've brought a pair of socks you left behind!'

Fiona, positioned nearby, said, 'Really, Jocasta!'

Julian pocketed the socks and muttered, 'That wasn't very tactful.'

When they got home, he looked quite drained.

'Thank God that's over!' he said.

'How was it – seeing Jocasta I mean?'

He frowned. 'What came over to me most about her was her depression.'

'Is she depressed?'

'Yes, I could tell.'

'She told me once she never gets depressed.'

'She tries not to let herself be. She runs around being busy.'

Just before they went to sleep, Julian suddenly said, 'Oh!' as if he'd been stung.

'What?'

'I've seen it. What it is that attracts me to Jocasta... you won't like it if I tell you.'

'Try me.'

'It's as if there's somebody really beautiful and good inside her, that's somehow been warped.'

Miranda said, 'I don't not like that. It could well be true, I suppose.' It was, after all, a basic theory of the Support Group.

He said, 'I did try to relate to her on that level. But she's totally nihilistic.'

Miranda lay awake longer than usual that night, thinking about the evening's events. And about Julian's dream of Jocasta's suicide, and Jocasta's remark about his characters only pretending to be dead…

*

Next day, Miranda phoned Judy to congratulate her on the play and found her elated. 'Finn really likes it,' she said. 'There's a small theatre company he thinks may be interested. He says it only needs a few tweaks.' Then she in turn congratulated the two of them on passing the Jocasta test. 'I'm sure she's quite over Julian now. After you'd gone, she said, "Isn't it lovely to see Julian and Miranda looking so happy?"'

Miranda recalled that Jocasta had said something similar to Fiona shortly before she filched Julian. But Judy went on, 'Then she actually said she felt rather guilty about all that.'

'Good heavens,' said Miranda. 'Well, so she should.'

She repeated this to Julian, who had been very quiet all morning. 'She does have a nice side,' he said. 'She was very kind to me at first, she used to say I was kind to her. She once said, "I can't understand how Miranda could let that go."'

'But you weren't being all that kind to me!'

'I didn't think you had any feelings for me… I didn't know you at all, really,' he said. 'I thought you were terribly strong. It wasn't till I came to the hospital with you, and you cried… I'd never seen that side of you before.' He frowned. 'It worries me, actually – when you were crying and looking so fragile, that really turned me on.'

Miranda decided to make light of this. 'You'd better be careful, I might play up to that!'

'If you were Jocasta you would. But she hardly ever

cries – it's rather shocking when she does. The first time we went to bed, she cried. She said people weren't usually as nice to her as I was – I suppose someone with her kind of reputation doesn't always get treated kindly by men. And she cried about Grant not wanting her. And when I went back to her after I'd been to the dental hospital with you, she was pathetically grateful…'

'Julian, then she does have feelings for you! You've always told me she's as hard as nails!' Miranda was alarmed at the portrait he was painting of a Jocasta who could be hurt. Sometimes with Julian she felt as if she was in a hall of distorting mirrors. 'I wish you'd said – I would never have wanted to put her through what she put me through!'

Her expression must have shown more than she intended, for there were sudden tears in Julian's eyes. 'Oh, Miranda, I'm sorry, I am sorry I hurt you!'

She said, 'It's all right, I'm not hurt now.'

After a long hug, Julian said, 'You know, it's a pity you and she can't really talk to each other. You're actually quite similar in some ways.'

'Jocasta is a lot bolder about acting out her fantasies,' said Miranda. She looked at him seriously, aware that he still had a strong pull towards Jocasta. 'I wonder which one of us it really is?'

He put his arm back round her. 'If I'm honest, I could still be attracted to Jocasta but I'd never want to get back into all the analysing and the depression and everything. Anyway, she ended things.'

'She seems to think you ended them, so does Fergus. Listen, Julian, I just want you to tell me if you ever decide to go back to her. I don't want any more ghastly shocks. God, here we are talking about Jocasta again. I don't want her here!'

'OK,' he said. 'Buzz off, Jocasta!'

They returned to their routine, Julian writing intently and Miranda typing his novel most evenings after finishing her own work. Realising just how badly he needed stroking and morale-boosting, Miranda renewed her vows to give him all the support he needed. But although he no longer mentioned Jocasta, things were no longer quite the same after their visit to the Pig and Apple. Cracks were beginning to show.

There were days when Julian's fragility re-emerged, when he was stricken by a headache or one of his inexplicable depressions. At these times he did not want to talk, but his hunched, writing back somehow demanded Miranda's attention, nor was she always able to sustain her ideal of being all-loving and all-understanding. It was, for example, extremely distracting to have her time-travel index interrupted by a plaintive voice demanding, 'How can I manage to take flower remedies four times a day as well as all my vitamins?'

'Oh, for goodness' sake, Julian!'

'I'm just expressing my feelings. We agreed to express our feelings.'

Julian, for his part, was irritated by Miranda's continued interest in matters spiritual. She realised belatedly that what she intended as interesting discussions he interpreted as attempts to convert him. Sometimes they were. Once, when he was tossing about in bed agonising about his wasted past, his unknown future, she tried to help him by extolling the benefits of living in the present.

'How can I live in the present?' he snapped. 'I'm a writer, I have to live in the past and the future, and my imagination, my dreams.'

'But you have to accept reality, too,' said Miranda.

'No, I don't, why should I if I don't like it? Don't tell me how to feel, Miranda!' Fifteen minutes later he was still tossing and turning. 'What's going on?' asked Miranda tentatively.

'The trouble is, when we have this sort of conversation… it spoils the romantic part.'

But these incidents were small shadows in a generally sunny landscape.

*

Miranda had been looking forward to reading the novel from beginning to end and learning what it was actually about, but even in its proper order it remained elusive. It was like a series of dreams strung together. The three main characters – a man and two sisters – wandered through barren landscapes and dark forests pursued by shadowy enemies and keeping from each other secrets they barely understood themselves. Miranda still believed, hoped, that all would become clear in the end. After all, there was power in Julian's writing, and poetry.

One evening, after reading aloud a section about the older sister, Maia, Julian remarked, 'Jocasta identified herself as her, you know.'

'And is she?' Did that make Miranda the younger sister, the one the hero truly loved – and betrayed?

'She even dreamed she was,' he replied. 'Once she called out in her sleep, "Oh, my little sister!"' Then he added, as if awarding Jocasta a brownie point, 'You never dream about being in my novel!'

He's missing Jocasta, thought Miranda, *whatever he says.* That night, as if even her subconscious was trying to please him, she dreamed she was in an adventure story, pursued by a faceless enemy. She was shot; she fell to the ground and lay still, pretending to be dead. A little girl approached; Miranda signed to her not to give her away, and the child smiled back, a brilliant, knowing smile. Her look said: 'It's all a game, really, we both know it's only a game'.

As she continued working through the novel, she had a curious sense that she knew what it was about better than he did. She thought, *but the hero has lost his soul! It's his soul he is looking for!* Did Julian know that? She dared not ask him. With the competition deadline approaching he had reached a stage when almost any comment came over as criticism.

One evening she came to a passage which created a cold tingle down her spine: a description of moonlight and clutching branches and swirling cloaks as a group of hooded people danced around a clearing in the forest. She stopped typing. Had they both had the same dream, or was this a shared memory? She said, carefully, 'Julian, these people dancing in a circle – did you dream this?'

'Yes. There's a lot of my dreams in there, I told you. What's wrong with it?'

'Nothing. It's very powerful.'

Some instinct prevented her from telling Julian about her own dream. She was sure now that they did have a past-life connection. The dream suggested that they had been involved together in some kind of witchcraft; probably Jocasta had been a member of the coven. Was this where it started? she wondered. Because she now felt certain that they had had other connections, other linked lives. They were tied together, the three of them, by invisible, powerful cords. Were they destined to dance in circles forever, changing partners, competing for power? She must talk to Cassie, soon.

3

DEPARTURES

With the arrival of March and the competition deadline ever closer, Julian became increasingly tense while Miranda felt increasingly swamped. She was doing all the cooking and cleaning and paying for most of their provisions, as well as typing Julian's latest draft in the evenings. More than once she recalled what Guru Chakrao had said about the dangers of getting what you want.

Any exploration of past lives would have to take a back seat. She was sure that Julian had no idea of the possibility – he would not have been capable of keeping it to himself – and she had no intention of complicating their relationship by suggesting it. But Jocasta? Jocasta was the one who enjoyed exercising power. It could explain why Jocasta had pushed her at Julian. Was it possible that she had drawn Miranda into their eternal triangle, whether instinctively or deliberately, to keep the dance going? Miranda wanted to know more; she wanted to remember. She would have liked to discover more through dreams, but she was too tired to dream. She wished she could talk with Cassie, but there was no time.

Meanwhile, the sheer logistics of living and working together for most of the week were now leading to clashes. It was impossible to meditate with Julian there, and Miranda badly missed those islands of peace. One-to-Ones were out of the question: how could either of them listen non-judgmentally to the person who was getting on their nerves? Try as she might to be all-accepting and all-loving, Miranda found herself regularly snapping at Julian, which did not improve matters. He did not seem to understand that you can love someone and still find them irritating.

Julian's dark moods returned in force. Miranda tried every which way to cheer him up, eventually to be rebuffed by, 'Just leave me alone! Jocasta was much better with my depressions, she just treated them lightly.'

'Thanks for the comparison! I'm only trying to help.'

'Well don't. I just need to be left as I am till I come out of it.'

'All right, I'm glad you told me.'

One evening she plucked up the courage to tell him she needed more space. He took this surprisingly well. He said, 'Look, as long as we're clear about it, it's OK. I'll go home a day earlier next week. I can just as easily write at home.' Then he added sadly, 'I wonder if I'll ever meet a woman who wants me there all the time. I am trying not to pressurise you.'

'Maybe we just need a break.' Miranda stretched. Her shoulders were aching from typing. 'Do you fancy going out dancing on Saturday? I haven't danced for ages.'

'Yes, all right, why not?'

'Lovely! That'll keep me going.'

But when Saturday came, at the very last minute, Julian was too tired to go out. 'Oh, Julian, I was really looking forward to it.'

'I've got a headache.'

Miranda was too disappointed to be nice. All her good intentions swirled down a black plughole. She flung at him words she hadn't even realised she was thinking. 'You don't want to give me anything! You're only here because things didn't work out with Jocasta, I'm just second best!'

'That's not true – I am here, aren't I?'

'It wasn't your decision, you weren't even happy about it!'

Then they were in a shouting match, Julian's face grey as he yelled back, 'You don't want me here, you won't commit to me, you don't care about me!'

'Oh, don't be ridiculous – you're the one who's missing Jocasta!'

They stared at each other. Miranda took a deep breath.

'We mustn't do this,' she said.

'No, we mustn't.' He held out his arms, and the sensation of his sweatered shoulder against her face comforted her.

She said, 'We mustn't keep raking over the past,' aware that she was the one who had brought it up. 'I suppose I haven't really got over the Jocasta business yet. It just seems accidental that you're with me – you didn't even make a choice. I do sometimes wish you'd take responsibility for your actions!'

'I don't feel responsible for my actions. I'm not an instigator, I react to other people.'

'But you're still responsible for what you do.'

'I absolutely disagree. I am what I am. And what I find hard to take about you,' he added, 'is your constant harping on personal development.'

'You mean you don't want it for yourself.'

'I do want it, actually. It's the way you keep on about it, you get so intense about it all.'

'I swear I've been trying not to.'

There was a pause while they stared at each other. Finally Julian said, 'What's really bothering me is that I've got two weeks to finish the book, and I just can't do it with all this friction.'

'Well, I can't work with all this friction either!' She took in his wan face, and her heart turned over. 'Look, I want to help you finish the book. I am committed to that.'

He said, 'I know. I'm sorry. We'll just keep trying, shall we?'

Later, trying to meditate while Julian went for a walk round the block, Miranda thought, *I don't want a relationship that has me worried all the time.*

In her head the reply came as if spoken by someone else: 'Then don't worry all the time.'

But she lay awake that night, listening to Julian's breathing and the voice of her own insecurity reminding her that he had danced with Jocasta and would not dance with her.

*

For the next week both did their best to avoid conflict. They saw less of each other, made love less often, and quarrelled not at all, possibly because they were too tired.

Suddenly the competition deadline was a week away. Julian arrived that Friday evening announcing that he had no money and had only eaten one piece of toast since yesterday. He had a headache, he would never finish the book in time. Next morning, as she struggled blearily out of bed, it dawned on Miranda that the pattern of the past few weeks had been controlled by Julian's unspoken conviction that because he was a creative genius her role was automatically that of subservient handmaid. Somehow she had fallen in with it. Perhaps in a previous existence she had been his slave.

If the novel really had been a work of genius she might have felt differently. But the more of it she typed, the more she realised that it was not. She concealed her thoughts, but could not give Julian the unstinting praise he craved. 'But where is the story?' she wondered, as his three main characters continued to wander arbitrarily through the alien landscape until they arbitrarily stopped. There was no shape, no catharsis, no conclusion. Then it came to her – Julian did not want to find the real story. He would have to delve too deep.

Two days before the deadline Julian reached the final page and Miranda typed it. At the very last minute they bickered over the placing of a semi-colon. As he set off to deliver the manuscript by hand, he barely muttered goodbye.

*

When he returned the following Sunday he looked tired, but he was no longer the snappy person who had departed so ungratefully. 'We ought to talk,' he said, as they embraced on the doorstep. Miranda agreed.

But talking was postponed. After lunch they lay down holding each other like two comrades exhausted after a battle. And Miranda was aware of a sadness in him – a genuine sadness, not the anxiety-ridden dissatisfaction she had recently been subjected to. She leaned on her elbow looking down at his tired face, his shadowed eyes. 'You're hurting somewhere,' she said.

Tears came into his eyes, and he nodded. 'What is it?' she asked. 'What's hurting?'

But he did not, could not, tell her.

In the morning he made love to her very tenderly, very lovingly. Afterwards, as Miranda looked at his now peaceful face she felt herself soften as though something rigid inside her was melting.

Julian looked up at her and said, 'You're really smiling at me, you've never smiled at me like that before.'

'Perhaps you haven't noticed,' she said. Then she said, suddenly knowing it, 'There's a lot of love in you!'

He looked sad again. 'Yes, there is. But it's difficult to let it out. It's so easy for love to get hurt.'

She thought, holding him, that there was someone in there whom she loved very much. And she knew it was not the whole of him; there was someone else in there too, who could betray her without a second thought, and moreover justify it to himself.

At breakfast the next morning he said uncomfortably, 'By the way – I went to the Circle on Friday. I talked a bit with Jocasta in the pub.'

'Oh?… How was it?'

'Peculiar… she was pleased I'd got the novel off. She wants to read it. She said you and I must go over sometime for a meal.'

'She must be joking!'

'I said we could meet at the pub but she didn't want to do that.'

During that week, as she approached the end of her index, Miranda's mind kept returning to past lives. Who had they been? What had they done? She remembered the strange One-to-One when he had spoken of having to keep his power restrained, and recalled Cassie saying to her: 'Perhaps you misused power in a previous life.' It seemed highly likely that they had both misused power in the past. As for Jocasta…

*

Two weekends later, although he behaved lovingly when he arrived, there was something evasive about Julian's manner. He didn't say whether he had been to the Circle again, and

Miranda didn't ask. On the Sunday morning, his mood was odd. Over breakfast he launched into a long and irrelevant monologue about vitamins. That morning everything Miranda said or did met with contradiction or criticism. Her enthusiasm for the daffodils lighting up the local gardens was banal. Her affection for Rollo was sentimental anthropomorphising. A comment she made about Judy's play showed a lack of literary judgment. *Here we go again,* she thought, overcome by an immense weariness. *He's feeling guilty.*

Finally, she said: 'Julian, I am tired of being put in the wrong. Is there something you want to tell me?'

'What are you talking about?'

'You're covering something up.'

'Don't be ridiculous, you're being irrational!'

Irrational was a Jocasta word. She looked at him steadily. 'Let's just say I'm not enjoying your company today,' she said.

He flushed deeply, his features tightened. He said, 'All right, if you don't want me here, I'll go.'

And he went.

*

The next day, with a sense of relief at returning to normality, Miranda met Fiona for lunch. Fiona's shock at learning that Miranda had been largely subsidising Julian shocked Miranda herself: she suddenly felt ashamed at the way she had let herself be used. As she described the last few weeks, Fiona's expression grew increasingly severe.

'Dammit, Miranda, you've been keeping him!'

'Well, to be fair, he is on the dole and he did chip in when he could.'

'Doesn't he mind being on the dole? It can't be very good for his pride.'

'He doesn't seem to. Anyway, it isn't the money so much as being totally taken for granted. He didn't lift a finger the last few weeks, he couldn't even empty his own ashtrays.'

'Miranda, why have you been martyrising yourself? The little turd can't be worth it! Where's your pride, come to that?'

'I don't seem to have any at the moment.' She was beginning to realise just how much she had been distorting herself in the name of love. 'D'you know, it feels as if I'd been hypnotised... I thought I loved him, maybe it was just sex.'

'Well, in the words of an American friend of mine, the screwing you're getting ain't worth the screwing you're getting!'

Miranda laughed. 'That sums it up, I'd say.'

'Anyway, it sounds as if you could do with a break.'

'Yes, maybe.' Perhaps she could visit Sally again.

*

After over a week's silence, Julian rang, his voice sounding cold and strange. He was sorry he hadn't been in touch; he had a lot on his plate. He was job-hunting. He had started a new short story. He'd been told about a weekend writing course in the country; he thought he might go.

'Can you afford it?' asked Miranda, sounding nastier than she intended.

'I can usually afford what I want.'

'Well, bully for you!' This time she meant to sound nasty.

'What's that supposed to mean?'

'Oh, come on Julian, I've been pauperising myself looking after you over the last two months! Do you know what it would have cost to have your novel typed professionally?'

'What a mercenary thing to say!'

'That was a lot of work, and you never even thanked me.'

'I said thank you, didn't I?'

True, the freshly typed sheets had been received with the occasional grunted "k'you". 'You may have muttered something once or twice. You could have written to me, sent me a card at least.'

'I didn't want to be beholden to you,' said Julian.

The logic of this defeated Miranda. 'But by not thanking me you are beholden!'

'I am not going to quarrel with you on the telephone,' said Julian. 'I was going to ask if I could come over, but I won't as you're in such a bad mood.' And he hung up.

Miranda heaved a huge sigh of mingled fury and relief. That was it: she wanted no more of him. How could she have loved this man? She didn't even like him. So, this was how it ended: not with a bang but a whimper. Good. No more Julian, no more Jocasta. She was stepping away for good and all. She just wished she'd been the one to hang up.

*

Fiona telephoned after the next Circle evening. 'Jocasta told me about your telephone tiff with Julian – he seems to have run straight to her for consolation.'

'I thought he would,' said Miranda.

'I told her I thought he'd behaved very badly, and Jocasta, said "But you don't know what Miranda said to him!" I said, "I don't suppose you do, either, if you only have

Julian's version." Which shut her up momentarily. Anyway, I told her you were fed up with housekeeping for two and paying for it.'

'And typing his awful novel, for no thanks at all, just to have him run back to Jocasta! Bloody man! Jocasta can have him.'

'I don't suppose he's getting much joy there – Kenneth is in residence. But I hear Julian's job-hunting, which is something. I rather resent my taxes supporting people like him.'

*

For the next two weeks Miranda's life seemed on hold. She had completed her index on black holes. All was silence from Daphne and Clive. Even the Guru Chakrao Fellowship had gone quiet, with no lectures offering spiritual sustenance. She had too much time to think. After her first break-up with Julian she had had something to fight for: now there was a nothingness. She had failed in love.

It was definitely time to visit Cassie, she decided. She was ready. But when she rang, a recording of Cassie's smoke-textured voice announced that she was away for three weeks: her acting career had unexpectedly revived and she was in Birmingham doing a 'cough and a spit' in a soap opera. *Well done, Cassie*, thought Miranda, feeling childishly let down. At least she had arranged to visit Sally the following weekend.

*

The day before she left for Sally's, the post brought an envelope bearing the logo of the Guru Chakrao Fellowship.

It contained a letter from Warren, a very sad, very solemn letter, announcing the demise of the Fellowship. Guru Chakrao had been behaving in a manner not only unbecoming to a spiritual leader, but positively criminal. His misdeeds included embezzling the Fellowship funds, seducing several of the young female helpers, and taking to the bottle. He was now in hiding abroad. Warren and the GCF committee were devastated, but would be available to give counselling to any of the membership who were equally devastated. All he could say was that everyone had human failings, and those who were furthest along the spiritual path had the furthest to fall.

Miranda's first impulse was to laugh. There was something comical about the all-encompassing nature of the Guru's misdemeanours, the discarding of his vows of poverty, chastity and abstinence in one magnificent bundle. Then she thought of all the devastated people who had trusted him, who had handed him their money or their bodies or their faith, and felt slightly ashamed of herself.

Her third reaction was sheer puzzlement. Why had he needed to succumb to such banal temptations? His spiritual power had been real, almost tangible; when he said he had come to heal the human heart he had spoken from his own heart, and Miranda's heart had resonated to his words. He had thrown all that away – and for what? She stared out of the window, trying to work things out. Finally, just as she had decided to give up, she heard in her head a voice that was simultaneously hers and not hers. It said: 'The music is universal, but you are the leader of your own dance.'

4

THE NUNS ARE SHOCKED

She decided to give Cassie one more try before leaving for Suffolk, and was surprised when Cassie answered the phone in person. 'You're lucky to catch me,' she said. 'I have to go back to Birmingham tomorrow for another week. How are things, then?'

Miranda hardly knew where to begin. 'I've got so much to tell you, Cassie, I really need to see you. But you'll be pleased to hear I've finished with Julian – I think I've understood what that's all been about—'

'I'll be back at the end of next week,' said Cassie. 'Can you come that Saturday?'

'Oh, yes, yes, please!'

'Right, Saturday afternoon. It's time... are you going away somewhere?'

'Yes, I'm going to my friend's in Suffolk this weekend.'

'That'll be good for you. You need a change of scene.'

*

It was good to be back with Sally and Harold again, in an atmosphere of sanity and good humour. From this distance, she could only wonder what she had been doing in that claustrophobic relationship: it was as if she had been caught in some kind of web. Perhaps it was nothing to do with past lives, perhaps that was all a fantasy. Sally and Harold were so normal; they didn't need past lives to live their current ones happily. She wondered how her life would have been if she had met someone like Harold when she was younger. She would probably not have been interested – she seemed destined to be drawn to difficult men.

'I hope you don't mind,' said Sally over supper. 'But we're going to have sherry with Bunty on Sunday morning. The rest of her family are away, and Bunty said she'd love to show you her paintings – she seems to have taken a fancy to you.'

Harold groaned. 'Bunty haunts us, she keeps popping round. Sometimes we hide behind the sofa when we hear her coming. You don't have to go.'

'I'd like to,' Miranda was intrigued at the prospect of viewing Bunty's paintings.

'It's quite an interesting house,' said Sally, 'but such a mess. They have a woman in, but I don't think her eyesight's very good. There are cobwebs everywhere.'

By Sunday morning Miranda felt her sanity returning. They had been for a long walk the previous afternoon in a countryside alight with the vivid greens of spring, talking about nothing much. That night she slept better than she had for weeks.

They walked to Bunty's house across muddy fields, Miranda wearing a pair of the boys' welly boots. As they approached the house it looked more and more like a fairy-tale house, ivy-covered, with a sagging red-tiled roof and deep overhanging eaves. Through the small windowpanes Miranda glimpsed black beams and the promised cobwebs.

When Bunty opened the door to them she looked even more unkempt and witch-like than before, her dark grey hair straggling down the sides of her face. Miranda had forgotten how tall she was.

'Welcome! Welcome!' Bunty trumpeted. 'Come in, lovely to see you, er…'

'Miranda,' Sally reminded her, as they trooped into the dark hall, where Bunty introduced them to a huge portrait of herself as a girl, in a virginal white dress. Large, soulful eyes gazed out, the odd-shaped nose was flatteringly blurred. 'Not one of mine – done by a real artist,' she explained. 'I was nineteen,' she said. 'I married the Colonel the year after – of course, he wasn't a colonel then.'

In the front room Miranda's eyes were instantly drawn to two great tusks from an elephant shot by the Colonel in India; above these the head of a wild goat glared from the wall. The ensemble resembled a satanic altar. Bunty introduced her visitors to other items of interest. 'This is a sedan chair, this side comes open, you see, to make room for the crinoline. They'd have needed six men to carry me!' She laughed, too long and too loud.

Harold laughed too, and Bunty wagged a gnarled finger at him. 'I said it first!'

Her art gallery consisted of two small, messy rooms at the back of the house, every wall covered with pictures mostly of flowers, thickly painted with a heavy hand but full of energy and colour. Proudly, Bunty announced, 'This is what I get up to!'

Miranda said judiciously, and truthfully, 'They're very original. There's so much life in them.'

Bunty said, 'I'm allowed to enjoy myself, now I'm old, wha'. Thought you'd like them.'

The paintings duly praised, she led her visitors to a large sitting room, whose beams only just cleared her head. Here she filled four not very well washed schooners to the brim with sweet sherry. Smeary glass in hand, Miranda found herself gazing in fascination at a quite massive painting, hung above the stone fireplace. It showed a group of children coming down a flight of steps accompanied by several nuns. In the foreground, three pigeons were examining a little girl, who had fallen down. The lower right-hand quarter of the canvas was filled by two nuns in extreme close-up, their robes heavy with black paint, and their eyes closed. It was crude, badly painted, but vivid.

'Why have the nuns got their eyes closed?' asked Miranda.

'They're shocked because the other nuns aren't looking after the children. The little girl has lost her ball.' She pointed out a round patch of red resembling dried blood.

'It's Rome,' she explained. 'You see, families all have eight or nine children, and when they've got more than they can manage they give them to the nuns to look after. Well, they did when we lived there. Perhaps it's better now, I keep forgetting how old I am.'

At lunch afterwards, Harold remarked: 'Bunty's never going to make the Royal Academy, is she? You were terribly tactful, Miranda.'

'But I really like her pictures,' Miranda said. 'They're a bit like a child's paintings. Uninhibited.'

'They keep her happy,' said Sally.

'I expect they do,' said Miranda, remembering that Bunty had not been encouraged to paint when she was young.

*

That night, despite a companionable and well-lubricated dinner, Miranda found it hard to get to sleep. Bunty's paintings floated before her eyes, particularly the picture of the nuns. 'The nuns close their eyes in shock, because no one is looking after the children.' *Why*, she wondered, *do people have children they don't want? Why are children neglected and abused? All the child wants, all everybody wants, is to be loved.* Miranda, Jocasta, Julian, even Daphne, they were all little children – even Miranda's mother, a howling, wilful child, demanding love by force because she knew no other way. And when they don't get what they want they pursue distorted means of getting it, because no one has ever simply held out their arms to give them what they need.

And then Miranda saw what she had been doing. She had been so busy rescuing the little boy she had forgotten to look after the little girl. It was time to look after herself.

*

Sitting on the train, Miranda wished she could somehow start her life again. To begin again, free of the history she had been dragging around with her for so long – how light that would be! She longed to emerge into a new daylight. But how did one get reborn without actually dying?

The movement of the train was making her sleepy; in rhythm with the wheels the words repeated themselves: 'The nuns are shocked… the nuns are shocked…' Revisualising the painting she thought, *But surely nuns don't wear jewellery?* In her mind's eye it was quite clear: around her neck one of the nuns was wearing Jocasta's pendant.

Miranda's half-closed eyes flew open. Bunty had got it wrong. It was not about the children. The nuns were shocked because one of their number had run away with a priest. It had happened in Italy, centuries ago. Before the couple could get far, one of the sisters had betrayed them and the errant nun had been punished by imprisonment in a tower of the convent. She had even dreamed about it.

It fitted: Julian, the priest; Jocasta the betrayer; herself the victim, starved to death for the sake of love. She let out a deep sigh. She was beginning to remember.

*

When she got home Rollo gave her his usual warm welcome, wrapping his soft body round her calves and purring loudly; Miranda's neighbour had clearly looked after him well. She bent to rub his head. 'Have you been a good boy?' she asked. Rollo blinked up at her, his eyes translucent gold and enigmatic.

How silly! she thought. *Cats can't be good; they have no concept of 'good'.* Rollo had a sunny nature; he purred at a touch or even a glance; he enjoyed life with feline gusto – eating, being stroked, playing with a cork or, as now, rolling onto his back presenting his soft, vulnerable tummy for tickling. She gazed down at the perfection of his markings, the sheen on every hair, his delicately carved nose – he was beautiful. What was more, thought Miranda, as his purr rose to a rasping squeak of pleasure, he was appreciative. But he was not 'good'; he was just himself, totally self-accepting. He had no need to seek warmth in cold places.

A spark of energy exploded in Miranda's middle. All her life she had been trying to be good, trying so hard, and always failing, doing penance for some unexplained guilt. And it didn't work; in fact, the harder she tried, the less it worked. She had exhausted herself trying to support Julian – and for what? What had she been trying to prove?

To Rollo she said aloud, 'I don't want to be a good girl! I don't want to be good anymore!'

That afternoon, her life began moving again. Clive booked her for a week's work, and a publisher rang about a new book to index. Her cousin James telephoned to say that her mother was coming to London next month for her hip operation. 'I just thought I should let you know – no one expects you to visit or anything. I'll go. I gather from Ma she's rather nervous about it. By the way,' he added. 'I may be able to put some work your way. I'll let you know.' More indexing, Miranda assumed.

She could hardly wait to see Cassie. Meanwhile, although she dreamed a lot, her dreams were scattered and broken, involving people she didn't recognise in places she didn't know. One of them reminded her of *Jane Eyre* – something to do with a Victorian governess – but it had gone before she could grasp it.

*

Midweek, she met Fiona and Judy for lunch at a pizza house near the British Museum. At first all three avoided the subject of Julian. Judy was in a buzz of excitement: her play was going to be put on in the autumn, in a small fringe theatre. 'I'm not going back to the Circle,' she said. 'Jocasta said she was happy for me, but she really wasn't, I could tell.'

Fiona said, 'She's actually been quite helpful with my novel. But of course it's a long way from getting published.'

Judy hesitated and then said, 'I wonder if Julian's novel will get published.'

'I shouldn't think so,' said Miranda.

'He looked terribly down last time I saw him,' Judy went on. 'We had quite a long chat in the pub. He said he was missing you.' Miranda managed to hear this without a twinge. It was over, it really was over.

'So he should miss you, the little bugger,' said Fiona. 'After all you've done for him.'

Judy went on, 'I asked him why he didn't ring you, and he said it was very difficult – pride, I suppose.'

'Isn't he with Jocasta?' asked Miranda. 'I thought he was back with her.'

'I thought Kenneth was still there – but come to think of it, he hasn't been at the Circle for a while. Goodness, how does Jocasta keep up with herself? Anyway, don't think of having Julian back, even if he asks!' urged Fiona.

'I won't,' said Miranda firmly. 'It's finished. Thanks, Judy, but I don't want him to ring me. Jocasta can have him.'

'D'you know,' said Fiona. 'I've been thinking, and I think I know what's wrong with Jocasta. I think she has absolutely no imagination. Hence all the note-taking, and battening onto people like Julian, and putting you and Judy down, because you do have imaginations. And the way she behaves without any regard for people's feelings – do you know what I heard her say to Fergus once? She said, "How does it feel to be the discarded lover?" I mean, honestly! I don't think she has any conception of what she does to other people!'

Judy said, 'Of course, that's it – no imagination. That's why she teaches instead of writing.'

All three considered the phenomenon of Jocasta in silence for a moment. Then they turned to other topics. As Miranda bit into her last piece of pizza crust, something terrible happened. She put her hand over her mouth, exclaiming, 'Oh, my God!'

Judy and Fiona turned anxious faces to her, visibly about to rescue her from an immediate nervous breakdown. Hand over mouth, Miranda had to explain that not only had one of her new tooth crowns come off, but she had also swallowed it.

*

Cassie greeted her with a warm hug, and the cats rubbed themselves round her ankles. Miranda sat opposite Cassie at the little cane and glass table. She had so much to ask her, so much to tell her – but Cassie simply said, 'Shuffle!', and thrust the battered pack of cards at her. Miranda shuffled. 'Now cut three times.' Miranda did so.

Cassie laid out the first pile in rows. 'Hmm,' she said. 'You're not quite there yet, but you're doing well. You've cleared a lot of debts. That's why it's been so hard – you had to clear the path so you can move forward.'

'Debts from past lives? That's what I wanted to ask – this thing with Julian and Jocasta...'

Cassie nodded. 'I know. They're telling me you're right, you've been involved with each other in the past. But you haven't got the whole picture. This triangle – no, it's more like a circle – it has to stop. It has to be stopped.'

'I have stopped it. I've finished with Julian. Really finished!'

Cassie smiled. 'Oh, it's going to need more than that. He's still standing beside you. He'll want to come back, but there'll be an ulterior motive.'

'I don't want him back!'

Cassie ignored this, and laid out a second row of cards. 'This circle, it's been going on for centuries... it's been damaging you all.' She looked into the middle distance. 'My, my, we have been a naughty girl!'

Miranda stared at her. 'Me?'

'Oh, yes, sometimes it takes three to tango! It was your choice. You three created the pattern between you; it's been repeated and repeated, and now you're all stuck in it.'

Miranda remembered one of her dreams. 'Did it start in

Ancient Egypt?'

Cassie considered. 'Yes, they're telling me yes. You were a child, you had gifts the other two wanted to use. They stole your true self. After that, you joined them. You still had a choice, but you joined them.' Her voice sounded different, deeper than usual. Her face looked different, too, sterner. 'All those lifetimes…'

'I've been trying to remember,' said Miranda. 'Was I a nun, once?'

Cassie closed her eyes as if remembering, too. 'That's right. I've got a name… Sister Maria Bianca… sixteenth century, I think.'

Miranda's spine tingled, she felt fearful.

'You were jealous of her,' Cassie continued. 'You wanted the priest for yourself.'

'What?'

'Yes, you haven't always been the victim, you know. They shut her up in a tower, she nearly starved to death. Don't know what happened to the priest – men get away with a lot, don't they!'

Miranda was shocked. She had been the betrayer? She wanted to know, even if it was bad, even if it was awful. 'What else?' she asked.

'Oh, there's been so many, dear. There was a coven in the Middle Ages – ah, you know about that one – that's when you made some sort of pact, the three of you. You vowed to stay together, but it went sour, it turned into a contest for leadership. It went on and on, life after life, all sorts. You haven't always been a woman. You were a poet in the fifteenth century, very attractive to women… you and your brother between you used women like paper dolls. That's why you chose to be a woman this time, to experience what it's like at the receiving end. There was an Edwardian family;

the father had an affair with a governess who bullied the children… your mother was one of the children…' Cassie looked at her quizzically. 'You certainly paid for that one!'

She turned over some more cards. 'Sex magic in the 1920s… Hmm, that was fun! More sex than magic, if you ask me. You've always been drawn to each other, the three of you, but you've had to play these silly power games. It's time to stop – but you know that.'

'Have I done – did we do – really awful things?'

'Oh, I've come across a lot worse. You weren't mass murderers or torturers. It's been about power, mainly, power over others and power over each other. People got hurt, certainly, yourselves mostly, in the long run. You've stopped yourselves from evolving spiritually. Which is what we're here for.'

Miranda was shocked. She had been as bad as the other two – possibly worse. 'I wish I could remember more,' she said.

'Remembering isn't important. What's important is releasing the pattern. You've been stuck in a loop, and that's not how it's meant to be. Souls are meant to progress, to learn and move forward, to use power in the right way. Humankind needs to be lifted on to a higher plane, especially now, and the darkness wants to prevent it. So you have to do your bit. The world needs healing.'

'I suppose I've been trying to heal Julian,' said Miranda. 'But I don't think he wants to be healed.'

'It's not your job to save him, or that woman. They are responsible for themselves. But you can free them.'

That was it! That's what she had come here for. 'But how?' she asked.

Cassie closed her eyes. 'The links are strong, dear… but you'll know when the time comes.'

Miranda's head was swirling. Cassie looked at her sharply. 'It's a lot to take in, I know. But don't worry, once you're free to be your real self there'll be a better path for you, a path lined with blossoms, with love at the end of it. Oh – they're saying something about luggage, does that mean anything?'

'I'm not sure… maybe.'

'Would you like me to give you some healing?' said Cassie.

*

When she got home, Miranda felt exhausted and overwhelmed. Cassie's healing had made her feel incredibly sleepy. She lay down on the sofa bed, and drifted off, coming to an hour or so later, with a dream still playing in her head. She was a child again, and she was happy: she had been given a toy, an old-fashioned Noah's ark, complete with carved and painted animals. She was placing them side by side in their pairs, saying aloud: 'The lion is for courage, the elephant is for trust, the horse is for friendship, the dog is for fidelity, the deer is for love, the dove is for the spirit…'

She awoke still speaking the words out loud, and understood why she felt so happy. This was the luggage she had left behind; it had been restored to her. And at last she knew why she had been so eager to be born: she had come here to break the circle. Now it felt as if she had known it all along. Even though she hadn't the remotest idea how to do it.

PART 7

SUMMER: ENDING
THE DANCE

1

PITY FOR THE WITCH

'When you pity her, she is no longer a witch.'
Paul Romer

After her session with Cassie, Miranda did a great deal of thinking. She had to break up the circle of three, for good. Stepping away from it wasn't enough. In fact, it may not have been all that helpful. Now she felt sure that in order to act she had to be in contact with the other two. Currently, she didn't want to be in touch with either of them.

Cassie had said she'd know when the time was right. She decided to wait and concentrate on her latest job, indexing a book on Japanese flower arranging, a relatively soothing task; the illustrations were beautiful. As she worked through it she felt herself becoming calmer. Fiona was keeping her up to date with Circle gossip; when Julian's name came up she felt not the slightest twinge. *I am changing*, she thought. *Soon I shall be ready.*

One evening early in May Miranda met her cousin James at a wine bar off Regent's Street. She was happy to see him; although they met so rarely he felt like an old, comfortable friend.

'I'd like to put you in touch with a publishing chum of mine,' he told her after ordering for them both. 'He's looking for editors for a series of children's books, and I thought it might be your sort of thing. Shall I give him your number?'

Children's books – that sounded nice, much more creative than indexes.

'Yes, please! Gosh, thanks a lot, James.'

'The other thing is, I thought you might like to know your mother's arrived for her op. She's having it done tomorrow. She's in a private ward – very swish. I popped in at lunch time.'

'Oh, James, aren't you good!'

He made a wry face. 'I had very mixed feelings about it, actually, feeling sorry for her at the same time as wanting to leave as soon as possible. She's… do you want to know this?'

'I suppose so. Go on.'

'She's turned into a little old lady all of a sudden, sort of small and frail. Quite pathetic, except you can't help wondering how much it's an act. She's fed up that Xavier wouldn't come with her. And she's already managed to antagonise the hospital staff, treating them like servants and complaining about the food, and ticking them off for calling lunch "dinner"!'

'I can imagine.'

'Anyway, she asked after you, quite kindly. Then she went all maudlin on me and said she'd had a good life and wouldn't mind if she died under the anaesthetic – it was rather yucky, actually.'

'Hip replacements aren't dangerous, are they?'

'Fairly major, I think, but not life-threatening. I guess she's just making a meal of it. It's my ma I'm sorry for, she's invited her to stay while she convalesces.'

'That's kind of her.'

'I'm afraid it's more duty than kindness. She'll hate every moment.'

'Gosh, James, it must be awful to be the sort of person no one wants to have around!'

'I suppose it would be, if she was aware of it.'

*

Later, stroking Rollo on her lap, Miranda thought about her mother. What sort of person would Miranda be now, if her mother had not disliked her so? She recalled an incident at the swimming pool when she was about five; her mother was teaching her the breaststroke, holding her up by her swimsuit straps. Halfway across the pool, Miranda realised that she was swimming by herself.

'How did you know I could swim?' she asked, paddling back.

'I just felt it was the right moment to let go,' her mother said.

How was it that she had been capable of that moment of pure, right instinct, and yet bypass any other moments of potential harmony? It must be hard to have a daughter who doesn't want to know you. Miranda could not feel guilty, but she did feel sad. Perhaps now, visualising the ageing body in a hospital bed, she could at least stop hating her mother. She decided to send her a get-well card, poor old bat.

*

That same week Fiona rang with news. Jean, one of the Circle members, had invited her for coffee the previous Sunday. 'And there was Jocasta, all red-nosed and bright-eyed after a major bust-up with Kenneth. He's been exploiting her, living off her and seeing other women. As a result, Julian is now the sympathetic person who's giving her a shoulder to lean on.'

'So are things back on between them?'

'He's certainly spending a lot of time with her, but I don't know on what basis. Anyway, apparently he's got himself a job.'

'Goodness. Doing what?'

'It's in some bookshop in Charing Cross Road. That should suit him.'

'Has he moved back in with her?'

'I'm not sure – I gather there's someone else in the offing, someone she met over Christmas.'

'I thought that was Kenneth?'

'No, he was later.'

'Goodness, how does she keep track?'

Miranda wished Fiona hadn't reminded her that Julian could be a sympathetic person. She had been doing so well; now her Julian feelings began to stir once more. She wanted him, not sexually, but simply to hold her in his arms. Why did she love him more when he wasn't there? She thought of the rhyme: 'As I was going up the stair, I met a man who wasn't there. He wasn't there again today. How much I wish he'd go away!'

Yes, that was Julian. Go away, she told him, but he wouldn't.

*

A week later, Miranda was positively dancing along the sunlit pavement of Great Russell Street, the skirt of her new, sky-blue dress swirling round her calves. Her meeting with James's friend had gone remarkably well. Her previous contacts with publishers had been mainly telephonic;

entering Alastair's sleek office in a sleek building, she felt she was at last entering the grown-up world. Alastair himself was pleasantly unsleek – a tall, fair man with a particularly nice smile. He explained that he was general editor for a series of anthologies for children on specific themes – school, animals, history, fairy tales and so on.

'Would you be interested in editing the fairy-tales book? What we want is an unusual slant – not rehashes of *Cinderella*, but lesser known stories, by good writers – De La Mare rather than Blyton, you know. Your job would be to make the selection, and then negotiate the rights to any that are still in copyright. And you could commission one or two new ones.'

'Goodness, what power!' said Miranda. She could ask Fiona to write a story. A pity she couldn't commission one from Julian – speedily she erased the idea.

Alastair laughed. 'James says you write, so if you want to write one yourself, feel free – I'd have to vet it of course.'

She came away a foot off the ground. Perhaps this was the beginning of the new blossomy path Cassie had predicted. She would enjoy working with Alastair. *He really liked me,* she thought. And why not? She was beginning to like herself.

*

'Alastair was very pleased,' said James, when he telephoned two days later. 'He thought you were just the right person for the job.'

'I'm not sure how he could tell,' said Miranda. 'He didn't ask me much.'

'Oh, he's quite an intuitive chap.'

'James, thanks a lot for the intro. I'm going to enjoy working on this!'

'That's good. Listen, what I actually rang about was your mother.'

'Oh – how is she?'

'Going back to France next week, much to Ma's relief. Not the easiest visitor! She was very touched by your get-well card, by the way. But – the thing is, when I last saw her, she gave me something for you.'

'Oh? What sort of something?'

'Erm, well, I'd like to give it to you personally – there's something I have to explain. I could bring it over to your place and maybe we could go out to lunch afterwards? But I'm awfully sorry, I can't do it straight away. I've got to go abroad on business for a couple of weeks. Is it all right if I call you when I get back?'

Miranda felt extremely curious, but clearly she'd have to wait.

*

When Daphne telephoned, Miranda was feeding Rollo, enjoying his noisy chomping and total preoccupation with his dish.

'It seems ages since we had a proper talk,' Daphne said. 'The thing is, I've got something to tell you. This isn't easy, but I wanted you to know – I'm probably going to die quite soon.'

'Daphne! Are you sure?' Miranda felt a sudden pain in her middle.

'Oh, yes, my body's been telling me so for some time, and there comes a point when you can't ignore it. I had a small heart attack a week ago, and my consultant says I'm liable to have more. My lungs are pretty bad, too. I've moved in with my parents, I'm more or less permanently in bed.

Anyway, it's a nice day, so I thought I'd give myself a treat and ring you for a long chat.'

It seemed tragic that Daphne's idea of a treat was to telephone Miranda. Daphne went on, 'I must talk to you some time about business – I need you to write a letter to my solicitor, but I've been putting it off. I was worried about upsetting you.'

Why should Miranda be upset? They had calmly discussed Daphne's possible death more than once; Miranda had even joked that Daphne would come back to haunt her. But this time, the dying was for real. And Miranda was upset.

They talked for nearly an hour. Not about death but about life: Daphne was missing London – had Miranda seen any good plays lately?

Miranda said, 'Maybe they have theatres and restaurants in heaven. You'll find some handy angel to do your bookings for you.'

'Are you so sure I'm going to heaven?'

'I don't believe in the other place.'

'I'm sorry I never met your healer friend,' said Daphne. 'But just talking with her did something for me. Whatever she gave me over the phone has stayed with me, it's made a difference.'

'That's good.'

'I'm hoping I can last out for one more piece of work. There's a small local theatre group who are putting on a play about being disabled. I'm going to help with the publicity.' Daphne launched into a detailed description of the company set-up and her plans for it.

Suddenly it was all too practical. Dammit, this brisk-sounding person on the other end of the line was planning to die shortly. 'Perhaps I could come down and help you,' Miranda offered.

Daphne said sadly, 'Oh, no. No, I mean – thanks, but we couldn't plan... I have to use my energy when I've got it. In short spurts.' She laughed. 'This call is my energy expenditure for today.'

Miranda's image of businesslike Daphne crumbled into something else. She said, 'I'm going to miss you.'

There was a pause, during which what she had just said became the truth.

Daphne said, 'You know, I really do value you. I've always valued our friendship.'

And Miranda knew that that was the truth, too.

It was all right, Miranda told herself, that Daphne was dying. There was nothing tragic about dying, even in your thirties, when you'd lived a full life and your body was packing up, and death was really nothing to be afraid of. So where did the grief come from? Why, after putting the receiver down, did she find herself shaken by a flood of noisy, racking tears which sent Rollo scurrying under the sofa?

*

Cassie said, 'You're going through a crash course, that's what.'

Miranda had come to Cassie's Muswell Hill eyrie for some hands-on healing. All that week she had had to stop whatever she was doing at regular intervals, overtaken by waves of grief – for Daphne, for the loss of Julian, even for her mother. After each bout of weeping she felt quite normal, but more tears kept coming.

'It's a clearing-out process,' Cassie said. 'Crying's good for you – well, you know that. You're letting go of a lot of old junk.'

She moved her hands over Miranda's head and down her back. 'You feel much stronger to me,' she said. She cocked her head, listening. 'They're telling me you've done well. You're nearly ready for the next step. You just need to learn to trust a bit more, and you'll be fine.'

'I thought Julian was out of my system,' Miranda confessed. 'But he isn't totally.'

'Well, maybe there's a reason for it.'

'I think...' Miranda tried to clarify her thoughts. 'I think, if the circle is to be broken, I have to see him again, and Jocasta. But I still don't know how I'm supposed to do it.'

'You'll find out; you have some powerful guides. They're saying it has to be final; it needs a ritual... Oh! That's odd, there's a man here in spirit I haven't seen before – he's a kind man. He's keeping an eye on you. You'll be all right, my duck.'

*

The following week, Fiona asked Miranda to come to the Circle; she was nearing the end of her novel. It was important because Judy had offered to introduce her to her agent, but she was uncertain about the ending. Jocasta had said she could read it next Friday, and Fiona would value Miranda's opinion.

'Julian won't be there,' she added. 'He said last week he'll be working late, stock taking.'

Miranda knew she had to go.

As she walked into the pub she had a dreamlike sense of entering the past. Flaxman and Fergus greeted her with cherubic smiles, Fiona with quizzical eyebrows. 'Do look!' she said. 'Jocasta's been raiding a basketball team!'

The seat on the right hand of Jocasta was occupied by a very tall, square-jawed, crew-cut young man, who gazed raptly and silently at Jocasta throughout the evening's proceedings.

Keeping a low profile, Miranda waited for Fiona's reading, but it never happened. Jocasta had either forgotten it or had simply decided to favour other students that evening. Fiona's expression became increasingly grim; in the bar afterwards she marched up to Jocasta to vent her annoyance.

Miranda decided to leave; she would catch up with Fiona on the phone. But as she made to go, Jocasta liberated herself from Fiona and swept towards her. 'Do wait, Julian's coming later!' she cried, as though offering a treat. 'He's working so hard, but he's coming on afterwards – why don't you wait and see him?'

Miranda said firmly, 'I don't want to see Julian, that's all over.' Behind Jocasta, Fiona was stalking out of the pub, her face full of fury.

'Oh, no, I'm sure it's not over!' Jocasta cooed.

'Listen, Jocasta, Julian hung up on me weeks ago. I'm not going to go chasing him.' She had to see him, she reminded herself. But she was not going to make things easy for Jocasta.

'We must talk about this! I'm sure there's been a misunderstanding.' Jocasta seized Miranda's arm and manoeuvred her into a corner on a bench behind a round iron table. Miranda could not escape without resorting to physical violence.

'It would be so nice if you waited for him. You see, he's staying with me – just as a friend – and Joseph will be coming home with me, and it's a little awkward with Julian staying. Joseph is leaving soon, and this is a really important relationship for me.'

The nerve of her! Miranda said, 'Jocasta, why the hell should I do you a favour?'

Jocasta flushed. 'That isn't what I meant. Julian should clear the air with you, you ought to be able to be friends after an affair, like he is with me.'

'I don't want to be friends with Julian.'

'Perhaps you don't realise that Julian was in a bad way after finishing his novel – it really took it out of him, all that intensive writing. The only thing he's said against you was that you didn't understand the state he was in when he was finishing the novel.'

Miranda said, 'He didn't understand the state I was in, Jocasta! I was working more than full-time, typing his novel, feeding him, counselling him—'

With what could only be described as a smirk, Jocasta said, 'Actually, he's had two counselling sessions with me, he had a good cry, it really did him good. He is such a good friend, he was so kind when Kenneth and I broke up. Don't you find him kind?'

'He can be quite unkind, actually. I felt reduced to nothing by the time he'd finished the book.' Close up, Miranda observed the tiny lines traced on Jocasta's youthful face and brow. How long did she plan to go on flitting from man to man? Lowering her gaze, she found herself staring at Jocasta's pendant; she couldn't pull her eyes away from it.

'But he has been changing,' Jocasta went on. 'Now he's got a job he's got more self-respect. And it's good for him to have some money, he's being very generous with it.'

As she spoke Jocasta began to fiddle with the pendant; it seemed to be irritating her. 'Goodness,' she said. 'This is burning! I must have developed a metal allergy or something.' She removed the pendant and laid it on the table, before returning to her theme. 'I still think you two should have a friendship, he's very fond of you.'

There was a red mark on her creamy skin, where the pendant had hung. Miranda dragged her eyes back to Jocasta's face, and said, 'Frankly, Jocasta, it sounds as if you get on with him much better than I do.' She would have liked to walk out, but she was pinned behind the heavy table between Jocasta and the wall.

Jocasta made a last effort to sell him to her. 'Poor Julian, I'm afraid he's been rather hurt by Joseph moving in with me. He's finding his new job very tough, on his feet all day, humping books around… anyway, he should ring you! I'll tell him to ring you.'

'Jocasta, will you please mind your own business!'

At this point Joseph arrived, and catching Jocasta's eye, nodded his head towards the door. 'Coming, sweetie?'

Suddenly girlishly submissive, Jocasta rose. 'I'll get him to ring you!' she said over her shoulder as she left the pub on Joseph's arm.

'Jocasta, wait – you've left your…' Released at last, Miranda squeezed herself from behind the table, and followed them to the door, the pendant in her hand. She was too late, they were nowhere to be seen.

As she made her way towards the underground Miranda realised that this was the first time since October that she had held a conversation with Jocasta without feeling scared of her, let alone standing up to her. In fact, she could almost feel sorry for Jocasta, lumbered with a Julian she no longer wanted.

*

Next day, he telephoned. 'I thought I'd ring you,' he said, as if Jocasta had nothing to do with it. Miranda braced herself against the seductive concern in his voice as he asked how she was, was she looking after herself, was she eating properly? She answered as briefly as possible. Finally, he came out with: 'Listen, I'm sorry I haven't been in touch. It wasn't very nice of me.'

She said, 'It really doesn't matter now.'

'The thing is… I'm still very fond of you. Can't we see each other, as friends?'

God, Jocasta had fed him his lines. 'Listen, Julian, I can't ever live up to your needs. Anyway, I gather you're friends with Jocasta again.'

'I've never not been friends with Jocasta, we have a deep bond. She says I'm very supportive.'

'How nice for her.'

'I've introduced her to One-to-One sessions. She's become quite anti-analysis now!'

Internally Miranda boggled. That was how she had 'counselled' Julian, was it? There was a pause. Then he asked, 'Are you going back to the Circle regularly now?'

'I wasn't planning to. Are you?'

'It's very difficult… about Jocasta, you see. I've been staying with her since Kenneth left, just as a friend. Only then she moved Joseph in, and he comes to the Circle, and it's very awkward for me.'

So it would suit you to have me back, to save your prideful face. 'That's really not my problem,' she said.

'Look, I would like to see you – couldn't we meet for lunch or something?'

'I'm very busy at the moment.'

'You always were. OK, well, I'll call again sometime.'

Miranda felt much better after that. The conversation had taken Julian out of the realms of fantasy and back into real life. He and Jocasta simply wanted to use her; she was not going to dance to their tune. She would decide when they would meet.

2

BREAKING THE CIRCLE

'Do you mind coming again tonight?' Fiona asked, the following Friday morning. 'Jocasta swears I'll get to read first. And she assures me Julian won't be there in case you are – apparently you weren't very nice to him on the phone.'

'Yes, of course I'll come.'

As well as hearing Fiona's novel, she should return Jocasta's pendant, thought Miranda, replacing the receiver. Or should she? Jocasta had virtually given it to her. Back home after the Circle last week she had taken it out of her bag – it was surprisingly heavy – and put it in her modest jewellery box wrapped in tissue. Now she took it out and held it again. She had the sense that it was full of history. *Whoever owns this is the leader of the dance*, she thought. She returned the pendant to the box.

On impulse, she got out her Tarot pack and drew out a card at random. It was the Tower Struck by Lightning. There they were, the two people falling out of the stricken tower – this time it seemed a good omen. She drew in a deep breath. A ritual, Cassie had said. She had an idea that a full moon was a good time for rituals. She checked her diary; the next full moon was on Sunday week. But that was too soon!

She wished she could sense her helpers as powerfully as Cassie could. After she had meditated that evening she asked them silently for help. There was no reply. But a memory came, of Warren speaking about the power of a genuine intention. She certainly had a genuine intention: she had to break the circle. That would have to do for now.

That week Miranda threw herself into researching fairy tales for the anthology. She was an editor now, she thought, with an inner leap of pleasure. Her own story would include a child and a witch, but so far that was all she knew. Reading other writers, however, was engrossing; in her local library she found both the familiar authors who had enthralled her as a child, like Andersen and Grimm, and contemporary children's writers who were new to her, and all the more interesting. She began to draw up a list, trying to create a balance between witches and wizards, princesses and dragons, Arabian flying horses, French talking cats, and Japanese dolphins. Her reading effectively took her mind off Julian, and wondering how to do a ritual.

*

On Friday night Miranda went to the Circle. So did Julian. He walked in after the group had already assembled upstairs, Jocasta still escorted by her American Joseph. The shock of seeing Julian was physical: Miranda found herself shaking as he took a seat near the door, looking enigmatic. Glancing surreptitiously at his profile, Miranda felt an annoying twinge of longing.

After Fiona's piece had been read and largely well received (with a few picky but insightful comments from Jocasta) Miranda decided to beat an early retreat. Just as she reached the door, Julian caught up with her. 'Are you leaving already?'

'Yes I...' Oh, God, she wanted to put her arms round him. 'I'm sorry I wasn't very nice on the phone.'

'Don't say any more.' He kissed her on the cheek and turned quickly away, leaving her with the soft touch of his cheek imprinted on hers and her insides turned to jelly.

When she woke the next morning her feelings for him had been thoroughly revived. She had planned to stay cool and uninvolved. Now she could feel herself being pulled inexorably towards something dangerous, like a space traveller drawn towards a black hole, to be sucked in for all eternity. Surely this longing wasn't part of the plan? But she had to see him.

At midday she telephoned Jocasta's number. Julian answered.

'Can you talk?' she asked.

'Miranda! Oh, God. Miranda. Yes – Jocasta and Joseph are out for the day.'

'Do you still want to meet?' she asked.

'You know I do. You knew it last night.' He breathed a heavy sigh.

'Is that so terrible?

'It's quite annoying, if you want to know. I've been trying to understand what the attraction is.'

'It's there, though, isn't it?'

'The trouble is, if we get together again, it'll be fine at first and then it'll get all over-intense again.'

Miranda hesitated. She wasn't planning on them getting together again, at least not for long. She said cautiously. 'Why don't we just meet and take it from there? No strings.'

'We could try. No strings, no pressures. But…' His voice became strained. 'Look, I'm still very involved with Jocasta.'

'But now she's got this Joseph chap?'

Julian gave a wry laugh. 'Actually, that really put my nose out of joint – but she says she loves me, she says I'm the only person she can really communicate with.'

'Good. If Jocasta loves you so much she can type your next novel!'

He laughed again. 'She wouldn't! She already does too much. The house is always a mess, she says she's too tired to clean but she's running round London with Joseph looking at art galleries…'

'Isn't it awkward for you, staying there?'

'She really needed me here after Kenneth left. And I've got what I wanted, which is a deeper relationship with her. At the moment she's spending a lot of time with Joseph, because he's going back home soon. She's going to need me when he's gone.'

'I see.' So why was he so keen to see Miranda?

'So, are we meeting?' he asked.

Miranda caught her breath. 'Yes, we're meeting.'

They agreed to meet on the following Friday evening, away from the Circle, and that they would do something 'normal', as Julian put it, like going to the cinema. *Solaris* was on at the Hampstead Everyman.

*

They never got to the Everyman. They met at Hampstead tube station and went to a local bistro in a kind of trance. Side by side on the banquette, they hardly dared look at each other. When their eyes finally met, the electricity between them was almost unbearable.

'I can't breathe,' said Julian. 'My breathing's gone all funny.'

Miranda, too, was gasping. She said, 'What's happening?

This isn't about sex.' This couldn't be right. Perhaps it was a test of her willpower, a test she was rapidly failing.

'It can't be,' he said. 'It's like – it's weird – it's like a drug heightening of the senses. When I met you leaving the pub the other night, I... I don't know, it came over me so strongly, like a wave.'

A waiter came to take their order. 'I'm not sure I can eat anything,' said Julian.

'Me neither. We'd better order something.'

They ordered paté and salad. Miranda asked, 'Does Jocasta know we're meeting?'

'She asked if I was going to see you, I just said we'd spoken on the phone. I told her I was going home for the weekend.'

'You see, one reason I was so cool on the phone the other day was that Jocasta had made it very clear it would suit her to have me take up with you again. And I don't like to be used.'

'I'm not going to tell her we've met,' Julian stated. 'I'd like some privacy myself, I haven't had much lately. And don't you tell Fiona. She had a real go at me, she was terribly angry with me for the way I'd treated you – I thought you must be, too, that's one reason I never phoned you.'

'Well, I was angry with you... you'd made me feel desperately small, as if you only wanted me for sex and typing.'

'Did I really make you feel like that?' He frowned. 'I'm sorry. I think Jocasta gave me the idea that everything must be subsumed to the creative genius at work. I'll make it up to you.' He laid his hand over hers on the table and a bolt of electricity shot up her arm.

*

Two hours later they were standing in Miranda's flat, several feet apart, gazing at each other. The whole room seemed to be vibrating. The blue and green curtains shimmered like sea plants under water. Miranda felt faint. Julian looked white and anguished.

She said, 'You look as though I was about to operate on you without anaesthesia.'

'I feel so strange!'

'I love you,' said Miranda.

'I love you,' said Julian.

Somehow, despite their state of total weakness, they pulled out the sofa bed. Somehow they undressed. At first Miranda almost didn't want him to touch her, her skin felt as though it had shed five layers. She thought, *I will burst like a balloon, there will be little bits of me stuck all over the walls.* How would she be strong enough to break their connection?

Julian went on, 'I feel tender towards you, I want to look after you.' He bent over her, and it began again, their strange and familiar rollercoaster ride.

It was as if they were under some spell, a spell that rocked them and shook them in a sea of sensation. As they moved together, Miranda could see atoms of rainbow-coloured light swirling and dancing behind her closed eyes, as if their lovemaking was taking place on some other, transcendental level. And she was aware of something expanding in her, something not connected with Julian at all, as if some energy inside her were pushing, pushing to get out and be born.

Afterwards as they lay side by side, Julian actually felt physically different, stronger, more present. Just before they finally gave in to sleep, she put her hand on his heart.

'That makes me peaceful,' he said. 'Your touch makes me peaceful. You have healing hands, did you know?'

She had never loved him so strongly. And at the same time, she could see quite clearly that their dance was about to come to an end.

*

The next day was sunny; after breakfast they decided to go out. They took a bus to Hampstead Heath, walked for a while, and then lay in the sun, holding hands, not speaking. Miranda gazed at his face, relaxed and peaceful. This was supposed to be their last time together; how was she going to manage it? He looked back at her, and his expression became worried. He said, 'It feels wrong. I can feel love coming from you.'

Miranda sat up. 'Why is that wrong?'

'Because we decided not to get involved – no strings, we said.'

'But we're not involved. You're going back to Jocasta.'

He hesitated. 'I'm not treating you very well. To be honest, I'd really like to go back to living with her and seeing you as well.'

Miranda digested this without comment. 'What about G.I. Joe?'

'Jocasta's talking about him marrying her, but it's all nonsense. He's got a wife and child in the States. At the moment she's upset about him leaving – he's going on Monday. I feel quite sorry for her. But she says she loves me. And the thing is, I need a permanent relationship, I need the security. For a bit, anyway.'

'You need a permanent relationship for a bit?'

He laughed. 'I know. But I do seem to be able to give her something. We're like brother and sister, really – you are the mistress.' *Not for much longer*, thought Miranda. 'And quite honestly,' he went on, 'she could be useful, she has contacts, she may be able to help me get the novel published. And she can get me some editing work. I don't want to work in that shop forever.'

'God, Julian, you're just using her!'

'What's wrong with that? She uses me. Actually, I'm not sure I do want to go back to her full-time. The kitchen's disgusting, I saw a cockroach the other day.'

Cockroaches now, in the gingerbread house! 'If it's so disgusting why don't you clean it yourself?'

'I couldn't, I'd be sick.'

'Anyway, just to be clear, you want both of us, as and when it suits you?'

He had the grace to look embarrassed. 'You make me sound like... I can't help the way I feel.'

He probably couldn't, thought Miranda. She had to get off this lunatic merry-go-round.

'I don't like this conversation,' said Julian. 'Let's go and find some lunch.'

They went to a café near the Heath. Somehow they stayed clear of the subject of Jocasta. As they waited for their food Miranda asked, 'Have you heard anything about your novel?'

He shook his head. 'I'm trying to forget about it. It's a bit like waiting for an exam result. Jocasta hasn't read the final version, I'm angry with her about that. But I'm moving on. I'm writing a new short story.'

'Good... I'm writing a story, too.' She told him about the anthology.

His response was: 'Miranda, when are you going to do something for yourself?'

'This is for myself!' she said, savouring the thought.

'OK. You must let me read your story.'

'I'm still mulling it over,' she said.

As they were drinking coffee, Julian said, 'Oh – I almost forgot, I can't stay all day tomorrow – I've arranged to meet Fergus after lunch for a One-to-One.'

'A One-to-One?' A seed of discomfort stirred in Miranda.

'Yes, he was upset about something Jocasta said to him, so I started doing One-to-Ones with him, and he's finding it really helpful. So am I – last time we worked on "powerlessness" and I really let rip about my parents – it was very liberating! Actually,' he went on, 'I'm thinking of starting a group.'

Miranda stared at him. 'A group? Julian, you can't!'

'Why can't I?'

'Julian, you've only ever been to one group. You'd need to go to a weekly group for at least a year, and then do a training course.' It was a crazy idea! 'You can't run a group!' At the same time, into her mind flashed an image of Julian as leader of a cult, whether a memory or a premonition or just her imagination she couldn't tell.

'I don't see why. I've been getting on fine without training. Why are you being so negative?'

'Julian, you can't go playing around with people's psyches without proper qualifications. It's not ethical.'

He went white, then red. His expression changed to one of pure hostility. 'You see! You see!' he hissed. 'I told you this wouldn't work, it's just like before – we get close, and then you have to ruin everything, you have to... to diminish me!'

Miranda remained calm. 'Julian, I'm just saying – messing about with people's emotions is dangerous, unless you know what you're doing. I'm not sure it's even legal.'

'Oh, don't be silly! Anyway, I do know what I'm doing.' He glared at her.

This was it, thought Miranda. The turning point she both feared and welcomed. Who was this man? He was like two different people: the loving, tender Julian of the night before had been taken over by someone she couldn't even like – the vain, touchy, narcissistic Julian who fed off other people and spat out the bits he couldn't swallow. And who now wanted to exploit the power he had been keeping restrained.

After a pause, she said coolly, 'You're right. This isn't going to work. If I can't be honest with you, as a friend, without you exploding, then of course we can't be friends. There's no point trying.'

She caught the waitress's eye. 'Can we have the bill please? Anyway,' she added, 'you've made it clear you still want to be with Jocasta, and I'm not interested in playing that game anymore.'

He said furiously, 'You have to put me in the wrong. You're the one playing games!'

'No,' she said. 'No more games. I don't want to see you anymore. It's best for us, for all three of us.'

'I'll pay the bill,' Julian said, through gritted teeth.

'Oh, good. Thank you.'

They walked to the tube, where she left him, saying she would take a bus home. He turned to her one last time. 'I can't believe this is happening,' he said. 'After last night…'

'It's for the best,' said Miranda.

Julian suddenly started patting his breast pocket. 'Oh, sod it!' he exclaimed. 'I must have left my fountain pen at your place.'

'I'll ask Fiona to give it back to you,' said Miranda.

*

When she got home she felt wobbly but strong. She had done it, she thought. Just in time for the full moon the next day, and for the ritual. She still had no idea how to carry it out. She sat down to meditate, but it was hard to calm her mind. Her conversations with Julian kept replaying in her head; she felt sad and angry, and also extremely relieved. Finally she spoke aloud to the helpers Cassie had assured her were there.

'I don't know what to do,' she said. 'Please show me.' Answer came there none.

She spent most of Sunday cleaning her flat very thoroughly, and discovered Julian's pen under a chair. She went out and bought some lilies which she put in a vase on her desk; she found three candles left over from the New Year and placed them in a triangle on the coffee table. In the centre she laid the pendant, Julian's fountain pen beside it.

It was nearly midsummer; it would not grow dark for ages. She went for a walk. She had a long bath. She played with Rollo. She scrambled some eggs for supper, but couldn't eat them.

At half-past nine she looked out of her window and could see no sign of the moon. She lit the candles on the coffee table, and spoke, feeling very self-conscious although she was alone: 'This is the end of the circle of three. It stops now!'

She waited. And waited. All that happened was that she began to feel extremely sleepy. She decided to go to bed.

*

She was simultaneously asleep and awake. She was curled up in her bed, and at the same time she was standing in an open space in what seemed to be moorland; it was night, and there was a full moon in the sky. She was not dreaming: she could feel her feet, shod in sandals, on the sandy earth; she could feel a breeze ruffling her hair and the robe she was wearing. She could feel the rough wood of the long stick she was holding in her right hand.

She knew what to do. With the stick she drew a large circle in the earth, and within it a pentagram; across this she traced the zigzag that crossed the pendant, and then placed the pendant itself in the centre. She stood back, and mentally summoned her soon-to-be ex-partners.

And they were there, within the circle, a man and a woman. In the moonlight their faces wavered and changed: they were Jocasta and Julian, they were two men in Ancient Egyptian garments, they were a nun and a priest, they were a soldier and a servant girl, a man and woman in Victorian dress, there were others, perhaps a dozen manifestations, and she recognised them all, all who had been part of the trio. She watched them in silence until they settled back into being the Jocasta and Julian she knew, facing her, silent and still. She saw that she and they were linked at the heart by chains of tarnished silver.

She told them, perhaps aloud, perhaps not: 'We are playing this game no longer. The dance ends now.' The stick in her hand had become a sword. With it she struck the chains linking them and they easily broke, shrivelling to nothing as they fell away. When the last chain had gone, she faced the other two and said: 'The circle is broken. Go in peace.'

The two figures shimmered, becoming as one-dimensional as paper before fading and finally disappearing. Miranda breathed out a heavy sigh, and stuck the sword solidly into the earth. A wind blew over the design she had created in the sandy soil, blowing it away until there was no trace of it left.

She woke to find it was morning, the sun was shining through the curtains, and Rollo was lying on her chest, purring loudly. Looking over at the coffee table, she saw that the candles had guttered down to nothing. Julian's pen still lay there, but the pendant had gone.

3

FULL CIRCLE

She had done it— she really had done it – with a good deal of help from the invisible world. It could have been a dream, of course, albeit the most vivid dream she had ever had. But the pendant had gone. That was real.

Common sense told her that Rollo could have knocked it off the table during the night. To appease common sense she made a thorough search round the room and under the furniture, and found nothing except some dust balls she really must deal with. Of course it wasn't there; it had gone back to wherever it had come from, or disembodied itself now that it no longer had a role to play. Besides, she felt totally different – lighter, freer, liberated from a heavy weight she had been unaware of carrying. She tested her sense of Julian and Jocasta and found she could think of them without emotion: no love, no anger, just a certain curiosity as to what would happen to them now.

She picked up her Tarot pack and drew three cards at random: the Three of Swords, pain and sorrow – that was the past; the Tower Struck By Lightning, with the two figures falling from it. That was the present. Third came Death, skeletal Death, signifying great change, transformation, and the letting-go of old values. With an unexpected pang it struck her that in letting go of Julian she had let go of love

– even the unsatisfactory, twisted love he had offered. She pulled out one last card. It was the maiden overcoming the lion, the card for Strength.

Shortly afterards, Cassie phoned her; she had evidently been kept informed by her discarnate friends. 'Congratulations,' she said. 'You've done it!'

'Thanks, Cassie. Yes, I really think I have!'

'You better believe it,' said Cassie. 'Now you can start being your real self.'

*

Shortly afterwards Alastair telephoned and invited her to lunch the following week to discuss how the anthology was going. Miranda was halfway through collating her chosen stories, and had yet to write her own; she had better get a move on. Then James called, proposing to come over on Saturday, bringing whatever it was her mother wanted him to give her. *Two nice, sane, grown-up men*, she thought. Such beings did exist.

Every now and then, she experienced a burst of happiness, as if all the happiness she had not been aware of was releasing itself in her body in little bubbles. At other times, she recognised that a part of her was on tenterhooks, waiting to hear news of Julian and Jocasta. She recalled their figures shrivelling to nothing in the night sky of her dream, or not-dream. What was happening to them now in real life? She would have to wait and see. Meanwhile she had her work to occupy her thoughts.

Towards the end of the week Fiona rang. 'What happened with Julian?' she asked. 'I thought you two might be getting together again but he seems to have gone back to Jocasta's.'

'Is he still with her?' asked Miranda. 'I sent him packing. I really meant it, this time.'

She was puzzled; if Julian was still with Jocasta, the breaking of the circle was not complete. Yet she was so sure she had succeeded.

'Thank goodness for that!' said Fiona. 'Perhaps you'll find yourself a decent man, now. Yes, he's staying with Jocasta at present, but I doubt it'll last. She hasn't heard from her American since he left, she's really pissed off about that. Anyway, she's invited me to one of her lunches next Sunday. I don't know who else is coming, but it could be fun – I have to admit she's a good hostess. Her niece is coming for the weekend, so I'm not sure if Julian will be there. Jocasta doesn't seem that keen on him at the moment. She said he keeps waking her up in the night to discuss their relationship.'

Miranda laughed. 'I look forward to a full report.' She couldn't resist adding: 'By the way, I don't want to put you off your lunch, but I have it on good authority there are cockroaches in her kitchen.'

Afterwards, Miranda thought how odd it was that of her own small social circle, she was the only one who had never entered Jocasta's lair, never supped at Circe's table.

*

'I like your flat,' said James, looking around. 'It's cosy. Oh, hallo, nice cat!' Rollo was demonstrating approval by rubbing himself around James's cashmered ankles.

'Coffee?' asked Miranda.

'Coffee would be great.' He seemed nervous. As he took his coffee he said, 'I'd better get straight to the point. Your mother asked me to give this to you. She hasn't read it, she's never opened it.'

From his breast pocket he took a manila envelope. From inside that he withdrew another, a blue airmail envelope. 'It's from your father,' said James.

In the gap between James's words and his handing her the letter, Miranda conjured up a whole scenario in which her father had never died, was still alive and well and writing to her from Canada. But the stamps were old, old stamps, bearing the head of King George VI.

James said: 'Apparently it arrived a couple of days after he died. Your mother says she didn't give it to you then because she thought it would upset you, and then she never found the right moment.'

'She's kept it all this time?' Miranda was horrified, furious. 'But it's my letter!'

'Maybe she forgot about it – I don't know, she did remember to bring it with her to London. At least she kept it, let's give her the benefit of the doubt. She may have been waiting for the right time all these years, and decided it was while she was on her sickbed. I thought it might be a bit of a shock – that's why I wanted to give it to you personally.'

Miranda turned the envelope over in hands that were shaking so violently that she couldn't open it. She stared at it, her heart pounding in her throat.

'I'm sorry – obviously, it is a shock.' James stood up. 'D'you want to read it on your own? I'll take a walk round the block and come back later.'

Miranda nodded. 'Good idea,' she managed to say.

When she opened the envelope, a small black-and-white photograph fell out: a smiling man with his arm round a little girl. The man was her father. It was the clearest picture of him she had ever seen. But how young he was – younger than Miranda was now. And the child was herself. She hadn't realised before that she had been pretty.

She unfolded the pages that had been folded for some three decades. The writing was clear.

My own little girl,

I don't know why – perhaps because it's a lovely sunny day here – I felt I must write and tell you that I love you. I hope very much that I'll be seeing you soon, and will be able to give you a big hug. Mummy and I have been talking about your coming to Canada to see me in the holidays – would you like that?

I'm sorry I have to spend so much time away from you. I'm sad to think of you growing up and learning new things and reading new books, and not being there to share them with you.

But as you may know, and are old enough to understand, your mother and I do not find living together very easy, and that's one reason why it's best for me to live abroad. People can love each other but still find it hard to be together. I hope when you marry you will choose the right person, someone you will be happy living with.

I can't tell you how much I am looking forward to seeing you and having you all to myself for a bit. I think of you lots, and send my love across the ocean to you every night.

This comes with all my love, now and always –
Daddy.

James took his time; when he returned, Miranda had splashed her reddened eyes in cold water and recovered her calm. She let him read the letter. When he had finished, she thought she saw tears in his eyes.

'He must have written it just a day or so before he died,' said Miranda. 'I wonder if he had a premonition.'

'Maybe,' said James. 'I don't know much about these things. He was a nice man, your father. I only remember him slightly, but Ma sometimes talks about him. She thought your mother didn't deserve him. He was a good man.'

Spontaneously, slightly awkwardly, he gave her a hug. Then he stood back and asked, 'Are you OK to come out for some lunch?'

*

Later that afternoon, after an enjoyable and expensive lunch, Miranda was free to weep again, which she did at length, cuddling Rollo who seemed to accept her need to grieve.

She spent the evening quietly, slowly absorbing the reality of her father. That shadowy figure in her mind had been a real person: Daddy, who sent his love to her across the ocean every night. If only she'd known. What she knew now was that her father had loved her; his absence was not a rejection of her, as a deep-down part of her had always believed.

Now new memories made their appearance. They came in little snatches: Daddy reading to her at bedtime – *Alice* and *Winnie-the-Pooh* – and once, when she couldn't sleep, laying his hand on her brow and telling her to imagine floating up into sleepy pink clouds in the sky. Walking in a park, feeding ducks, her small hand in his big one. Riding piggyback on his shoulders… she had forgotten all this – or had she simply not wanted to remember what she had lost? She still had a lot of grieving to do, she realised.

And now, as if her mind had been given permission to remember, another memory shot unbidden to the surface. She was lying surrounded by bars, the bars of a cot, and above her loomed a woman's face, distorted with frustration and fury, screaming at her, her hair hanging down over baby Miranda's face... no wonder she had always thought there was something wrong with her. But there was nothing wrong with her; there never had been.

*

On Sunday evening, Fiona telephoned.

'How was Jocasta's lunch party?' asked Miranda.

'Rather dramatic!' said Fiona. 'Julian walked out on her yesterday morning! It was all very peculiar. After the Circle on Friday I was with them both in the pub – he was complaining about a tummy ache, and Jocasta said it was his own fault for eating at some dubious pizza place. Then she said, "Miranda can cope much better with Julian waking her up in the night, and he ought to marry her." So I said, "What does Julian want?" and he said, "I don't know." Miranda, where is Julian? Is there a real person in there? It was as if he just wasn't there, somehow.'

'I know what you mean. Fiona, I don't know who he is.'

'Anyway,' Fiona went on, 'apparently he was complaining all night, and in the morning nothing Jocasta could do was any good, and he yelled at her and just walked out. So the lunch party was rather dominated by her complaints about Julian and what a terrible person he is. So it wasn't much fun, and the meal wasn't very good. Poor Jocasta was in quite a state, what with Joseph not writing and Julian creating a scene... I didn't spot any cockroaches, by the way, but her kitchen could do with a good clean.'

*

Two days later, a letter arrived in the post in Julian's black handwriting. It was written from his parents' home.

I am writing to say that since our last meeting I have been thinking things over and you were right to decide we should finish. I could never live up to your needs, and I cannot take your constant criticism and discouragement. You want too much from me, and whatever I do doesn't make you happy.

Miranda had to admire the way he had turned round her complaints about him.

You may like to know that yesterday morning I slammed the door on Jocasta. What tipped the balance was that while I was staying with her for a couple of days I was ill, and she was totally uncaring. She tried to make me take aspirin, which makes me sick, and then accused me of rowing in front of her niece. As I have never rowed in front of others I simply walked out. It means I am depriving myself of work and possible help in getting the book published, and I'll lose the companionship of the Circle, but so be it.
'I hope you don't feel too badly about me.
'Love, Julian.

So the ritual had worked. He had left Jocasta of his own volition. Good. The circle was truly ended now.

Miranda got out her cigarette lighter and slowly burned Julian's letter. Watching the paper blacken and break, she thought back over the last eighteen months and wondered what she had been doing with this totally unsatisfactory man. What a waste of all that love! Though perhaps love was never wasted, perhaps it was absorbed into the atmosphere and recycled, like an etheric compost, to nourish those who needed it.

*

She wanted to finish her story so that Alistair could read it before they met. She knew it was about a little girl who longs to dance, and a scary witch who lives hidden in the attic of her grandfather's house, but that was all. Now it came, flowing easily on to the page. One day the little girl decides to overcome her fear of the witch, and speaks to her through the keyhole. The witch explains that she is locked in and longs to be free. The child finds a silver key to the attic and frees the witch, who gives her a pair of silver shoes and teaches her to dance and then to fly.

Yes, that was right, that was how it was. The witch was not evil; she was the power Miranda had been afraid to use, she was her anger, and her creativity. Together they would fly.

*

She was typing her final draft when she heard the front gate click. She looked up and saw a woman coming up the path, a woman with fading red hair, wearing a long green skirt and a dark embroidered cape twinkling with mirror glass insets. At first glance, oddly, Miranda didn't recognise her. At second glance, she realised that Jocasta had come to call.

She considered ignoring the doorbell, but curiosity overcame her. On the front step, standing slightly below her, Jocasta looked smaller than usual and slightly uncertain.

'I didn't phone beforehand,' she said. 'I thought you

might not want to see me. I know you broke things off with Julian, but he may be back in touch – Fiona may have told you about his recent behaviour. I want you to know what really happened. I was coming in this direction anyway, so…'

'You'd better come in,' said Miranda.

'I won't stay long… what a nice flat, what a nice cat, I adore cats!'

Rollo sniffed briefly at her skirt and loyally walked away with his tail perpendicular.

Jocasta seated herself on the sofa without removing her cape, and launched into her story.

'I think you ought to know what kind of person Julian is. He's been staying with me on and off, just as a friend. Well, last Friday I didn't want him to come back with me at all, I had my niece staying and it wasn't convenient. But he had a stomach upset, he was in bed at my place all Friday, moaning and groaning – and Miranda, it was quite worrying, he was going on in a monotone about a cosmic virus! It was quite scary. He was well enough to come to the Circle, but afterwards he insisted on coming back with me, and he went on moaning and groaning all night. I did everything I could, but nothing seemed to be enough for him.

'Then, in the morning, I was scrambling eggs for Jenny and he came into the kitchen, still complaining of feeling ill. I offered him an aspirin and he said that would make him sick, but he'd like some scrambled eggs. So I said, "If you're really feeling ill, you'd better not have scrambled eggs."

'And then, Miranda, he let out this great howl! Like a child having a tantrum, only a grown man – can you imagine! Jenny went quite white and I said, "You'd better go," and he did, slamming the door hard enough to shake the house!

'The thing is, now I can understand a lot of the things you've said about him, which I've never believed before.'

Miranda said, 'But I've never known him behave like that, it sounds weird.'

'I thought I ought to warn you about the state he's in, in case he tries to get in touch with you.' With splendid self-contradiction Jocasta added, 'It's a pity he's not with you, Miranda, because he needs a friend, and you're much better at coping with him than I am. He's been really difficult this last week, wanting to do counselling sessions with me all the time, including in the middle of the night, and trying to push me into places I don't want to go, and putting wrong interpretations on things I say.'

'You're not supposed to interpret at all in One-to-Ones,' Miranda put in.

'I think he uses them to manipulate people. Fergus seemed terribly shaky on Friday, I think whatever Julian's been doing with him has been bringing stuff out of his subconscious that ought to be dealt with by someone properly trained.'

Miranda said, 'Quite,' simultaneously feeling worried for Fergus and remembering all the times when Jocasta had poked around in her students' subconsciouses.

'Still, I think dear little Fergus will be all right,' said Jocasta. 'I've persuaded Judy to keep an eye on him – they could have something really nice going between them.'

Oh, no, Jocasta, are you still at it?

'As for Julian,' Jocasta went on. 'He was completely irrational! I'm afraid he's having a nervous breakdown.'

This thought had crossed Miranda's mind, but something told her he wasn't. 'I suspect he was putting it on,' she said. Could it be an effect of the ritual?

'But you know, there's always been a streak… his novel is so – by the way, I think it's been rejected, though he hasn't said – but it's so depressing, with such a perverse attitude to women.'

You never said so during Circle readings, thought Miranda. She said, 'He told me you hadn't read it.' What other lies had he told?

'Of course I read it, weeks ago! and when I pointed out all the flowery bits he should cut he got terribly offended.'

'Then you can imagine,' said Miranda, 'the flak I got when I corrected his spelling and grammar.'

'Yes, yes, I can, I can understand now… And all this hypochondria! Apparently he told Fergus that as soon as he left me his stomach ache got better – as if I'd given it to him!'

So now she knew what happened when he got ill at Jocasta's. Miranda said, 'Actually he wrote to me, his letter sounded sensible. Childish, but not crazy. I think it's quite healthy for him to be clearing his decks.'

'I'm sorry, I don't agree, I think people should live in the moment.' Jocasta couldn't bear clear decks, Miranda realised. Her next sentence confirmed this. 'When I get home, I'm going to fill in a computer dating questionnaire – why don't you try that?'

'I'm not that desperate for male company,' said Miranda tartly.

Ignoring this, Jocasta looked directly at Miranda and said, 'I want you to know something. I'd never have started an affair with him if he hadn't told me things were really bad between you two.'

'A pity you didn't check that out with me,' said Miranda. 'I thought things were going rather well. I've come to one conclusion about Julian: he doesn't want to be happy, anyone who tries to make him happy is wasting their time.'

'Yes, well, I just wanted to make things clear.' Jocasta rose and adjusted her cape. As she walked to the door she said, 'I'm planning to go dancing after the Circle next Friday, you'd be welcome to come along.'

Join in another dance with Jocasta? 'No, thank you.'

Miranda watched as Jocasta set off down the road, no longer a witch but a small, middle-aged woman dressed as a hippie, off to fill in a computer dating form.

*

Soaking in the hot bath that suddenly felt essential, she thought over Jocasta's account. Who was Julian? Where, as Fiona had asked, was Julian? This was not the wounded child, seeking love, the innocent Peter Pan. Was he a weak man genuinely torn between two loves, or a parasite, battening on the emotions – not to mention the eggs, bacon and typing services – of love-hungry women? Or was he simply an actor who had lost his script and could only respond to the cues fed to him by others? It didn't really matter, now. It was over. Julian was out of her system, like a virus.

That night she dreamed she was riding a white horse down a wide country road. She passed Julian standing on the verge: he was dressed as the joker in a pack of cards, which in many games can represent any card in the pack.

*

The next day she walked over the already browning grass of Hampstead Heath. Everything looked clean and clear, as if a mist had been wiped from her vision. Above her, colourful kites clattered and tossed against the bright blue sky. She thought about her father, and wished he was walking with her. Perhaps he was.

On her way back to the bus stop, she stopped to watch a group of young people sitting round the remnants of a picnic, happy in each other's company. She saw a man playing ball with his little son, and the child was laughing and laughing with pure joy. Near the ponds she passed a family, the father lying down in the sunshine, the mother sitting up on the grass. Her breast still open to the air, she was holding the baby she had just fed, and she and the baby were gazing into each other's eyes with such an intensity of love that Miranda could hardly bear to take her own eyes off them.

As she turned away and walked on, she became aware of a growing sensation that she, too, was loved. It was not the love of a person, but a sense of love expanding inside her. It seemed to fill her whole body with a kind of smile that grew from deep within her, filling her and filling her until her entire being became that loving smile.

This book is printed on paper from sustainable sources managed under the Forest Stewardship Council (FSC) scheme.

It has been printed in the UK to reduce transportation miles and their impact upon the environment.

For every new title that Matador publishes, we plant a tree to offset CO_2, partnering with the More Trees scheme.

For more about how Matador offsets its environmental impact, see www.troubador.co.uk/about/